"Because first, blessedly, I am an animal."

– Arielle Greenberg

"We have all been here before

We have all been here before

We have all been here before

We have all been here before."

– Crosby, Stills, Nash & Young, "Déjà vu"

Lech, lecha.— לֶךְ-לְךָ

"Go forth. Go for you."

– Genesis 12:1

LECH

LECH

Sara Lippmann

Tortoise Books

Chicago, IL

FIRST EDITION, OCTOBER, 2022

Copyright © 2022 by Sara Lippmann

www.tortoisebooks.com

ASIN: B09TDFFCMJ
ISBN-13: 978-1948954693

for Rob, who held me to it

PROLOGUE

The hills of Sullivan County squint into the sunlight each June. Pleasant enough, they are no great beauties, and even the fullest bloom can't mask the mediocre wonder of nature; then again, it's often the subtlest landscape that's known to take root. If these hills could talk—the region has seen it all. Nothing is how it was (only of course it is). Beyond that line of trees the fox and hare still perform their timeless dance to remind us that for every prey a predator; every history a ferocity of ghosts. Sliced down the center, these hills reveal a layer cake of Western civilization, from the Lenape to the Irish to the borscht-drunk Jew. Who's laughing now? Industry has been lost. Seasons turn. Road signs wage a battle of red over blue, the color of blood outside or in, and it's unclear what is won by winning. The year may be 2014 but this is an old story. Here in upstate New York the median per capita income is $28K. Farms lie fallow and for sale. Religion ransacks the fitful heart. What's left are gun shops, a broken roof, the faint smell of stretched hide from centuries-old tanneries, long closed. Ponds are called lakes. There are lakes galore. All through the county, a river wends. For some it's a haven, for others it's a trap. Just ask the people.

NOREEN

When the phone rings, Noreen Murphy is minding her Monday at Sullivan Sales. Zero foot traffic, spit of rain. She blows on a fresh coat of polish: *Can't Elope*. Her nails look like candy corn. She ears the receiver. All men are honey.

"Depends," she says. "What is it you need?"

Everyone's looking for something, but these men are so and so and so and so. They want land, water, they want and they want, and Christ on commission, *You've come to the right place!* She bounds out of her chair. Just like that, it's happening.

Real estate boils down to location, and Noreen's the only one physically there. *Tell me more*, she urges. If it all sounds too good to be true, she doesn't doubt them. Somehow she remains a bright-side-of-things person. For all the bum cards she's been dealt, Noreen is not one to fold.

Play your hand, said the elderly guest where her parents worked, can't remember which, there were so many hotels, with hedges and lawns and a thousand salad forks, the man's accent thick, his eyes big as a jewel thief's. She was four, no more than six, small enough to move about the resort undetected.

He found her beneath an eight-top on the veranda busying herself with lost things: a stray golf ball, scalloped compact, iridescent beads loosened from sweaters. A clutch of men penned her in with their black socks and pale knees, hairs curling from calves like frayed wires. Their language, unknown to her, shot from the gut, consonants crashing in a tower of plates, but it was no kitchen accident. This was not even shouting. This was how men spoke in their mother tongue. This was the friendly four o'clock card game.

Every hotel had one. Many had many, going all hours.

Employees were not supposed to bring children to work, but Noreen did not want her brother looking after her. Patrick either didn't look or gave the wrong kind of look. At the hotel she could disappear among the bottomless buffets, meat fanned on lettuce, vegetables carved intro cranes. Her palms buzzed from flocked wallpaper. Ladies twisted lipsticks and pressed themselves with a kiss. She had such a watchful eye the manager occasionally let her peel potatoes beside her mother or ride the mower with her father or hand out towels in the powder room where satin poufs made every guest feel like a movie star, provided she did not disturb.

Decks smacked, shuffled, fell.

"A-ha. Just as I thought."

The word "thought" came out as "taut." Noreen gnawed her kneecap.

"*Pitzele*, let me explain you something."

He offered her a candy, hard outside, jelly in, ends folded in like a present. Her legs did not reach the floor. "Everybody cheats. The trick is not to get caught."

The old man pulled a coin from her ear.

"How'd you do that?"

"Life's an illusion." He shut the oily metal into her palm, taught her gin and blackjack with a casino deck stamped in blue winged babies, hole punched through the heart. Practice, he said: get good at math, and a fast calculation might be her ticket. *From where to where?* That's when he opened his sleeve. Rolled his cuff once, twice, until it revealed a crooked row of ink. Noreen thought it was a phone number or secret code. "No mind-reader could have imagined." *What?* She didn't say.

"The inhumanity of humanity," he mumbled, which sounded like a riddle. Then he covered up. "What's your story?"

No one had ever asked her. She thought about her brother with whom she shared a room. Nine years older, Pat was practically a man, hair sprouting everywhere, his body a Chia Pet, the way it grew, the way he grew when he made her touch it. In the bathroom he asked for a trim around the shaft, no bumps. Noreen was deft with scissors. He smelled like vinegar and fern spores. Told her to put her pencils you know where, measured how many she could fit. When she got to six, he said: good girl. Now you're ready for school.

The old man waited. "You know, I knew once a girl your age," he said, but she just stared at his liquid eyes until he regained himself. "It's okay," he patted her head. "Next time you'll tell me."

Only there was no next time. What did Acapulco have over the Catskills? As hotels closed, her parents floundered. In the off-season her father took odd jobs, clocked hours at the mill, thrashing and hauling seed as needed. Eventually her mother got a job at the state hospital cooking vegetables until they lost integrity. Noreen no longer asked to be brought in to work. She got older. Pat moved out. Her parents died.

For years, Noreen took the expression *play your hand* to mean accept your station in life, but no: it meant stop waiting around for that ace. Use the cards you're dealt. Be smart, don't bleed the fan, and you, too, can hustle the table.

If only he could see her now! How she's dreamed of this moment: a big call comes in. Just like her online real estate course. Noreen glances over her notes—Steven Frank and Ed Messina—doodled with vines and stars. Frank & Messina: kissing in a tree. Their address is on Madison Avenue. Has she heard of them? Of course, she says. She hasn't. She pictures Penn & Teller. Will one be large and the other slim? They're scouting for new opportunities.

"Murmur Lake!" she blurts. That it's not on the market is a detail she keeps to herself. That it belongs to two different owners; that it's occupied, comes with baggage—let's face it, a death cloud—no one would touch, but reputations can be reframed. Letting the property rot like a roadside shrine hasn't done anyone any good. Noreen had been a teenager when the drowning occurred. Wasn't there a statute of limitations on grief?

As the men talk opportunity and expansion, Noreen can't keep up; theirs is a private language of catch phrases ("new dev" sounds like a shampoo); static cuts in—are they eating?—jaws working overtime as they carry multiple sidebars, hold the mayo, which makes her wonder who else is there, is she being broadcast into a midtown conference room or limousine, these men with their booming voices and business speak, do they wear shirts with the contrast collars and cuffs, pinky rings and hair greased in waves? They're not talking with her but at her, as if she's inconsequential, uh-huh, she says, because that's what people want to hear, agreement, echo as opposed to interaction, they want to know you can supply their demand.

Pitzele. What'd I tell you? She can almost hear the old man.

"You're going to love it," Noreen says. "A jewel of a place. Beauty to die for, with its very own lake." When she lobs a price— ludicrous, the cost of a small country—she holds her breath. They've muted her, she can tell, but when they return, their voices have dropped an octave. They're interested. The truth is, Noreen has low-balled. Who doesn't want a steal? Who could call a three-and-a-half-million-dollar price tag a steal? Steven Frank and Ed Messina, that's who.

Now all she has to do is get the sellers to sell and the buyers to buy and the banks to close the deal. That she's never done this before, that she's flying by the seat of her pants doesn't faze her. Noreen is not one to follow protocol. Authority has nothing on her. She whispers a prayer to the universe, to her card shark of yesteryear who never did share his name. Maybe it's not faith, but gratitude. Hell in a hand basket, she's already won.

Well water or county water? No sweat. She'll find answers on acreage, zoning laws, tax info, the latest from the gaming commission. Tourism numbers and market trends. Anything Frank and Messina want she'll get. She uses the word "jiffy."

The senior sales employees are Sally Roux and Christopher Prig. Chris lives in Brooklyn and comes up on weekends. Their website has experienced a 33-percent spike in activity over the last eighteen months, consistent with the reported uptick in secondary aka "go-homes." Sally is more of a seller's agent, but even with signs pitched throughout the county, rainbow sheets draping the boarded up pub, there hasn't been a need to staff more than one person in the office at a time. Noreen will need another job if she doesn't sell something and soon. No way she's splitting this commission. Noreen shuts her desktop and collects her things. Her beat-up Toyota is on the street where she's left it. A good sign: her daughter Paige has not run off with it. A bad sign: Why isn't the kid at work?

Lately Paige is in a mood, Noreen never knowing what she's going to get. Tommy Potts coming around with his boots and his tin can, and that's when he's got a job. By the time Noreen was Paige's age, Paige was almost three, in underpants because accidents cost less than disposables. Lunch was split pea soup, dinner, sliced frankfurter over soup, but she had a daughter who belonged to her only. No one could touch that, the love she felt, particularly those early years: baffling and bursting. If only love paid the bills.

When Paige's phone goes to voice, Noreen hangs up, slings her studded fringe bag across the passenger seat. Life spills out: Lotto stubs, scratch coins, assorted nips. She lights a cigarette off the dash, cranks the A/C. The sticker on the windshield long expired. It doesn't take a mechanic to tell her she needs new brakes and rotors, her tires bald from last winter, nor does it take a genius to crunch the math. Inspection will have to wait. At the traffic light she twists the top of an amaretto and shoots it. The bottle is fit for a doll. She turns left out of town, headlong into the blunt iron sky.

Thirty minutes is nothing in the country, Noreen on automatic pilot, though it's been a while since she's driven out to Murmur, a rocky, unsettling climb, as if the bottom might drop out beneath her. Fifteen years since she lived out here, up the dirt road and around the bend. Kole is not home. Not working the fields, at any rate. Corral's empty, the pasture untamed by wind. Late to start running the compressor. Already he should be breaking the cut into bales. If he applies the same neglect to grain, it will go to seed, and Kole will miss the harvest. The Holsteins have strayed out toward the road where the growth is richer, and Noreen slows to watch them stewing in their patties of shit, flies on noses slick as river rocks, tails swatting wire fencing as if trying to break free.

The farmhouse is older than she remembers but so is she. Clapboard once white, now overcast, fallen shingles exposing dark squares like an unfinished puzzle. Satellite dish bent over the roof in defeat. Noreen fixes herself in the rearview. Her face is broad and hard, her nose never quite healed, eyes set like they can't decide which side they are on, torn at odds in a tug of war. She's in work clothes: lilac blouse with minimum boob, hair fixed in combs. From under the seat she pulls a concert tee, hacked at the sleeves and neck. Better to give the people what they want. She redraws her eyes. Her rose tattoo blooms on her shoulder. She has her daughter's birthdate stamped on the inside of her forearm: 081891. Tacky, Paige says, *appropriative* or something, but the lease on Noreen's body has expired. Paige no longer has claim to it. Cinder blocks bolster the porch against the earth's pressing hunger. Noreen flakes her cigarette off the ledge. Every week she quits anew only she's lying to herself.

No one comes to the door.

The house is unlocked. She could march upstairs and slap Kole from his slumber, haul him into the tub, but Noreen's moved on from all that, for the most part. He has his wife Kathy now. Still, a suffocating familiarity returns, as if she's been shut inside a jar of fermenting pickles. Down the hall Mrs. Troller's room is empty, wheelchair gone; all that's left is the commode the color of tombstone. Noreen can smell the bowl is full.

"Kole? Kathy? You decent? I got news, a proposition for you."

Mark is where he always is: at his post by the window. She's never known what to call him, Kole's brother; locals, if they called him at all, called him mute or worse; what to call his quarters—parlor, TV nook, bedroom, living room. *Salon.* His posture admirable in wood-pulp flannel, his gaze fixed toward the lake, hair, thick as ever, as if a pair of squirrels has taken up residence between his ears. He palms the armrests. Visiting Mark is like attending church—calming, infrequent. It fills her up, to watch him watch over Murmur. How she wishes she were the kind of person to instill that kind of loyalty, living or dead.

Noreen coughs in the doorway, mentions the weather, each word an intrusion, she is practically shouting, a ridiculous adjustment, he can hear her just fine—if he chooses.

"Kole on his way home? I can wait."

Mrs. Troller never wanted Noreen to stick around that long winter. That long winter which turned into four long years.

"A girl is not a kitten. You don't just give her a bowl and a place to do her Christian. Noreen Murphy is not your problem. Take her in, and she'll rob you of all your best years."

Kole was gawky, then, with lots of hair, fiery in a boyish way, not built to be taken seriously. Noreen almost pitied him. Mrs. T was cranky but right: Noreen was not worth the headache. Noreen with Paige in her lap. Noreen with an island-size scab on her lip. She looked walleyed at Mark but he would not look at her. She zipped the Velcro of her daughter's shoes and stood. Which is when Mark stepped in, Mark the beautiful, Mark the broken, Mark the silent son pushing out the words: "Let her. Stay."

"Maybe we'll see some late day sun." Mark does not turn. The sudden light makes the water look warm although Noreen knows it to be cold. Across, on the other side of the dock, she can make out the outlines of two figures: mother, child. Summer people. She cups Mark's shoulder, his muscles rigid beneath her touch.

"Would you like to go down?" Meaning the water, a closer look. Frank & Messina wanted images, and the sky after the rain is just right.

"Take a walk with me?"

The lake stirs with life, the swift tail of a fish.

"Whaddya say?"

Mark doesn't. No need. He's not going anywhere.

PAIGE

The fuckers are coming. No stopping their big cars belching exhaust from here to eternity where the road ends, dust kicks, where options dwindle. Where signs point: camp or more camp. Every summer, tourists invade, plastic shells humping roofs like suspicious growths. They take over the diner. Paige Murphy watches it all from the parking lot. This summer, she swears, will be her last.

Key fobs click and beep, safeguarding sleeping bags and brushed metal canteens. Doors slide open. Children tumble out in orthodontia, in an assault of tie-dye. Parents steal shirts into chinos and stand in approval of their offspring huddled together like a special unit, a purposeful molecule, as if they were close, as if they really loved each other and were not just trying to milk the last minutes of screen time from their shared devices before they're confiscated in accordance with overnight camp policy.

Paige aims her cleaner like a weapon. Behind the glass, she mists, clears a graveyard of midges from the sill. At twenty-two, she is impossibly old. Her T-shirt pops up. Sweat feathers her brow. She will have to work fast to maximize turnover, to accommodate the rush already yanking on the railing that's come loose. One father will bust through the door, aghast.

"Fix that before you have a lawsuit."

Shaped like an Airstream, an aluminum pill too large to swallow, The Breakstone Diner swells hot and loud and important. The revolving fan can't compete. Diane, with her hip, is in the weeds, hobbling to and from the hostess stand, leg clicking at her side like an ice cream scoop. These people are not used to waiting, but they know how to tip.

Paige arranges her face. "How many?"

Sunglasses slide onto heads. They are four, they are six, they smudge the dessert tower of éclairs and black forest cake, they leave their condensation on the glass. Children paw a dish of powdered mints shaped like baby teeth.

"That junk has been sitting out all winter."

"You don't know where people's hands have been."

"This way," Paige says and they walk ahead like they own the place, pausing in front of the mirrored wall to smooth their hair as she indicates their table—

"Actually, we'd prefer a booth."

As she gathers the filmy stack of menus and guides them to a booth, kids stomping on fallen forks, mothers and daughters still fixing their hair. There are barrettes in their jaws, tiny fangs, glossy manes swishing, which they lift off their long necks and loop in a way to look casual, accidental, as if they did not spend a fortune on color and keratin.

"Do you have anything bigger?"

Paige plops her menus onto the original round meant for six. These people pay whether she smiles or not. They never run out on a bill. Sometimes, they tip more the grumpier she is— imagining her home life, her prospects, dire straits. *Arnie, how would you feel?* They whisper as if Paige is not right there, she's invisible, too dumb to process. *And such a young girl.* They say *to boot.* They worry it's not just pudge she has but pregnancy. This, too, translates to bigger tips. If Paige can keep her wits she will earn enough to get the hell out of Sullivan County by September, so she stomachs their chatter: how long the drive's taken, the extended fifteen-day forecast. *Didn't such-and-such-hotel used to be around here? Dinner rolls light as pillows!*

Children want hot fudge sundaes at ten in the morning. They want cheeseburgers and a side of bacon and a basket of fried chicken and root beer floats.

"Fatten up the little pigs before sending them to slaughter," fathers say. *Dad!* Protests are ignored. Fathers want eggs—here comes the wink—*over-easy.*

Mothers want fries but order egg-white omelets.

Daughters want coffee. Mothers want their daughters to eat. Daughters want their mothers to stay out of it. Fathers jump to their defense, as if mothers need defending.

Paige says, "How about a side of fries for the table?"

Harsh, maybe, but she has no time for nice. To think: once she looked forward to this time of year, the Neversink flush with snow melt, the air rife with moss and butane. Dragonflies hummed, and she and her mom played cards—spit, palace, bullshit, hearts—the radio antennae crooked skyward for signal. Every cookout had a burger to spare. Winter was long. Paige didn't ski or skate or partake in any of the regional attractions stamped on brochures. The thaw was brief. Perennials jumped the gun or slept through their window. Spring, her mom said. Fickle, unreliable. There was no trusting it.

Tourists still arrived for autumn leaf-peeping, providing just enough economic stimulus from maple syrup to carry the county to ski season. Her mom, Noreen, colored herself like a Muppet, and charioted Paige from corn maze to monster mash, lollipops sucked thin in a parade of masks and capes, of children pretending to be other people, as if that were possible in a place whose year-round population topped out at 350.

Then Paige caught on to the heist of summer. Coach buses conquered the dusty hills. Paige remembers faces in the glass, aware of how her life in the husk and tassel might seem to outsiders: uncomplicated and carefree. She was five, six, she was always older. The farm grew her up quick. Paige would wind herself in the tire swing Kole Troller tied to the sycamore, a violent hinge, drilling herself into the earth—crust, mantle, core— as if it all that twist and release might transport her elsewhere.

Night, she listened to the freight howling toward the hamlet of Narrowsburg. Sometimes, she slept through. At the Trollers', there weren't always footsteps, Kole's breath at the door, and it wasn't always bad, to be raised in the shadow of a lake dubbed Murder and all the talk that went with it. Despite the stories, Murder was pretty as an ink spill. Paige never asked about it, never gave much thought to Mark Troller in his window, or why no one ventured into the water for a swim. She had other worries. Chickens, a skinny-ass goat. Kole counted on Paige to sweep up loose feed. Maybe he'd send her to fetch a beer. Once he brought her a Big Wheel but she was already too big, so he brought her to the hayloft, her body sinking beneath his red-faced weight. *Animal, vegetable, mineral.*

Fuckers, everywhere.

By high school they'd chuck rocks at river canoes, kids singing songs, sometimes in Hebrew, the foreign tongue echoing in the white-capped valley like a spell. Flash their tits to whole rafts of families, sneak into campgrounds for pie irons and Swiss Army blades. They rotated road signs nailed to trees, Camp Neshama this way, now that, dumped Kool-Aid into Camp Yad V'Yad's ("yadda yadda," they called it) heated pool. When Tommy Potts sliced swastikas into the sides of the boys' bunks, Paige said he'd gone too far. But she understood. Life was a con. The season no longer belonged to people like her and Tommy, but to the influx of outsiders who transformed the Dairy Barn and Pizza Town into kosher joints through Labor Day, mandating weekly closures from Friday through Saturday evening, condemning Paige and her friends to the slab of sloped concrete beneath the overpass.

At the Walmart, where she also worked, summer people looted the aisles, loading up on hammocks and kiddie pools like they'd won a shopping spree, then deserting half of their merchandise by the register for her to re-shelve.

"Nice shirt," a customer said.

Paige fed the scanner. "Buy one, get one free."

"Couldn't pay me to wear that."

The whole county bent over like the president was coming. Streets swept, playgrounds painted, traffic lights re-strung, menu prices jacked. Bartenders stopped carding. The fountain in the square spouted on the ten like Shamu the whale. It was crackers to feel like a stranger in your hometown.

"Watch, hot plates." The grabbing begins, a battle for salt, Tabasco. No one says thank you. Easy, maybe, to lust and hate the same thing, but Paige doesn't want what they have, she only wants to stack as many miles as she can between her and here. Florida is her answer.

"Refill?" Paige lifts her pot.

Finally, they turn. "Wait. Didn't we have you last summer?"

Tables clear out, crumpled bills, clot of ketchup swirling in a water glass. Paige picks at her shorts as Tommy's truck thunders into the parking lot. Stupid antlers on top. Saw it in a movie, he told her. Paige doubts he shot the buck. Probably pulled the horns off a dead stag or traded the pair for dope. Tommy leans against the grill, lights a cigarette. From the way he's twitching she knows he hasn't slept. Tommy is a fucker too, but he is her fucker. Bells jangle her heart as he plows through the door.

"Get you something else, folks, or are you all set?"

IRA

She is twenty. She is forty. To Ira Lecher, the woman seems almost a child, hair bunched in buns like teddy-bear ears, standard white T-shirt betraying—if it betrays anything—only a lack of imagination. Cut-off jeans, fringed at the thigh, give way to legs, long legs, legs that hook fast to hips, legs that have known their geography but that seem somehow lost, out of practice, ill-defined, unaccustomed to sun. From this vantage point, he can't be sure, but with girls, it's never a stretch.

What matters is: she's here.

He ducks down, chest first, arms pumping at his sides, as if the ground is a surfboard and she is his wave cresting toward him. It is the same each summer. His property becomes his own wildlife park, a controlled environment in which he knows exactly what he'll find: his new tenant, right on schedule.

Half a mile away Ira heard her round the bend, expecting the usual: black SUV, third row, essentially a minivan but without the stigma. Instead it was one of those gas-efficient cars, light as a toy bouncing over the pebbled drive, struggling to come to a stop. His ex-wife Vivian had the drive installed from the quarry when she'd come up alone with the girls to ensure no surprise visitors. The grass tickles his neck like a hippie's full bush. Supposedly, that's the rage again; what's old is new, life itself one smug circle, but Ira has little use for trends. His eyesight isn't what it used to be, either. Add that to his stunning list of inadequacies. But if his vision is weak, his body is strong, strong enough to support his own weight as he army-crawls toward her, fifteen, thirty paces, elbows pressing into the earth. There's nothing sinister about it. He's but a boy! Reliving his days at Max Mendel's, deep in the land of pretend. He's a sniper in the trenches, a hunter tracking a duck or deer, some real-life Elmer Fudd. Oh, come on. Joke. This is 2014. She is not the hunt.

"You should be ashamed of yourself," Viv would say, "preying on anything with legs." At 66, Ira is long past shame. Who's preying? What harm was fantasy? When has loneliness ever killed anyone? That's not even funny.

She has a child. The good ones always do. Ira remains confounded by his own adult children. Heather and Hillary. He's nothing to do with them. Kids complicated matters. Kids came between perfectly decent people, but this kid—honey curls, bare feet—Ira understands implicitly: the boy speaks his language of want. He wants to be put down, but she whisks him up and over to the tall field by the side of the house adjacent to the outdoor shower he built, a simple pine box, akin to what he buried his parents in, door with a rusted hinge. The boy sneezes. Mom stops, drops, peers up the kid's nose as if it contained all the world's answers, at which point he breaks free, falling back on the lawn as if onto a mosh pit, as if life were a trust game on which to be buoyed by infinite, cheering hands. As if. The kid beetles the air. Uproots a fistful of dandelions whose fluff he casts with profligate, reckless abandon. A ribbon of dust sails behind him. How the world speaks to the young. Ira feels it in the *kishkes*: To have one's whole life ahead! The joys! The sorrows! Next season, his property will be foolish with weeds.

The mother makes trips. Astonishing, what fits in that baby-sized trunk: suitcases, rice sacks, bricks of toilet paper. She feels around the back for stuffed animals, picture books. Dumps everything onto the ground like it's meant to be tagged and sold off by the piece.

His own mother packed the car to the gills for their bunga-low summers: quilts and trivets and blackberry preserves in chamois jars, a collapsible ironing board. His father would thrash through the gates, ditch their belongings on the picnic table, jaunt off to a quick Sunday card game, then hit the road. Why a sweater salesman would be in such a hurry to head south? Who hankered for his wool in such weather?

This mother seems similarly stricken by kitchen-sink syndrome. As if the Catskills were some charred nuclear pit and not the fertile crown of New York State, she's brought every provision down to the water, like she's too good for the tap.

Summer people. Over the years, names escape him but faces cement, faces he's catalogued, taking them down from the mental shelf periodically like collectibles to dust: a birthmark here, the weepy glass blower in clear braces from last season. Viv kept records. The first time they rented it out, Viv leased to Scarlett Station, the indie jam band, but they trashed the place, prompting her subsequent ban on musicians. Since then, they've housed a Swedish mime troupe, a gay couple with twins. There was Sylvia, painter of life-sized Saint Bernards; and Latrice, the lyric memoirist, who kept to herself but whose benefactor roared up on weekends in a classic car like some kind of Gatsby. One time a Wall Street slick secured the place then gallivanted off to Saint-Tropez. No one came that summer. It was awful. Ira, all alone. Like a falling forest tree, did he even exist in the absence of company?

It hasn't always been smooth sailing. His place has a past, don't we all. A person drowned here. People drown in lakes all the time, but Murmur Lake is Ira's lake. A woman died—not on his watch, mind you, before they even began leasing—and Viv blamed him. Nearly twenty-four years and counting. That July morning he'd gone to visit his ailing mother, but when the body turned up like a polyhedron in an eight-ball, it became his unlucky fortune. He'd let the girls down; somehow, he'd let everyone down. Should've been him to find her, not his children. Like their goldfish floating belly-up in the bowl on New Year's morning, this was a father's job.

"What kind of man shirks responsibility?"

"But my mother—" Ira said.

"You and your mother."

Thus was the mark on his property. The rift in his marriage. Like any proximal horror, it was nothing and everything and that's all there was. They'd gone back and forth on transparency, hosting siblings with a taste for the macabre, paranormal paramours, forensic hobbyists who roved the grounds with headsets and metal detectors for other morbid pearls, but those tenants gave Ira *tsuris*, so Viv dropped prices and cast about for the clueless, outfitted the powder room with fussy, wrapped soaps.

As for the others. A father drops dead from a coronary, an aunt throws a clot to the lung. Takes over a half hour for an ambulance to arrive out this way. Two unfortunate deaths in two-and-a-half decades wasn't terrible, three counting the drowning. Chaya Bloch was her name. Plus animals (one family dog, a mischief of field mice, a pink-fingered shrew.) Eventually, death comes for us all, but it's easy to get hung up on numbers, easy to forge a pattern, easy to think it's all about you; the place, somehow jinxed—or chosen. Statistically, for each strike on his property, Ira gets a bye, which means, he can't help but think, *who will be next?*

Ira watches his tenant. A quick scan of her surroundings is all it takes—no rats, no broken glass—for her to turn her back on her child and devote her attention to his house.

Her house. As of today she will inhabit his rooms, obtain shelter from his roof, safety from his walls; she will sleep in his bed, cook in his kitchen, rinse her lather down his drain. She will be his very own Goldilocks, a moment that thrills him, year after year. Like jumper cables to the soul, the energy of another body, another presence in his space, another being living—*living!*—eating sleeping fucking; trimming fingernails with their teeth. They are intimates, yet strangers. The best of both worlds.

She begins. His door—her door—stays open. Ira re-stained it after the cold winter, iron knocker welded into a rakish grin. She schleps from car to house to car, her steps swift, determined, the tethered laps of a domestic kept on short leash. Airs out the funk of the place; the windows, operated by crank, jut out from the custom stone exterior like stunted, awkward wings. Viv insisted he replace the casements, splurge on air-conditioning in three energy-conserving zones. Her upgrades all top-of-the-line, but Ira can't live with them.

In recent years he's given up the main house entirely. It's a hassle, shuttling back and forth with his toothbrush and moccasins. When the weather's a nasty hell, he'll surrender for a few nights, hunker down for better insulation, then return to where he belongs: out back where it's simple, his parents' summer bungalow transported by flatbed from Max Mendel's Mountain Village when it closed, hauled into his woods for posterity. This is comfort: among the milkweed and pine, the sexy white birches. Maybe Viv would feel a tinge of pity if she knew: *poor Lech*, destined for the doghouse. But he never told her. They don't discuss details. She keeps him afloat with rental income; he spends all year in Sullivan County. If they were rotten together, they are better apart.

Already layers are flying off. A cream camisole suctions her ribs, flaunting the flinty lust of her shoulders. She slams the trunk, slams the passenger side with her hip, scoops up a small pair of shoes, red, round in the toe, slams them against her thigh three times like the tambourine player of a folk band—useless, but gentle on the eyes—calls to her child once more but he does not come. She calls again. *Zachary! Ryan! Chase!* Their eyes lock, mother and son; it's a standoff, quick draw, Ira mildly amused, until along comes a bunny. The nervous twitch. Who can deny a rabbit?

The child whoops an echo and runs.

BETH

Beth bleeds as she drives. As she drives she lists: After-Bite, age-defense cream. Behind her, the city is shrinking, the cotton canoe between her thighs expanding, absorbing more of her, of what might have been. Over the George Washington Bridge, the radio spits Foreigner, Taylor Swift. Her son can't stand product placements, apathetic disc jockeys, any interruption to song, whereas interruption is the air she breathes. *Welcome to motherhood.* She could kill herself, if only she could complete the thought.

"That's not how you spell come," Zach says as Quiet Riot flashes across the dial. Not yet five and already reading, which fills her with pride and annoyance. Zach is a preschool tyrant, his a reductive world of right and wrong. Not that he's above poop. That's his gray area. He poops to the beat. She tells him to close his eyes.

"I'll wake you when we're close."

"Promise?" Her son is always making her promise. Like Doug, they feel owed. *Can you at least promise to try?* Smile, buck up, brighten the long face with toner, with wrinkle repair, with smooth, supple lists: Zach's EpiPen, his favorite lovey, his spare lovey of his favorite lovey just in case.

"I promise."

The trip upstate is a last-minute decision. A two-month lease will last through August. After that is anyone's guess.

Two days have passed since the D&C about which she's told no one. (The procedure sounded like a mall shop for tweens. *I love your top. Did you get that at D&C?*) Not that Doug asked. She was at the clinic and then she was on the couch, but she was often on the couch, housewives uncorking their lives on reality TV.

Doug came home from work.

"What is there to eat?"

"Check the fridge."

"Are you in the mood for anything?"

Tweezers, Off!, sunscreen. Lists keep her grounded, a balloon on a string, tied to the task at hand. Lists stave off the dark beasts of thought that encircle and creep, sniffing out her susceptibility like scent. Her problem, she's been told, she's too much in her head. "Don't overthink things," as if thinking was like scorching herself on the stove, or worse, burning another. They've gone through it before: You're a mother. As if she'd forget. Restless? Make yourself useful. Volunteer! Beth is no joiner. Take time for yourself. Take up a hobby. Knit, decoupage. Get a haircut. Get some exercise. Get out of town. This is not what Doug meant but it was the opening she needed, so she took it, which is what brought her here: in the car, this June morning, barreling into the glare, visor down, destined for—what?

Summer. Beyond that, she does not know. All she knows is foot on the gas, hands on the wheel, eyes straight ahead, eyes checking mirrors, checking on Zach who's fucking the glass up and down until she engages the child lock.

"Are we there yet?"

"Nope."

Poopee. And so on. *Now?* Later. Zach has no concept of time. Beth counts the seconds. In the city she sets a timer for everything: hard-boiled eggs, morning coffee, she is punctual, she is late, she has missed it all, slacker. Where she's headed there will be nothing but time. Nothing to do. Her mind churns: did she unplug the toaster, shut all lights, twist the faucet hard enough to curb the endless drip? At home she keeps lists on her nightstand, smeared on receipts, she pours items through her mental centrifuge, falling asleep to their tumble and whir.

She has what she needs. She has cleaned herself out.

Beth is vacant. Hollow. Empty. Void.

Zach, at last, has conked out. There are songs. Blackbird, Beast of Burden. Books. *Harold and the Purple Crayon*. People make good lists. Better on paper than in high school: girls with matching head tilts, boys with cereal breath, which brings her back to B. Beth Barkman, your epidermis is showing. Hot shame followed by fury. Barking up all the wrong tress. Bent over like a bitch in heat.

With boys, the list is long. Eric Saltz on the living room sofa, the hump, dry; the sectional, plush beige; the coming, like biting into a Chewels. Jeremy Gibbons in his indoor hot tub, jets sputtering, boxer shorts ballooned like a flotation device. Mouths swollen red in the front seat of his Ford Falcon, chlorine trapped in her tights, Beth believed they were soul kissers, she actually believed, then, they could go on like that forever. Joel Fischer in his little brother's bed shaped like a Corvette. Everything cool, down there? Joel leaning back all proud until someone knocked fast and sloppy on the door and hollered out, cops. Amy waiting up for her, high on mushrooms, and how nice it was: to be sisters for a minute, and not sluts, just the two of them, before Ivy was born, watching *Fantasia* and spooning Cool Whip together, straight from the white, plastic tub. Martin Pith in his basement that smelled of piss and beer and splooge, Beth unable to count how many bodies there were, here a flannel, there a hole in the knee, mattresses damp as inner thighs that muzzy first time.

What else was there to do? This was late 80s suburbia. People shed virginity like winter coats.

Ryan Chase on a dare. Down a cup of canola or ask Beth Barkman to prom. Her social status on par with cooking oil, his exalted by athleticism and good looks, Ryan from Home Economics, on her doorstep with his girlish eyelashes and cummerbund, checkered Vans, no socks. Beth's fringe dress looked like a carwash but at least she was dressed and at least she was going, her father said, launching a clumsy baseball analogy to which Ryan assured him, *Dick*, amazing that Dick was still a viable nickname, not to worry, he'd look after his daughter. "I know you will, son," Dick slapped back, Beth's skin flaming from the flask she'd downed before descending, half-floating, half-dragging her sloshed body out to the street where the Winnebago was waiting with the starting lacrosse team, keg in the back, Solo cups tumbling down the aisles, surround sound pumping Thunder Road. The Garden Palace with its tablecloths and frosted balloons, Ryan smelling like eucalyptus, like muscle cream. He pulled her close and they swayed to that Clapton song about his child falling out the window. Later, in Atlantic City, Beth finally was part of it all, in a seashell motel swishing tequila like mouthwash. She could be whoever she wanted when she was wasted, and that night she did just fine as Ryan Chase's girl.

In the morning they were strangers. When Ryan rolled to the Pancake House she bolted. Beth ate funnel cake on the boardwalk and fingered the chokers of cowrie shells dangling from nails at open-air kiosks, took a casino bus home. At graduation, they shared a pat-slash-hug in gowns and Ryan said, "Looks like we made it," and she said, "Guess so," and he straightened her mortarboard tassel. "Well, take it easy." The cowrie stuck out from her throat like a jeweled hairless cunt. She never saw him again.

Add to the list: others, in college, over summers, dates before internet dating, when she'd stumble upon people, nameless, in a bar, waiting in line, waiting for a train, waiting for it all to begin; her life, buzzing, the stuff of sitcoms, young, single, messy-eyed in the city.

September 11th was a bright, clear morning.

Now it is only Ryan. In the face of Doug, in the face of her child. Why is it that those who are supposed to stay leave, and the people only passing through get lodged in it? If she owes anyone anything, she owes Ryan Chase, meaningless prom date, the sum total of her adult life. For all her escape fantasies, she's forever bound to his brother Doug.

The highway ends. It is replaced by routes, lettered iterations of the same road. 17 to 17 to 17. The digital voice connects and she does as she's told, gives herself over to GPS, to experts. Beth is good at following directions.

She is brilliant at creating distance. Measuring gaps in the rear view: this is Beth at her best. Ninety miles under her belt, a lifetime from New Jersey, where Doug wants her to be, if she doesn't sharp-end it into a ditch. Her palms prickle. A pickup rides her tail. The landscape shifts from rye grass to tire swings, asphalt to uncapped silos, stock barns caving onto themselves like mouths without teeth. Everything feels both worn and familiar. There must be a word for it, false nostalgia, phony déjà vu, believing you yearn for what maybe you don't, something German, maybe. Lanes narrow, turn to rock, then dirt. There is no shoulder. Wind pushes in. Her cup holder rattles to the rhythm of the unpaved road.

Beneath her is a thin blue pad, the kind used for housebreaking puppies; the nurse at the clinic gave it to her, along with a drawstring bag for personal items: wallet, phone, shoes.

The nurse said, "Do you have someone waiting for you?" In recovery Beth drank sweet tea in a paper gown with beds all in a row. It felt like a nunnery. Beth called a car service. But she's okay. Discomfort she can manage. She has Midol. She has the radio. Merciful quiet. She has her lists. One glimmering child, terrifically alive.

Two hours later, she is here.

The house at Murmur Lake looked better in pictures. A patchwork of wood, brick, and stone, as if the builder ran out of materials then cobbled together whatever scraps he could find. Walnut door framed in forsythia, circular driveway of pulverized bulk. After Beth's mother left, her father would send Beth to retrieve the daily paper from the edge of their driveway. The asphalt cut her feet.

Dick said, "Wear shoes if it hurts."

Beth abandons her sandals in the hall. Maybe all it will take is a house. Vaulted ceilings, high beams, the great room stretching out toward the waterfront drenched in sunlight thanks to an expanse of windows along the eastern wall. Wedged into a corner of exposed brick, the wood-burning stove, cast-iron pipe screwed to the ceiling, cold to the touch. Beside it sits a crosshatch of firewood; beside that, a stack of newspapers. Walls host a large abstract canvas splattered like the upshot of a paintball battle, a stag's head, tapestry of the American flag; the furniture, a curated hodgepodge of plaid and cherry. Embroidered throws, chenille rugs. A coven of kitchen witches straddle spoons on a bookshelf; dated enough to feel hip. Preserved. Like Betsy Ross's house. Before Zach was born, Beth accompanied a group of second-graders on a Philadelphia field trip. "You call this a museum?" they said as they wound the narrow stairs, Beth afraid the swell of her belly would catch and she'd be stuck, lodged and pregnant for eternity between floors. A game of hot potato broke out over Sammy Blau's ski hat until it flew over the ropes and settled on the bed Ross shared with her third husband, triggering the alarms. Beth quit teaching shortly after, her pay a fraction of childcare. For a while, she thought she'd do something, become someone else. She'd only been a sub, anyway. If she couldn't control a classroom, how could she possibly manage a child of her own?

For a second she almost forgets he's here: Zach outside playing. In Manhattan they may pay too much for their dismal box in the sky, for proximity to sights they never see, for a city that takes as much if not more than it gives. Murmur Lake makes no such demands. The grounds ripple out like a Gymboree parachute. Here comes her son, breathless and sweaty, "Mommy, I'm home," like they're an old couple, like they've been at it forever.

Zach sets to work exploring closets, popping drawers like they're flaps of his advent calendar, cheeks stamped with the joy of discovery—a pinecone, a lone hairpin. Dead moth. The Christmas countdown she can swallow, more than she can swallow Jesus. Doug loves Jesus and Jesus, Doug assures her, loves her, too, despite her love of smoked salmon and Sunday night Chinese. It's not like Beth has divine faith in anything, but atheism requires a devotion she lacks. Her life has been built by default. Stick with what you know. (See also: New Jersey.) For Doug, the impending move is a kind of homecoming. They've outgrown their walls, the apartment a kennel. Doug says, "Can you picture how tight it would feel with more kids?"

She'll call him. Hello, goodbye. Doug is the talker. They'd talked already. From the rest stop on the Thruway—yes, she had enough gas; yes, she'd bleed air from her tires to accommodate the gravel road; yes, she'd call when she got there. She'd call every damn day. His nature would be sweet if it weren't suffocating.

Only at Murmur Lake there is no cell service. No signal, roaming. Beth is completely cut off. She can do...whatever. Like the first time she babysat her half-sister Ivy, chugged a dusty pint of rum and enacted the hot parts from Cinemax with the neighbor next door. Dream big, kiddo. She is free as that.

The landline works fine but Doug does not answer. He is with the guys; it is Saturday so he's playing basketball in his wick-away sleeves, mesh shorts so long they look religious. Doug is as committed to his friends as he is to his fitness. A corporate coach, an esteemed team builder, he speaks in soundbites: "Loyalty is the currency of power."

At the beep she reports, "I'm in a dead zone."

The kitchen is a relic, yellow as ever, like one might style a baby's room, streaked in the colostrum of second-wave feminism. She unpacks Zach's special crackers, pasta alternatives. He fists a box, sucks a dry lentil noodle until it whistles. The overhead skylight is obstructed by leaves, dulling out the afternoon. Empty baskets of macramé dangle from the ceiling, awaiting ficus or jade, their spider plant, Wandering Jew.

The house needs to breathe, but otherwise, it's perfect. It is everything Beth wants. Dick took them all to a place like this as a child, before Ivy, before her stepmother Angie, when it was just her mom and dad and sister Amy, no more than a week or two, the days hot, nights cold, and laughter easy. The whole family bobbed in a rowboat. How could she possibly have guessed how fleeting it would be? They were happy, she knows it, her rainbow heart undies pinned to the line, where they flapped to the beat of Amy's taunting like ghosts in the wind.

The layout is an upturned chair, bedrooms housed in the legs off the living room, a loft reached by custom stairs that enchant Zach like a shiny, new toy. The master bedroom is dressed up like something pure, white and king-sized, eyelet curtains. She does not deserve it. A bathroom connects the other bedroom where twin mattresses lie topped with needlepoint pillows: SLEEP TIGHT and DON'T LET THE BEDBUGS BITE. She flops onto BEDBUGS.

When she awakes Zach is poking at her thigh with a stick. Her body curls inward by instinct. The second Beth sits she can feel it: she has bled through the bed.

"Mommy, I'm hungry."

The spot spreading beneath her: a dime, a nickel, a seeping fist. "Okay, love. I'll be right there."

TZVI

How he's ended up here, on everyone's speed dial, rolling bones in a converted barn, is both long and short. The short is it's a summer gig. He's got couches in Williamsburg to crash on through winter. The short is he's got cash but no urge to settle. The short is people find each other, and he's found a lost few, *apikorsim* all of them, and if they can stick together, that will make all the difference, if only for his mother, Chaya Bloch, of blessed memory.

No one told him but he knows. His mother was trying to leave. He knows this like he knows the warm smell of wool, a static heat that makes his nose itch. He was three when she died. How dare you tarnish your *mame*'s memory? his father says. But three is not too young to remember.

Herschel is his name, consecrated by his father, who hasn't called him in ages. A year after she drowned, his *tate* remarried. Had kids. Six on top of four but it's superstitious to count, hard to keep track. Of the original children, Tzvi is the middle. First one estranged, last one forgiven.

Still, his mother comes. A mist in the air. In the outline of strangers. He'll make eye contact and his lids will water. It's not like seeing a ghost. His *mame* is no *dybbuk* but an aura. He does not need to be high to feel it. To feel her. Makes no sense but then what does.

The long of it is more tangled and confusing. It trips him up. Tzvi still clings to the rituals into which he was born out of habit, as an insurance policy, to ground him in all that's unknown. He's been told not to question. There are blessings for everything. He unclips his phone from his belt, lays it on the table beside a sandwich of bills. Again he washes, right hand left hand right left right left, returns his two-handled cup beneath his bed, his beard trim, his *payos* twisted yet tucked, allowing him to keep one foot in each world. Like this, he passes.

Trouble has always followed. Maybe it began when his mother's immodest body was found, when his *tate* found a new bride, when his siblings arrived. When they all squeezed into one room, when they shared three to a bed. Maybe it was when Freya got burned. His younger sister, the baby, hot oil dissolving the skin on her limbs when a pot tipped over on Shabbos. In every act the hand of G-d, as if it weren't a case of no one paying attention. Who would marry her now? When one rabbi had enough of him, he bounced. From yeshiva to yeshiva. No one could touch him.

His first sin: empanadas. Then: fried shrimp. Tzvi removes his *kippah* for *treyf,* but the rest of the time he keeps his head covering on, even beneath a baseball hat, even when dealing, which is nothing more than a business transaction. He is servicing a need. Better him than a *shegetz.* Despite his crisis of faith, despite what happened to his mother, the Satmar community remains his connection to her. Three times a day he prays; that is, he moves his lips. Like the secular world with their lyrics to American Pie. The song comes on, and without thinking, you sing it.

IRA

Sleeping in—*at his age?* Ira is up with the birds.

Jewbirds, he's taken to calling them, with no small satisfaction. He aims his binoculars at the potato-hued flock congregating in his age-old oak. Sparrows, most likely, restless and chatty. Neurotic birds. Little yarmulkes on their birdy heads—beanies, the neighborhood boys called them, filching his velvet saucer by the tip and scooting down Cabrini Boulevard with their spoils in a whirl of dust and glass. Their squabbling pleases him, a lone grackle screeching above the fray. Fighting over territory, no doubt. What else does one fight about? Power. That's all there ever is.

Ira is a man of few tricks. Mornings go like this: wake, watch, coffee, shit. Shave whenever. Stay active, the marching order. Thirty push-ups. Tuna in a can. Sometimes he drives to the bookshop; he doesn't think about it, really. Time passes regardless. A family of deer grazes in the early fog, white tails stiff as the middle finger.

At some point, he'll go for a swim, pace the edges of his property down to the crossroads. He walks with a rainstick from the new age shop in town. It makes a tinkling sound that aggravates his prostate; every other second Ira has to whizz. He'll pick up bananas: potassium. More and more the city has been seeping out to the country. There's now a bagel bakery selling blueberry bagels, a luxury candy store. Yoga galore, some overpriced bondage trick called CrossFit.

He's tried yoga, winged his thighs but his knees cramped into stiff peaks. Who can articulate their tailbone from the hip bone? What was sacred about a sacrum? When the instructor said, "Embody the moment," he took it personally. Ira takes everything personally. In his life, he's embodied plenty of moments, thank you very much.

Solitude, like obedience, is overrated. Ira's no island. He drops in on whoever will humor him: Morgan Barnes, Stan Logan in Liberty. Noreen Murphy. Sometimes they crack a few cans. Occasionally, they get frisky. Noreen has a generous, open laugh, and a way of absorbing his moods like a quicker-picker-upper; he could get used to having her around. Leigh Cunningham at the general makes a hero with hot peppers to last him through lunch and dinner. While she wraps his foot-long, he leafs through the carousel of bumper stickers where the fracking debate plays out in bitter invective. A couple snaps a selfie with a jar of hand-crafted deer jerky, field goaling the tongue. Ira picks up watercolors and an art tablet from the crafts section, beards a paintbrush across his chin.

Once he had ambitions. He'd write a book—true crime of Murmur Lake. But he never got far. His efforts felt canned, melodramatic. Facts eluded him and he had no stomach for fiction. He did his diligence, cut the clippings. *"We're treating it as a suspicious death," Sheriff Jeff Johnson said.* No shit, Sherlock. A dead girl, a naked Hasidic woman—*Chaya Bloch, 26*—doesn't just spring forth from the well. Something happened, but what? Her body had been zipped off his property. *Bloch, a member of the Satmar Hasidic community, lived in Brooklyn but spent summers in Monticello, some 33 miles from where she was found.* No sect was more closed-off than the Satmars. He was no private eye. When life gives lemons, sure, but wasn't it wrong to lemonade someone else's tragedy?

Briefly, he'd considered a juicy tell-all of *Man's World* magazine, where he'd worked for 25 years, where staffers fancied themselves stars and behaved accordingly, with outrageous tabs at the Chateau Marmont. He's never even been to the Marmont. Editors lived a vicarious life. *Man's World* was parasitic, but it was all he knew. Parasitic symbiosis: I will eat you as you fuck me, the buzz of late capitalism. But no one read anything anymore. *Man's*

World closed last year to little fanfare. Instead he jots bits, sketches when words fail him, writes letters to his daughters. *Dear Heather. Dear Hillary.* Occasionally, he mails them. Receives nothing in return. He waits for inspiration to strike. A half-baked poem. An off-color joke. Ira dabbles. The day passes. Days pass. Years. Almost thirteen.

When he dings through Sullivan Sales, Noreen does not look up. Phone to her ear, pen in her lip, puppy mug stuffed with scissors. Her ridge of bangs softens her face though he's got a good twenty on her. She ought to sit up straight. The wood paneling puckers around the cooling unit. A watermark on the ceiling is shaped like a giant phallus. The entire world was cast in genital signifiers, his daughter Heather said one Thanksgiving, stabbing the patriarchy as yams slid a sweet mash down his throat. Here a cock, there some balls, a graceful cunt in bloom. Ira hadn't a clue what she'd meant by the hegemony of heterosexism and he wasn't about to ask. His own college yearbook editor hid a chesty centerfold, Jayne Mansfield type, in their pages as a prank and later became an award-winning cartoonist. *Man's World* profiled the guy in 1988, Ira commissioned it, but the subject—his classmate! Class of '69!—had no recollection of him, compounding Ira's shame: how painfully forgettable he was.

He helps himself to a chair. Reenie's nostrils flare like freshwater gills as she yammers on. He unwraps a mint and flips through the binder. Slim pickings: a mobile home near Roscoe, a 600-acre summer camp, a log cabin in need of a septic system, so he moves on to her mug, drumming a pair of highlighters against the edge of her desk. When it comes to attention, he's like a toddler—*the world does not revolve around you.* Viv again.

"How about it, kid?" He rolls out the ventriloquist number on her stapler. "Let's blow this joint. Are you a cake or pie person?"

Over the receiver, Noreen mouths: *I'm working.*

"We could catch a minor league game, a movie matinee. Senior passes come with free popcorn *and* soda."

She doesn't answer. He takes the hint. Pushed to the outskirts of another life, no hard feelings, but he doesn't want to go home, not yet, when there are still so many hours ahead, so he pops upstairs to her apartment where sure enough, Reenie's kid Paige—not much of a kid anymore—is standing there in the kitchen nook without pants, pudding thighs, Miami Dolphins tee. Cabinets flung wide like they might take flight. She pours him coffee.

"That's what I call service."

"I'm not awake. Don't fucking talk to me."

There's a family resemblance, but something not quite formed about her, like maybe it's congenital. Paige looks like the koalas from the Bronx zoo, heavy-lidded, a vanishing chin.

"Why the hell are you smiling?"

"You remind me of someone."

His daughters loved the zoo until they hated it, until they grew wise to its cruelty. *Why would you subject us to this, Daddy?* World's a cruel place, kids. Paige marches off. Door slams. The apartment shakes. A calendar of aphorisms swings from a nail. Ira tears a pleat of sugar packets into his mug. Left alone, he tackles the dishes, scraping oatmeal with his thumb. The single traffic light blinks from red to green, but the thoroughfare remains silent. You could bowl though it. There is nobody, no one, a stray cat, an all-terrain Ford.

On TV a panel of women dish celebrity weddings, offer the studio audience a year's supply of protein bars. At Murmur Lake Ira doesn't have television, not out of principle but willpower. Everything sucks him in, spots for dish soap and hair replacement. Whatever is put in front of him he can't look away.

"Party's over, pops." Paige's boyfriend comes out, skinny, littered in Bugs Bunny tattoos like some sad grab at childhood that almost chokes Ira up.

Back home, another day fades across the meadow, sun slipping behind the mountain wall, which isn't true, of course, Copernicus, Galileo, the sun stubborn and fixed as Ira himself; the earth flirting around it in reassuring repeats. His tenant's car is there, dinky as a Monopoly pawn. Yesterday he dozed on a bed of clover hoping for a peek, but she never materialized, which filled him with fresh yearning, like water rising into a toilet bowl.

Initially, Viv thought he was kidding. They'd been in their East Side apartment putting out bagels for the upstairs neighbors when he dropped the bomb. Weeks later and still, the death cloud spread north from downtown. Ira felt like a goose being primed for slaughter only it was not grain but ash and soot on which he was choking. He could not sleep, could not eat. He could not endure the machinations of brunch with the Glicks in 6F. The towers had collapsed; New York was burning, and he, Ira Lecher, was dying.

"I should be so lucky."

"This isn't a joke."

"Shall we order up a CT? Scan for self-pity on your MRI?" On a fish-shaped platter Viv plated the salmon, oily and translucent. Lox was the color of Fort Lauderdale. Foreskin at $30 a pound, he'd interject around the buffet at ritual circumcisions; to which Viv would remind him there's a difference between bad and funny.

"Viv, I'm a goner."

"Why am I not surprised?" Viv pushed a poppyseed through the slicer. "Company's coming, but you'd rather go off the deep end than make yourself useful."

Bagels passed through the guillotine. At work, a thirty-year-old named Redmond was the new top dog. Redmond called everyone "bro," with a shoulder squeeze for bonus condescension. Last week, Ira got the squeeze in the elevator. The kiss of death.

Why stick around for the inevitable? Ira could no longer feign interest in peaked lapels and custom brogues, could no longer convince himself *Man's World* sold anything that made men better. Perhaps if he left, his daughters would talk to him again. So he quit. Stopped shaving. Numbed himself with talking heads on TV, images on perpetual loop, as if the repetition might inure him to the fact that these were not shadows but loved ones spiraling to the ground, lost for eternity, recovered without rescue. Like images from concentration camps, gaunt faces of Buchenwald: exposure became desensitizing. Everyone knew someone or had someone or told a story. Yet, still people dug; still people searched, there were tapestries everywhere, tied to chain link, bled out by rain, pleas for information, prayers of hope, as nights turned to days and more awful nights of waiting and digging, the black hole smoldering, an infinite pit.

"What are we doing? For what?" They'd done this life; done it to expectation, more or less. Went to school and work and married and cheated and had two kids. Sometimes, he and Viv even loved each other. But those days were over. Hillary and Heather left for college, for field studies and co-ed naked parties. He was demonized in dorm rooms like all the other fathers. The girls carried cell phones and his credit card.

"Not we, *you*."

"Are you happy?"

"You expect too much." Viv picked up seeds with the pad of her finger. Upstairs in 6F the Glicks plodded on parquet floors. Ira once asked them to remove their shoes. "Over my dead body," Harry Glick said.

Downstairs, the Lecher kitchen screamed white in track lighting. A bowl of overripe figs leaked on the counter. Viv kept her back to him, her jet-black hair cropped at the neck, her Navajo sweater hanging from her like something made for a horse.

"Ira, you're delusional. You're deluding yourself." She popped a tub of cream cheese and stuck a knife in it, arranged an

Olympics logo in sliced tomato and onion.

"Life isn't a fairy tale." She spritzed her succulent. "It's dead up there. Almost winter. You're going to die."

"We're all going to die. It's dead here. I brush my teeth and spit soot. There I actually might live a little."

Ira wound his arms around her waist, nuzzled his cheek into her neck. "Come, try with me."

"Do I look like *Little House on the Prairie*?" Viv slipped from him. Flipped the lid off the coffee maker and added water. The machine sprang to life. Gurgle, belch, hiss.

"What will you do?"

"It's not about doing. It's about being."

"Christ."

They already led separate lives. Viv converted the girls' bedroom into a home office. Ira woke before dawn to hit the pool, tiptoeing around like an intruder. If pressed, they'd agree: they were stuck in roles not meant for them. Leave marriage to other people. Marriage was a garment from the bargain bin, marked "as is," the collar too tight, the armholes baggy. Nothing fit.

Their apartment had been paid up. The Second Avenue subway would cut through their building sooner or later.

"Ira, will you ever grow up?"

What he had not anticipated: all that he'd miss. Neckties and martini lunches, office girls with their message sheets in curvaceous script, pitches over the transom, skincare samples of bergamot and sandalwood. Those first months of isolation he beat his chest in atonement. *What have I done?* There was a term for his suffering—skin hunger, he'd read—and Ira Lecher was starving. Meanwhile, Viv moved on with swift detachment. In this way she was like his own mother, Ruth, who'd evacuated every last pumice stone and pair of suspenders from their apartment on 183rd Street before Ira's father's body turned cold, leaving a closet of wire hangers. Oh, Ira. His mother removed her hat, tucked the ends of her sash into her coat pockets. What is stuff? Stuff is only more to carry, more to store, more to keep track of, more to lose.

Viv's lotions and calendars and grooming scissors and diet sugar cubes and felt-tip pens: that's what Ira missed most. Objects promised return, radiated a collateral heat, they warmed him right up, like the hot water bottle his mother would tuck at the foot of his bed. Meanwhile, his daughters continued to rebuff him.

"Get a lovey," Viv said when he complained.

How long must he wait for a glimpse of the gal? Another day gone, Ira retreats to his cabin, assuming his post on the front porch, as darkness cloaks the sky, as clouds meld into one insufferable cloud, each tip of his rocker a metronomic beat, and—listen, wait, there is only ever waiting.

BETH

A change of scenery can't change everything: It's still her life. Beth was never cool enough to entertain any option beyond a prefab path. Parenthood had been sold to her like the wedding industry—gussied in ribbons and bows, to disguise the ugly truth: tedium was a killer. Of all the crap found in books: how to swaddle, how to soothe, how to parse the rainbow of poo, manage anaphylaxis, assuage a child's fear, not one mentioned the monotony. The ordinariness. Or the erasure.

Her older sister Amy eats it up, uses parent as a verb, guzzles the fizzy pop of ballet recitals and bounce houses. The most important thing you'll ever do. Beth just aborted her most important thing.

As for regret—there are only days.

She and Zach secure wipes to their feet and gloss the floors as if they're skating; buy glassware from the side of the road, $8 coke bottles because vintage. They snatch up a life sentence of potpourri, a compost bin, a mausoleum of Tupperware, wheel it out behind the house where it's sitting ominous and ignored, like climate change. Gather pamphlets on rafting, blueberry picking, a Biblical zoo. Beth tries to make french fries but gashes her finger on the mandolin. The blood is delayed, like a baby's cry: nothing, nothing, then a gush. When she's staunched the wound and finished frying Zach says, "They're not the same."

Belly down, they lie on the dock, Beth fighting the urge to fall in. Zach would follow, then what. It's too chancy. She doesn't have enough faith in herself to rescue him.

"What do you see, Zee?"

Fish and stones. Stones and fish. A ladybug on his hand.

"Make a wish," she says and he blows.

At night, she can't sleep. Gone is the buzzy comfort of late night taxis, drunken voices laddering up from the street. In the dark all she hears is

Lighten up

Don't be so hard on yourself

Don't sweat the small stuff

Why must you make everything a big deal?

Who do you think you are?

Your problem is

You should be grateful

You think you're the only one

Bitch

Once a mother always a mother

Quiet brings a new hell. The fridge whirs, floor creaks, the ceiling arranged in post and beam, a tightrope she'd have walked had she actually dated and not merely fucked that contortionist in college who joined the circus dressed in her favorite leotard. She rolls onto her stomach, seesaws her hips, grinding her sheets with the verve of a teenage boy, as if she might fuck her way out of another misery, as if that's ever worked. She's a mother who wants to be fucked by a stranger. Her wants are not allowed. Her son is beside her. In the haze she traces the bow of Zach's lips, a symmetrical pink dip, like Ryan's. Sometimes, it takes her breath away how much he looks like Ryan.

Why had she shown up at Ryan's memorial? Maybe she wanted to feel outside of herself. To feel, period. The scale of public terror afforded her a certain thrill where she could partake in the collective mourning without risking herself. Doug saw her and believed his brother had loved her, believed she was more than the booby prize of a dumb dare. He looked at her like she was worth keeping, so she let herself be kept.

How easily her life—*Ryan's life!*—might have gone another way. It was miraculous. Well, it was physics. In school she never paid attention to the laws of the universe, random selection, cell biology, how insignificant we all are. Everything born from an irreparable shattering. One prom night and boom: her son's damp head on the pillow, slick as a newly hatched bird.

That September morning she sat glued to the television. The more she watched the realer it became and the more unreal it felt, horror washing over her, but a voyeuristic, disassociated horror. She ate Cheerios by the fistful only it was not her fist, not her mouth tongue throat, ate the whole box, the wheat paste muffling sound. Did Ryan have time to be afraid? She tries to conjure his smell, the contours of his body (athletic, hairless, pancake brown) but bodies run together. What, then, is memory? Before Zach, love was a word reserved for songs and movies. She considered herself impervious, incapable, like that part of her, the loving part, the lovable part, was missing or stunted or had suffered frostbite, blunting her nerves.

She curls herself around Zach, his skin tender and thin as an animal's underbelly. Exhilarating, to watch a person sleeping, at their most vulnerable. It gives her a sick sort of power. Watching now touching and breathing him in, there's no greater clarity. What she feels is primal: love, driven by hunger and need.

She deals his body a tight squeeze. "Morning, starshine."

Zach blinks. Fishbowls. Ryan, Ryan.

"Mommy." His arms reach for her. "I'm awaked."

Today is a wash. The sky opens, angry sheets, and Zach clambers onto her reading *This one has a little star. This one has a little car* until her thighs fall asleep. Rain scolds the roof. *You whore*, it beats, scaling higher, lighter, becoming tinny, like laughter, spattering against metal, dropping softly into the muck. The principal from her last job cornered her against his desk before firing her, which was almost laughable, how expendable she was, how scripted everything is, sitting and snuggling, the celibate sound of rain.

"No sleeping on the job!" A pair of plastic people creeps up her thigh, one in a hard hat, the other with snap-on hair. "Want the good guy or the bad guy?"

"Whichever," Beth says.

After the rain, a rainbow.

"Fake," Zach says gravely, "illusion," and her heart sinks. He's not yet in kindergarten.

"How do you know?"

"Everyone knows. It's the light playing tricks."

"Well, it's real to me. And do you see that, a double—that's practically magic." She stands in the window, but he's already ceded his interest to toileting, a new independence. She calls after him, "Do you know how lucky we are?"

"Can we com-pose now?" He returns, shorts bunched at his ankles.

The compost bin is where they left it, next to the cooling system, beneath her bedroom window like a peeping Tom. Beth clips the instruction booklet and Zach takes it, sounding out microbe, optimal, aeration. When her mom died, they didn't wait for nature to take course but hastened the deal, from dust to dust, scattering her remains along the shoulder of Route 66 by Flagstaff, russet and ash turning to paste on Beth's fingers, the occasional chip of bone.

The demonstration at Hand's Hardware had won Zach over. "We eat greens bred on yesterday's garbage," an employee in a tangerine polo explained. "Nothing truly dies."

"It all turns to poop!"

"Imagine a future without landfills."

Imagine a *future*. As a child, Beth never pictured herself grown. All she pictured was a black hole, felt pad slapped to the wall, a cartoon portal through which a chased mouse escaped. To where? She did not know. Maybe this was it, there was no other side.

But the kit was on sale.

"Where does our garbage go?"

"Staten Island."

"Fresh Kills is dead. They killed Fresh Kills."

How he picks up this information. He's a magnet to lead shavings, like there's a little man inside that body. Fresh Kills reopened after 9/11. Maybe Uncle Ryan is at Fresh Kills.

"Prepare the blood meal," Zach commands, flying off in an imaginary cape for sticks and leaves, chanting *Be smart! Do your part!* She bridges her eyes but it's unclear if that's a deer or spire of glare or her landlord cresting the hill. Shapes can be deceiving. The compost bin resembles a bingo wheel. She grabs the crank and it's a game show feeling.

"Round and round she goes. Where she'll stop, nobody knows."

"You're doing it wrong. Here."

A robin's egg, smooth and blue, cracked with a hairline fracture.

"Where did you get this?"

"I got it." She shakes the shell to her ear but it's a dud.

Tonight there's no moon, only stars. They've been to the planetarium, but this is better, this is great, wide, swallow-you-whole sky. Lying on the grass Beth feels the earth tilt and pull.

Gravity, Zach reminds her, his head warming her center as it rises and falls with her breath. She knows the Big Dipper. He knows Cassiopeia.

"A shooting star!"

"That's an airplane."

Eventually, it's bed, bath time. The water chokes in brown bursts from the well, like something blocked, out of practice, before turning clear. The clawfoot is built like a trough. In New Jersey they'll have two bathrooms, plus a downstairs powder. Doug has the place picked out, nine miles from their high school on Lancet Lane, a cul de sac designated for new construction.

Stock model named Chestnut Barns. Doug said she could customize the countertops and molding.

He said this like she should be excited about her choices. She goes to lift Zach out of his clothes.

"I can do it."

"Of course you can."

Beth can parade around in her underwear, drink straight from the carton. If she wants to pig out on the couch she can pig out on the couch. She can—she chews a thumbnail. She'd heard about a woman knitting a sweater from her vagina. Yeah, nope. Not even in college, when she pierced her clit and inked a shaky poke and stick on her thigh, a smiley face of all things.

She rubs the mirror with the heel of her hand. Sometimes people stopped her on the street thinking she was someone else. She has that look. When she is unhappy she looks like a different person. She forgets what happy looks like. She goes in close, flattening her nose to the glass until her vision blurs. She is neither pretty nor ugly. She is another brown-haired girl from New Jersey. Let this be her great rebellion: they'll do whatever they want, and Zach will love it, Zach will love her.

Beth shuts the tap, swishes around a puck of soap. She lowers herself onto the toilet seat, rolls her maxi like a bale of hay. She's almost done bleeding. In the bath her son paddles, his hair matted to one side, his body so pale it is almost blue. Above him, a skylight frames the night.

"If space is black why isn't the sky? Will the sun burn out like a bulb? Will the planet get so full it explodes? Where will the animals go? Why are you so hurt down there?"

Beth yanks up her shorts.

"Does the water make you old?" Zach holds up his fingers.

"Out." Terrycloth flaps. "Raisin brain. Time's up."

At the Garden of Earthly Delights, Beth flips a sack of organic dairy-free chocolate morsels into her cart.

"YOLO," she says. "Let's really go to hell."

Alone, she'd go for a bucket of hot wings and a clamshell of pierogis, but she is never alone, and Zach's allergies have robbed her of pleasure, though he seems unbothered by his diet of rice cakes and squeaky artificial cheese. He wears alligator rain boots independent of the weather. He's at the age of *why*, and Beth is short on answers. Fifteen bucks for a pound of cricket flour? Slap the word *sucker* on her face, but what Zach doesn't know won't kill him. If she can get over the insect factor, the horrendous rip-off, she'll frost him a goddamn cricket cake.

What else is there to do? They've rumbled over bridges connecting the dots from town to town, but nothing connects. Six miles can take an hour. They've lost their way without realizing it. Everything looks the same. The country is like another country. Confederate flags and dumpster porches and boarded-up barns. They've maxed out on *CandyLand*, *Hungry Hippo*. She's shit out of ideas.

While Beth unpacks, Zach plays checkout, designing a make-believe conveyor belt and gnawing dried mango large as a pig's ear. He cages her feet in avocado netting.

Beth claps, "Nap time."

Though he is old for naps, she's not ready for him to outgrow them. As he talks himself to sleep, she rinses vegetables, carrots the size of walking sticks, pitches everything into the pot. Without a recipe Beth will improvise, let impulse steer her, the free-spirited way she assumes people do things out here, but when she goes to fire up the stove the burner just clicks and clicks.

Ira Lecher's door is wide open.

"Excuse me?" Beth knocks. Her landlord's place is a bunk, as if it'd been airlifted from a previously charmed life at a performing arts camp and plunked down between the shadows of hickory and pine. Built on stilts, his cottage tilts to the left. Flecks of green paint the size of Texas chip off the side.

"Anyone home?" She's winded, having run. Inside she hears water, the hiss of pipes.

A cough, a creak, the plodding of feet, the slow whine of Neil Young—*there is a town in North Ontario*—the abrupt scratch of a needle.

"I can come back."

"You are here now."

"Sorry to disturb."

"I'm not disturbed. Are you disturbed?"

His lumbering figure emerges from the dim cabin light. At six feet, despite a hunched posture, he swings his hands, hairy thumbs. There is something strikingly familiar about him, tired yet twinkly, as if he's a washed-up actor, late-era Nick Nolte or relative on her father's side nobody talks about anymore. It's destabilizing. He's got the face of that writer, the one who wrote about fornicating a steak (raw hamburger? liver?) that circulated dogeared in college. She's seen him—in town, on that poster outside the library, featured local comedian at the annual County Fair, his headshot shining like cheap metal, penetrating stare, fingers threaded through the loops of his Western buckle. The posters must be a decade old. Now he's wearing a faded blue City College T-shirt with khakis, the adventure kind you can unzip for versatility, but everything is twisted, stuck to him, wet. A gray ponytail drips down his back. The welcome packet on her kitchen table contained a map, hand-drawn to his X-marked hut, accompanied by a childlike scrawl, all caps: NEED ANYTHING CALL.

"May I borrow a match?"

"Never borrow, always take." He blinks like an animal accustomed to life underground.

"The pilot light. I'm in the middle of...my son's napping–"

Heat spatters her neck. She can't remember if she's brushed her teeth. She hasn't even unpacked her bras. When she speaks, her voice goes up, as if she's not sure who she is.

"I'm making soup."

"I love soup."

His eyes roam her calf stubble, settle on her pajamas doubling as outerwear.

"My son–"

"Right." He looks like he might say something else. He could be her father's age. Not that Dick could live like this, without his loafers and eleven o'clock news. Age has made her father paranoid. He's acquired a handgun, Angie confided. His politics are no longer what they once were.

Ira dips inside, then down they go, three steps and into the woods. She trails behind him through the thick of evergreen and rock, into the clearing of Queen Anne's lace, the Neversink rushing into the valley below.

"You hear that heaven?" Ira closes his eyes. Beth paws a clump of gorse then remorsefully tries to put the little flowers back on the bush.

"Getting along?"

"Great."

"Hot water?"

"Plenty."

"Found the extra comforters?"

"It's not cold."

"So why aren't you sleeping?"

"*What?*" She fumbles her keys.

He is standing so close she can feel the expanse of his chest, camel-hued trousers hiked up the crotch to carve out the humps of his balls. As she worries the door, his shirt brushes her elbow and it's soft, the kind of broken-in cotton that says, *Come. Rest. Dream.*

"Welcome to the boondocks. No one's dropping by except maybe a skunk or raccoon, but then they don't tend to use the front door."

"That's reassuring."

"Middle of nowhere, kid. No one locks anything."

Her cheeks burn. "Habit. Zach—my son—is sleeping."

"You know what they say about habits."

She doesn't prompt him and he doesn't lob a punch line. He makes for the kitchen. Lifts the cage off the burner, hits the gas.

"Poof. You are lit."

PAIGE

You better be dead Paige texts but doesn't send. Tommy is late again. Tommy is on Tommy time. Paige is pissed, not needy. She checks her watch, looping the ambulance circle, as if each lap might bring him closer. Her throat's an ash can, but if she goes back in for another Cherry Coke she might miss him, and then what. Tommy won't stick around. She lights one to the next, wishing she had a sweatshirt, wishing for a rocket to the moon but she has only her hospital pinafore balled inside a limp string sack. She loosens the knot in her shirt that shows her belly. Tommy likes it. Sometimes Tommy puts his tongue there. She has a skinny girl's stomach, dough that won't rise, punctuated with an opalescent stud.

Tommy is her ride. She's not about to call her mother. Her mom wants to be wanted and Paige will not grant her the satisfaction. Noreen has told her never to count on a man. Men are good for one thing, if that. Noreen has urged Paige to make something for herself, but not too much. Get a head and people will cut off your feet. By people, Noreen means Noreen. She has conditions. Be sharp. Finish school, provided school's no farther than Scranton. *You're all I've got, pigeon. How would you feel?* For starters, Paige wouldn't be dumb enough to have a kid at nineteen. But she's not sticking around. People in Neversink only like you when you're down. Take Tommy. He feels good when Paige is bad, as if that might offset his shortcomings.

Next to Tommy, Paige is a goddamn prodigy. She wants to shake him like a Magic 8-Ball. Will you ever get it together? *Reply hazy, try again.* Paige has learned to hide away parts of herself: clever parts, ambitious parts, any sparky, formidable part, so that no one can take away who she really is, what she might become.

Soon as Tommy Potts shows his stupid face, she'll start. Her pockets are full, the night hungry.

The emergency lane is empty. County isn't equipped to handle more than run-of-the-mill hunting wounds, rabies, opiate codes. Anything serious gets sent up to Binghamton; tourist trauma is airlifted to NYU.

It's the chronic care unit that has Paige coming back. Twice a week she moonlights at Sullivan County Community Hospital. SCCH. Pronounced *Suck*. What began as 120 hours of court-ordered community service for defacement of school property has become the most stable part of her life, the one thing she anticipates after work. Maybe she never had living grandparents, but Mrs. Schroeder and Mr. Riley make decent understudies, as does Bailey Smith, whose diabetes has turned necrotic. Their eyes light up at the sight of her stripes. She reads to them: *To Kill A Mockingbird*, *Great Expectations*, *The Good Earth*. Less than minimum wage, but Paige would fluff pillows and dump bedpans for free. It's an awful thing to be sick, to be old and dying, trapped in a body that's betrayed you. Once she made the mistake of trying to explain this to Tommy, but he was in a bad way at the time, having spent a jittery, uncoordinated afternoon removing a family of possums from Mrs. Cunningham's crawlspace, so she gave up, fished in her bag to give him something, then rocked him to her chest until he stilled.

If she can restore some shred of dignity to Lance O'Brien, who'd been transferred to hospice in a diaper the size of a pontoon, then it's worth it. She doesn't fear death. Once she gets to Tampa she'll do more end-of-life care, perhaps go to nursing school when she's not at the mermaid lagoon. She's read all about it. Tank mermaids are a dying art, but there's no shortage of old people in Florida. No shortage of housing, either, the surplus keeping down the cost of rent.

In Florida she'll work and work—*and swim!*—and dream. The shitty thing is, life can eat away at you even when you're young and healthy.

Kole Troller stole her childhood because he could. He was the father/brother/uncle she never had. *Didn't she love him back? Didn't she want to sit on his lap?* Her mom did not notice. Her mom chose not to notice. Kole bought Paige a Beanie Baby stitched to a heart that said YOU'RE MINE. She lit it on fire. The plaything was replaceable. You could buy them at the pharmacy. Soon Paige had a shit ton of Beanie Babies, from calico cats to purple pigs. Each one Kole offered up like a lock of his hair. She took them like they were her purpose. You don't look a gift horse in the mouth. What you do is stuff the synthetic plush against your jaw, wet fur on tongue, teeth grinding plastic pellets until it's over.

At 7:25 Tommy pulls up. His face is wrecked but the suck of cheekbones and the ice of his eyes are sexy. He gets first dibs. Amazing what she can take when no one is looking. Keys to the narcotics box right off the charge nurse. Like other hospital systems, SCCH is dedicated to pain management. Patients are asked to scale their discomfort. Staff can't let them creep above a three. Paige reaps the benefits, the Vicodin, which Tommy crushes with his fist, snorts off Paige's hand. They park near the river and push back their seats. Paige runs her fingers along the mats of his sideburns. After, he stows a bag in the glove and they slide down the slope to the boulders that forge a cliff. The light is falling, golden cords off the Delaware, the river narrow but deep, good for jumping, but they are not here to jump. Or fish. They are here for real drugs.

Tommy says it like that. Real. As if everything else is bogus. People live in sleeping bags on the rocks, still warm from the afternoon, smooth as the years that have shaped them. Tommy knocks them with his boots until they stir, their faces turned like thistle bending toward remnants of the sun. It's Richie and Lara, Janelle. Tommy's tweaked out cousin Silko.

"What do you want?" Richie asks.

Tommy gives the nod, and Paige crouches, her skin popping out of her jeans like a biscuit can. Janelle—her eyelashes now burnt to ant-like bits—had been in her homeroom.

"The air feels so silky," Lara says. Hunched in their bags, noses punched red, they look like lamprey eels. *What could they possibly feel?* Tommy takes her stash and barters. She has warned him street stuff is garbage but he doesn't care. Purity is relative.

No matter how many times she's seen it, she dreads this part. Paige has rules. She'll snort anything once. No needles. Tonight when Tommy takes out the tourniquet, she winces.

Paige has watched too many YouTube videos. Her life has begun to resemble one long video. Every other minute there is another article or obit. Jenna Rose loved dogs, volunteered at the humane society; Willard Pike was a big-hearted older brother. In winter, they occupy the deserted hotels until they are busted, then return to this spot along the river. Addicts are like Whack-A-Mole. Like roadkill on Route 191, stricken and convulsing. She never goes anywhere without Narcan.

"Do you mind?" Tommy asks. His arms are a blundered mess and she's a practiced phlebotomist. She can perk up the weakest vein. Her stomach flips as she releases the dope into his bloodstream, filling him up, and watches for his look of drift. In her lap he's at peace, and she gets it, she has brought him here, to this distant place. Where there is no anger, only calm. The river glints in the summer light. These are the stolen hours: the sun bursting in a wild bouquet of color. Purple, orange, electric pink. She coils the belt and eases out from behind him, making sure before she's gone he's propped up good and steady.

TZVI

Wednesday night is men's night at the Bowl-A-Rama. The place is alive, chewy with heat, funk ripe as a basement minyan. There is no need for a *mechitza*, for separate lanes. He scans the room. For a certain energy. A side glance. On Wednesdays, no women are allowed.

When he came of age, he endured the usual meetings, but from the start it was a reluctant effort to arrange a *shidduch*. Tzvi was no scholar. There were marks against him. He was thrown the old maids, the cross-eyed or lame, the ignominiously divorced. He sat at one kosher cafe or another, ordered the requisite sodas, spoke little to his matches.

It's not that he was actively thinking of men. Of the debasement of mind and confusion of body, the contradiction between what he'd been taught and what he'd learned, how he felt with himself in the dark. What he was thinking was anywhere but here. Across the sticky table. Beneath the harsh fluorescence. He sat. His shoulders hung. Sometimes, a waiter wedged a matchbook beneath an uneven leg.

There was one candidate with an elbow clipped to her side like a broken wing. With burn grafts, just like his sister. She barely met his eyes. What a thing, to be groomed for a life of housewifery. He wanted to reach out, squeeze her raw, pink hand. Whisper, as no one had whispered to his mother: *go, run, live.*

As he moves through the crowd white shirts brush against him so wet with sweat he can see their four-cornered under-garments. On every man: an obligation. He fingers a ball he has no intention of bowling.

That girl with the new skin growing over her dead skin? He married her.

NOREEN

Like any good story, it starts with obsession.

When Noreen is seventeen Mark Troller is God's gift. She's in class with his younger brother, Kole, and they get on the way you do with someone you've known since kindergarten, who's stood beside you on the risers for choral renditions of Silent Night. Mark is the heartthrob, dark and trim, while Kole is bread white and ginger. There's an intensity to Mark, like he might strangle or swallow you. He reminds Noreen of that movie star, brooding and remote, without even trying; the cool one, what's his name.

Mark runs Bait, Tackle & Fly down County Road, the fishing outpost built by Mark Sr., who understands that his son's heart belongs in a boat, belongs just about anywhere other than mowing checkerboard rows of drab and light. There's an unearthly quality to Mark that makes him ill-fit for land. People, too, though people never tire of looking at him.

Only Murmur Lake is too small for serious fishing, and the store brings a slew of bad luck: the silo fire, his father's heart disease, his mother's stroke. Mark holes up in his lean-to all summer long. Girls come in swinging their fathers' tackle boxes, wrists tucked into sleeves. The place smells like fish guts but it could be roses for how they linger. Men come with coolers for ice, the line trailing out the door. Noreen says, "Fill me up," worrying a pimple as Mark counts out nightcrawlers for Patrick. Feather lures look like butterflies. Girls slip him phone numbers on bubblegum jackets while he makes change at the register, cracks coins, quarters tinkling into trays.

The morning the body is drawn from Murmur Lake, the town of Neversink springs to life. Nothing ever happens here until something does. News like this makes people forget their own problems, and people want to forget, need to forget, so the mystery around it glows large and bright as an orb. Even Pat and his buddies get in on it, their talk graphic and gruesome, of bloat and rigor mortis, what it must feel like to fuck a cold, flayed fish.

Noreen wants to see for herself. She pitches Pat's three-speed and ducks beneath the tape where she finds Kole crouching in the mud, pinching baby frogs between his thumb and forefinger, skipping them across the water like stones.

"Who did it?"

"Ask them." Kole flicks his chin. "They think they know everything."

Summer people. On the other side, the dock bobs with float tubes and life vests. A woman carries drinks out to reporters. It looks like some kind of garden party except for a pair of girls hunched like vultures, shivering in terrycloth robes.

Noreen scoops a frog, strokes its gold-flecked skin.

"Shit stirrers. Stirrers of shit, yet no one comes over to ask us, to talk to me about what we did or didn't see, we ain't important enough."

"Why, what are they saying?"

"That's besides the point."

Kole opens his fist to the amphibious mash of the animal he's squeezed to death, popped like a water balloon; he wipes the guts on his jeans. All day she burns for Mark. The hours are endless. If she sees him she'll feel safe; if she gets close enough, she'll know the truth. She waits for the lake to be dredged to avail itself of secrets, but it reveals only leech and freshwater eel. Men with megaphones and flak jackets throw their weight around hounding neighbors, fouling the investigation. Kole starts drinking. Maybe she gives him false hope, but hope of any kind is better than none. Maybe love can only be won by proxy.

Nothing turns up.

"Too bad."

"Bad for who?" Kole says.

Noreen doesn't care about the drowning victim. Whoever she was, she didn't belong here, and besides, can't help anyone once they've left the living. Murmur is a private pond, not a public swimming hole. What was a summer person from one of those strange, closed-off, long-skirted communities doing so far from home? And where were her godforsaken clothes?

As facts frizzle, rumors churn. Wouldn't Noreen have noticed someone like that hanging around Bait, Tackle & Fly? Noreen used to station herself outside, track comings and goings, but the shop's closed now, the soda machine dark, the waste bin out front knocked on its side and rolling, thunder in the wind.

That fall, fur hats march down Main to the courthouse, white socks and black pants, coattails flying behind them like forked tongues. Police swarm both sides of the property. When they bring Mark into the station, Noreen feels the sirens speed through her heart. Kole can't get enough of the drama. Handcuffs! Red lights! How his brother does not put up a fight but stares down the lake waters as if some mythical creature might rise from it.

"Why are you crying?" the officers ask.

"Why aren't you?" Mark says.

Cops push his head into the patrol car. Senior year, Kole grows his hair like Jesus and has his pick of homecoming dates because girls eat up the story. But every horror has its expiration. When Betsy Harrison torches her estranged husband's Fallsburg home that November, her news takes center stage. There's insurance money but also children inside. Mark Troller is sent to the state place for crazies; after that it's a ten car pile-up of one thing upon the other, well beyond the reaches of Murmur, foreclosures and shuttered storefronts, grazed bullets in hunting season, bust-ups in basement dens: homemade bombs, demon cults—this is the '90s. People fear Satan. Satan takes priority, certainly over Jews, a dead Jewish girl. What's another dead girl? People have enough on their plates. Noreen has her brother's assault charge, her parents' deaths in rapid succession. If life's unfair, death can feel lucky. The first day Noreen moves into Pat's mobile, he won't lay off her. She gets a second job. A third.

Fifteen months later she is tending bar when Kole brings Mark into The Lion's Den.

"Reenie, be friendly and give my brother a good pour."

Noreen's been drinking, so she's all flush and teeth and heavy on the doubles.

"Long time no see, Mark."

Mark doesn't answer. Noreen clears their glasses. She is young and in her body, swinging her hair, but he just goes on studying his thumbs as if they're tying imaginary flies.

"At least be a gentleman and lend me a hand." She cinches the trash and heaves it over her shoulder like Santa fucking Claus. Mark follows her. Noreen backends the screen, tosses the night's empties onto the dumpster.

He says, "That's a lot of garbage."

"We go through more than you think." She takes his bags and then she takes him in her hand. He is sad and limp, but she is driven, determined; it's only natural, Noreen is drunk and here is Mark Troller, at long last, in her grip. Even if it's like wrangling a greased pig. It's not that she doesn't know better; it's that she knows this best. How many times has Pat wrangled her? Mark's skin is slick as a water wiggly. She tells herself he needs it, needs this, needs her.

"Relax, I got you," she says, spitting into her palm until he fits inside her where she holds him against the cedar shake as a rusty nail bloodies her thigh. Later, she will scar, she will get sick and think tetanus, she will be wrong, wrong about so many things, but at the time all she feels is the brush of their bones, flint to fire, as he shuts his eyes and she wrings him out with her solid, high hips.

"That a boy," she says and it's done.

Today Kole Troller is still at the bar, three pints in. It is barely noon. In the years since high school, he's puffed up so much his head looks shrunk, like a pin shoved in a sewing cushion. It's been a while. Maybe he's been here all along, a fixture at The Lion's Den, but she's not always looking.

Noreen fingers his flannel. "You do know it's June."

"Do you have any idea what the hospital charges for gelatin and mashed peas? Never should have admitted my mother. Should have just let her go, at home, in her own damn bed, how it's meant to be. With dignity. Would have done it too, in good faith, if that home aide hadn't squawked, 'She's having a fit, Mister, what you going to do about it?' Keep turning the woman like a roast on a spit."

"What about Kathy?"

"You really don't know anything, do you?" Kole turns to her, unshaven. When she'd first moved in, he'd taken an electric razor to himself twice a day, his cheeks a hopeful pink. "Last I heard she was at her sister's in Schenectady."

Noreen lifts his hand off her thigh. "We need to dry you out."

"Since when do you care?"

"You know I care."

"A battle against bedsores is no life. If death don't kill her first it'll surely kill me. You try to do it. My heifer has mastitis, rotary's on the fritz. Soon as I catch my breath, I'm ten feet under again."

"Well, then, let me throw you a raft."

She draws her stool closer, lays it out. Frank. Messina. Maybe she inflates things a smidge, makes it seem as though the sale is farther along, much farther along, buyers at the table. Chris at the office swears by vision boards to manifest destiny, he's all about intermittent fasting and cold brew, the man's never wrong, and Kole could use some manifesting. Noreen had known the farm was bad but not the extent of it. Knows firsthand how a place can all but crush you.

When she names the price, Kole pounds the counter. Other patrons give him the stinkeye. *Quit your holler, you dumb drunk.* They can't hear their own talk of Mexican influx, even though they mean Dominican or Guatemalan. His eyes narrow suspiciously.

"What about the other side?"

"Whole kit and caboodle."

"You know how I feel about those people."

"Even Steven or it's a no-go."

Nancy Maclean, tending, measures out two shots. Once the whiskey hits, Noreen feels right again. Kole hops off his stool for a pitiful sort of jig, dungarees slipping beneath the swell of his stomach. He looks tiny from the waist down, as if his bottom and top belong to two different people. Noreen laughs. He was, after all, more of a brother than her own brother.

"Cut the slobber. I won't have you jinx it."

"Let's celebrate. Steak and eggs?"

"This isn't The Breakstone, Troller."

"Then fix me whatever you've got. Plate for Reenie, too."

"None for me, Nancy."

"Now you're a monk? What about for old time's sake?"

Noreen taps out a smoke.

"Supposed to take that outside," Nancy says, sliding over the ashtray, a pair of bologna sandwiches in wax paper. Reenie peels back the bread, removes a slice of lunchmeat, bites a donut hole through it. It's just the kind of ill-mannered thing she'd harangue Paige for: *You want people to think you were raised by wolves?*

He burps, low and sour. "Hope you know what you're doing."

"Do me a favor, Kole. Shower. Mow the goddamn lawn. Look like a hobo and people will treat you like one. Nobody needs to see that pecker poking out of your fly. My buyers could drive up any time. How's your brother?"

"Bears still crap in the woods."

"Wouldn't mention any of this to him just yet."

Kole crumples his napkin in his fist. "You can trust me."

IRA

At nightfall, he sets out for the main house without a flashlight. Skunks be damned. This is a distance he knows by heart.

She's on his deck facing the lake, having started without him. At the crunch of his footsteps she turns, her hair so shiny it seems almost wet. Her glass calling out for a fill. He's brought a bottle of something. The smell, always, before or after a rain. He doesn't yet know her name, the business of leasing left to his ex-wife.

"Mind if I join?" Ira says. And so it begins.

PAIGE

Last night she cleaned up. Apparently, the Jewish people loved their drugs. Opiates, sure, but lesser narcotics, too, uppers and performance enhancers, little blue pills. Birth control.

Paige is not sure how she'll get it all but she'll get it. Five years at SCCH and she knows her way around floors, knows who has what, orderlies hook her up, patients hoard, security could be reckless. There were a number of ways to score. Duplicates to the narc box. She can pick a lock. Nail a pharmacist if necessary.

But she'd have to be careful. Fentanyl was fucked. Morphine, impossible. There was a count on Oxy. It was important not to raise suspicion. Percocet would have to do.

The bowling alley had been a gamble. In summer, Jews with their strange hats and straggly strings monopolized the lanes. Tuesday was ladies' night, Wednesday for men, and on Thursdays, couples clogged the center lanes, forging a human divider between the opposing ends where single sex groups bowled safe from temptation. They paid for privacy but wanted a bargain. The way Chuck Petrillo, Bowl-A-Rama's manager, described it, he had the whole Breakstone doubled over, his voice mocking and nasal, *Can you arrange for me a special price?* They brought their own food, their own DJs. They ululated. They left a goddamn mess. It was unkind, maybe. Wrong to laugh, the way it was wrong to mock the retarded. Like, maybe they didn't know better. But Paige had guessed correctly—they did not bring their own drugs.

Paige showed up on Thursday. Petrillo gave her the nod when she walked in. She dealt mainly through one guy. Tzvi had cratered skin, sparse beard and no hat, which meant, Petrillo explained, he'd been married at one point but was no longer. His side locks, tucked behind ears, meant he was the go-to guy for secular, worldly dealings. This, too, Petrillo explained. So much of these people could be explained through their hair. He had a rotted tooth, putty-colored and twisted, like a door swung half-open. They met in the bowels of the alley, crept into the crawl space where the mechanics or hydraulics or whatever were exposed in a complicated arrangement of wire, chute, and hinge. It smelled of WD-40 and wax and feet. Every few seconds balls rumbled through, pins sweeping in and out. When Tzvi spoke, he scratched his forearms. An addict's scratch, though his skin was covered in milky patches Paige recognized as eczema. She'd had it too as a child, hid her elbows in the silky white gloves of bell choir, soothing herself with a nimble rendition of Amazing Grace.

Eventually, she outgrew the condition.

Maybe he just scratched, maybe, unlike Tommy, it merely gave himself something to do with his hands. They had laws against touching, laws for everything. Rather than meet her eyes, he studied his sneaker shoes, rocking from toe to heel, his voice lifting in half-song. As she spoke, he tallied up names, numbers. She wondered if he took a kickback. Tzvi paid from a jellyroll. Bonkers, how much cold cash he had. Eleven hundred. She crinkles each bill in her fist, her hands smelling like money, and shuts it all into a tackle box.

When Paige steps out of the shower, her mom is at the table smoking and eating a diet bar.

"Who do I have to fuck for privacy?"

"I've seen it all before, pigeon."

Paige tightens her towel. A celebrity weekly sprawled on the table. *Stars: They're Just Like Us.* They drink coffee. They wear plaid. The way her mom sits there twisted up like a swizzle stick, Paige is sure she is onto some new scam. Vitamins, self-sharpening knives, placental cream. Noreen is an easy target. Infomercials preyed upon people like her. And those were the legal ventures. Paige drowns a bowl of flakes, the milk expired but not too tangy. She flattens the box.

"A girl your age grows only in one direction."

Paige drops her bowl in the sink.

In the car, her mom talks pressure fast, like she is auctioning off a prize steed.

"You're not going to believe it but—"

From which follows the same story: Their life is about to change. As if a pair of real estate moguls might swoop down upon them, in a private helicopter, no less, and gobble up a few hundred acres. Even if such a pair existed, who's buying an inch from her mother? Her only listings were a couple of trailers down Route 105, the sinking split-level in town.

"Have you even met these people?"

"By phone. We exchanged emails, they sent over a package. Check out their pens."

Paige twists the neck and a pair of corporate heads pops up. With the Trollers, Noreen may not have paid rent, but she'd paid. Everything came at a price. What her mom did for a bed, for fresh eggs, she'd do again, if needed. No pretense about it. Noreen washed one hand with the other.

"Make sure they're for real."

"I Googled them. These guys have millions to burn. Imagine: a world-famous casino. The Catskills are back, baby!"

"Is that what they're planning?"

"What else would they do?"

"Oh, gosh, I don't know. A gazillion other things."

"Play our cards right and we'll land plumb spots in hotel management."

"Baller."

"Why aren't you thrilled?"

"I am—for you."

"For *us*."

Paige stares out the window as if she's already halfway to Tampa. The postcard she'll send: *Orange You Glad It's Florida*. She pushes in the lighter fuse, waits for the click.

"You really think you can sell Murder Lake?"

"No one calls it that anymore."

"No one calls it period. What about Ira Lecher? You'll need a forklift to budge the man."

"Leave Lech to me."

IRA

Beth marches out, armed with purpose. Does he have a hammer? A clutch of nails? Would he like a square of gluten-free carrot cake? Contribute to her compost bin?

As a matter of fact. He swings bags of coffee grinds, banana peels. Carries his ladder like a cross, bulb bulging in his pocket.

Presumptuous—her light is not out, merely weak. He noticed one night. He could fix it, if she wants. She has hard lemonade. He has weed.

The field is what separates them, acre and wood, but not really. After the first day, there's no division. He doesn't question the mystery of attraction, their discrepancy of age or symmetry, the often reported beauty gradient. Their connection makes sense to him. They're two people alone in the hills.

"Beth." Saying her name is like spitting. "Parents weren't exactly creative, huh?"

"Actually, my mother wanted to be an artist. Died trying."

"Happens to us all eventually."

On Saturday a car passes through. The husband, Ira assumes, but he does not stay the night. Next morning, when she lets him in, Ira stumbles onto a chaos of toys. Puzzles underfoot. She backs into him with a laundry basket. Then there's the kid.

"Hey, kid."

The kid dandles a Hot Wheels. "Stranger or friend?"

"I'm your furry pal Ira but you can call me Lech."

"Race me, Wench."

They cock wheels and rip. Ira makes sounds he didn't know he had in him. Beth folds clothes. They keep crashing until the socks are balled and Beth appears with brightly colored bowls.

"Snack time."

She clears a heap from the couch. Ira can't tell if she's still unpacking or just a slob. The fuzz on her cheek catches the light, a mammalian reminder, as she gazes out on the middle distance, that we're nothing but animals in clothes. Zach comes across Ira's collection of vinyl. Stares at *Some Girls*, fondles the *Sticky Fingers* zipper.

"Gentle, kid, it's a first edition."

Day blends into night. It is summer and it is vacation, for her, Tuesday, for him, all the same. He doesn't grill her, doesn't say, *and where, pray tell, is Mr. Beth?* Her drinking speaks volumes. Tough to keep pace with all the pitchers of Bloody Mary. Too much pepper. The kid eats raw radishes on the rug.

"What kind of child abuse is that?"

"They're delicious in salt."

"Taste." The kid shoves a walnut-sized radish toward Ira's nose, so he takes it and bites and sure enough, it's not awful, like the canned discs of water chestnuts he picks out from Chinese, not interesting enough to finish, so when he puts down his half-eaten root Beth demolishes it. That's a new intimacy. She pours her tomato soup in a glass. He fishes out a sword, plucks olives with his tongue. It is quiet as they chew, then too quiet. She emits a low burr like satisfaction, but it's short-lived, her energy skittish; she pops up, goes to the window, pausing on a family photo: all four Lechers in ski jackets, fluorescent stripes. No helmets. Viv, him, the girls. She scoops up another frame. Hillary and Heather with hair sky-high, an alligator stitched over his nipple. They are in Disney, the Magic Kingdom.

"Land or World?"

What's the difference. One puked on Magic Mountain, the other wailed through the spinning teacups, condemning the place as torture. *Disney!* You had your childhood, Viv defended them. Can't you let anyone else have theirs?

He puts down his drink. "Let's talk. Ask me anything."

The pause is interminable. Not a trick question, even if she isn't the sharpest tack, or can't see past herself. Clearly, there's some hurt there. The husband came, went. Maybe it's generational. His own daughters are little narcissists. When he said as much, they called him a "micro-aggressor," which sounded like one of Viv's dermatological treatments. They stopped calling. He's felt sorry ever since. A father's job is to shut up and listen, cheer from the sidelines, never impinge or comment on Facebook, not that he has a Facebook. Still, this is awkward.

"Don't be shy."

At last, Beth speaks. "Do I have a string? I feel like something's stuck, a shred of celery, piece of pulp, it's making me nuts, but I can't get to it."

She pulls her cheek like a curtain. Ira peers inside.

BETH

When Doug surprises her for the night, she nearly socks him with a fry pan.

"You can't just come here."

"Why not?" He's her husband, the father of her child. Is that not his entitlement?

"I wasn't expecting you." Her stomach seizes. "You could have been anyone."

"Like who?"

"It gets insanely dark."

"But I'm not just anyone."

He steps toward her and she clenches. If she looks at him, she will soften, and she wants to hold onto her anger, ride out its surge. To him, she is "either bitchy or depressed." One thing to abort in college, when it's French-level chic, something to dismiss over cereal and cigarettes, but mothers are judged, mothers are unforgiven. How could you? Doug will say. How could you do this—to *me*? Sure, he'll mean well. Everyone sees the world through their own lens. It's not paternity. Nor is it Malthusian, although the planet is taxed, the planet is full enough. What it is, is—

"I need space," she says, so he leaves.

Now he calls and calls.

"How are you doing with your space?"

Why must she justify her choices? Her tongue is a sponge, expanding against the roof of her mouth, a Magic Grow capsule, puffing into a lopsided giraffe, a foam fish.

"Making friends?"

"By the bucket."

"You should put yourself out there."

"Thanks for the tip."

"Just trying to help you be your best self, Beth."

In bed she sweats and worries it's perimenopause, which it's not, but someday will be. Someday she will shrivel up and drop off, her eggs going the hard, blackened way of umbilical scab. Someday she won't have to worry. She will be only her best self.

"Have you been tracking your Happiness Quotient?"

Doug's trying to get the term trademarked. The self-care industry is all about buzzwords, so he's testing out the mileage on her. His empathy has a viral following, his appeal linked to the arc of his personal journey. Doug's connectability boils down to losing his younger brother Ryan in the Twin Towers. Companies employ him to teach them how to rebound from despair. Everyone loves a meaningful tragedy.

"Where would you say you are?"

"What?" Where is she?

"Where would you fall, Beth? On a scale of one to ten?"

A rating. He wants her to rate herself. Her happiness.

"Seven."

"Good, good, good." He speaks in three's, another rhetorical strategy. "Can we talk about the house? I'm meeting contractors this afternoon."

"Hold on, here comes Zachary."

"Daddy!" Zach holds the receiver like a walkie-talkie. She pours another drink. On the other end she hears, "Howdy, champ. Guess who misses you the most?"

Doug is a good father. They play checkers and airplane and horse; they play all the things Beth does not play. They fist bump and maraud around shirtless, Zach the parroting shadow of Doug's masculinity, so textbook it seems fake, at times, as if he's working off a manual on how to be a man. But that's Doug—

normal to the point of strange. Her head feels suddenly heavy, the way a seemingly innocuous object, a hollow vase, can surprise you with its unexpected weight. She wants to lie down but she has company. She has Ira. Not that he'd mind. The first time she met him, he rubbed a birthmark with his thumb. She cupped her cheek. *Thought you had*, he'd said. The spot couldn't be removed. Still, it was a gesture, like composting: where intention was everything.

On the deck, his bald spot shines beet red, his ponytail snaking to one side. His posture rotten, as if there's a dead animal strapped to his back. He's an old man. But curiously, in a matter of days, he's become *her* old man.

Zach's on a roll. Rattling off carbon to nitrogen ratios, two parts brown, one part green. Did you know, Daddy, matter never dies but keeps changing form. *Contractors are coming.* It's really happening, then. New Jersey or bust. What shape might bust take? She pictures herself on a Saturday, childless, window shopping in Williamsburg, her rescue pup stuffed into a sweater vest. *Who's this Wench?* she hears through the phone.

Not that Doug is the jealous type. He's far too secure. Besides, if she's learned one thing from marriage it's that fidelity fit like a pair of discount leggings: stretched out, prone to tears. Not that she is looking to bone Ira Lecher. He's part of the landscape, an amenity that comes with the place. But there's no denying the comfort, the thermal heat, as if she were a grab-n-go burger beneath a food lamp silently begging an extended, anonymous hand to *pick me*. Thus was the allure of strangers. Strangers feel safe. Strangers don't know her enough to judge. Ira shows up, licks his lips, not sleazy but perennially chapped. A faint halo blooms at his mouth. She is either home or not. Usually, she's home.

Zach slides on the hardwood. He runs everywhere, city and country. Through parks and crosswalks, as if some great urgency awaits. Daddy says he loves you. Daddy says he'll call later. Daddy says take care.

Hours later, she'll find the phone off the hook, spinning from its cord like a body.

"Who was that?" Ira asks.

"No one," she says. "My husband."

TZVI

His union did not last long. *Halacha* is clear. There are grounds in which a wife may ask for a *get*, for which a divorce is warranted: If a husband is derelict in fulfilling basic marital needs. If he commits adultery—with another woman; with another man, an abomination. If he is lecherous. If he is irresponsible. If he causes her a bad name. If she feels repulsed. If he abuses. If he forces himself upon her during her monthly bleed. If he has an intolerable stench. If conditions are deemed unbearable. If she does not get pregnant. If he is sterile. If he is impotent. If he is a deviant, a *mored*, and does not lie with her. If he no longer wishes to lie.

IRA

Honestly, she's almost too easy. An abandoned hole sits in her nostril awaiting consolation: *It's all right, kid.* Everyone regrets their choices. Her face, fractured like a knockoff Picasso, contorts with alcohol, and Ira won't let her go at it alone, even though it's eleven o'clock in the morning. The kid yips at his leg, dragging Ira like a chew toy out to his little science experiment by the side of the house where it gets academic in the show & tell. Composting is an adding machine—input garbage, output soil—and Ira's into it, he's tight on breath, heck, he wishes he'd thought of a sustainable means of sowing the future from the rot of the past. Beth trails behind with her vodka and ponytail; that is, she's not dressed like a mother, much less a wife. He's not alone in detecting her weakness. Mosquitoes are having a field day.

"Me, I'm passed right over."

"Didn't think they'd be so vicious up here."

"Viciousness is everywhere."

"I'm an all-you-can-eat buffet."

"Take the compliment." Ira takes her forearm and turns it over, cutting x marks into her welts. "As I was saying —"

Beth has not asked for his life story, but here she is, a warm body in a chair. The truth is, sometimes he talks just to hear himself.

"You're Jewish." A statement as opposed to a question. Beth has the look, though she's gone to some trouble to hide it, and he has the lilt of those who approach pedestrians on Broadway to shake the *lulav*, wrap *phylacteries*, listen to the *shofar*'s riotous trumpet.

"I'm nothing."

"Even the nothings were gassed."

In Manhattan Ira saw a therapist like the rest of the populace. If talk didn't cure him, it thinned his pockets. Dr. Mantel specialized in people like him, whose parents survived the war, survivors once removed, but he had no interest in diagnosis. If he was plagued by moods, well, he was who he was.

"My mother, can you imagine, had a cousin who owned a doll hospital in Queens. After they fled Europe, they fixed broken limbs, glued eyelashes and repainted cherry lips until my father joined the *schmatta* business. We were short on a lot but never sweaters. My father never more at peace than inside the armor of his Buick, bags packed by the door.

"Some people get trust funds, I get secondhand trauma. Six million became a catchphrase, orphaned of meaning. At recess, I traded Nazis like baseball cards, Roger Maris for Mickey Mantle, Eichmann for Himmler. Nobody talked about it. At home, I'd sit alone by the radiator, play with my pet fish."

"How do you play with a fish?"

"Lonely people can play with anything. Come summer, it all changed. The bungalows gave my mother what the road gave my father. In the Bronx we lived on top of each other. A polio epidemic in our tenement could finish the Fuhrer's job, whereas the Catskills evoked the hinterland with its fresh air and lupine. Max Mendel's was not exactly the hotbed of luxury, but for my mother it was paradise. This is how I picture Ruth: shoulders gleaming in the sun. Sherry on her breath. Best of all, she didn't have to drum up entertainment. I had Sy Newman, Eddie Fisk. She had everyone else."

"Your voice is incredibly soothing."

"Mother always said I should do radio."

"Why didn't you?"

"Should've, could've, would've."

"Were you drafted?"

"I'm uneven. One leg shorter than the other. Slight, but you can't go to Chu Lai with orthotics. Instead I became a hotel waiter, a real *macher*, with the napkin folds and dancing daughters. Once a week we had open-mic night."

"They must have loved you. You could read the phone book and I'd listen."

"Listen or *schnatz* through?"

No answer. In the distance, fireflies wink out their morse code. On his mother's *yahrzeit*, he fasted, the habit born from longing more than anything. ("Longing," according to his therapist, "is faith minus doubt.") Kaddish covered all dead. He conjures the flair of her dresses, alligator snaps misted with 4711 cologne. How she'd say, "My son's gonna be somebody," over the roar of the custodial vacuum in the grand hall. He asked, she came. That, to him, was family.

"Still with me?" Ira says as Beth's breath quickens, as though ragged from pursuit, but he can't tell who's hunting or being hunted, if she's dreaming, if she's fighting to come up for air.

PAIGE

Paige is pushing a cart down the palliative care wing when she hears Kole Troller's voice. "A sign from God." The tenor unmistakable, as if he's being held at the throat, hounded for change, as if finally someone has come to collect what he's taken. "Noreen Murphy is going to save us all."

Paige halts, feels around her pocket for something to even her out, to get over the sound of Kole's sniveling., Even shitbags could be good to their mothers. She tries to scoot. Her wheels give her away.

"Speak of the devil. Mother, we have a visitor."

Paige can picture the old woman's skeleton without any imagination. It feels almost indecent. Her chin sprung with hairs, wig aslant. But Paige's used to it. Dying people look alike, just as babies do.

The old woman has a double to herself. Paige cups her frail hands, nails caked in dirt or feces or chocolate.

"How's it going, Mrs. T.?"

"Been like this since Thursday," Kole says. "Stubborn as a mule. Not taking food or water."

"I'll have the nurse come and tidy." She's learned never to let patients see their smell in her face. Not that Mrs. Troller is alert to any of it. Paige smooths out her folds of skin. "Switch out these sheets."

Mrs. Troller emits a low sputter, like a car struggling to turn over. Paige refills the pitcher with ice chips and instructs Kole to glaze them over his mother's cracked lips.

"Blinds open or closed?"

"Sit with me a minute," he says. "I've got nobody to talk to."

His big hands clip her waist where her apron is tied like a present, like peppermint candy. When she resists, he takes hold, when she says not now, he says be nice, leaning back as if she's tugging on his fishing line. I mean it, she says, squirming. Me too, he says, reeling her in, nice and steady, that a girl, come to your Kole, and flops her down smack on his lap.

NOREEN

The library is a little-known haven with free Wi-Fi. It is here Noreen completed her real estate course, shopped for slacks, a sweater shaver, and the frame for her online certificate, which hangs proudly above her office cubicle.

Thanks to junior-high typing (boys had shop), Noreen does not need to glance at the keyboard. In another life, she might've been a hand model; another gender, and she'd have carved a lamp base in the shape of a duck, shellacked golden honey. But this is the life she has.

Noreen inputs a search for Sullivan County, New York. Gaming laws. Tax laws. Property laws. Property history. Ira Lecher purchased his land for $180,000 in 1977. No receipt of the Troller deed. It hasn't switched hands. There are different tax codes for working farms. Exemptions apply. Frank & Messina will have to devote at least thirty percent acreage to crops in order to maintain the tax break, although she doubts that's an issue. Nevertheless, she jots everything down.

Ira's acreage is listed at 189. The Troller plot is a mirror image, like a valentine heart. Not much by farming standards but too much for Kole to manage alone. She'll have to go to town hall for his records. If she wants them, that is. She's not sure. Consult Sally or Chris and they'll take a cut or steal the deal out from under her. She wants this, needs this, for herself.

Frank & Messina, she anticipates, want the full monty: Investment value. Feasibility. Precedence. Interest. Returns. Noreen antlers a pair of pencils through her hair, hooking her ankles around the chair to pull herself closer. The New York gaming commission has been granting licenses for years, seeding the region with growth. She'd been right about that.

A 1.3 billion redesign of the Monticello raceway is well underway. The developing team—more than a dozen fast-talking suits, architects, planners, food people, spa people, salespeople, money men—chitter through the video she's clicked, promising everything short of space travel: gilded casinos, steak houses, wellness center, waterpark, golf course, a racetrack for Italian sports cars. Frank & Messina, no doubt, already know all of this.

She's getting carried away. At only (*only!*) four hundred acres, Murmur Lake cannot hold a candle to the sprawl of Monticello. Frank & Messina's plan will have to be smaller in scope: an adventure aerial park, a new energy farm, those awful wind turbines that compromise the view. An organic meat plant would bring jobs but it's not her business. If it were her business—and shouldn't she be prepared just in case?—she'd suggest a boutique hotel. Where guests are treated as family, as they were at the old establishments, claiming the same rooms each year. Staff knowing who wanted turndown service, who an extra butter wheel.

Unlike, say, Vegas. On a lark Noreen had entered one of those sweepstakes and won, a winner at last, but the win, as revealed in fine print, was hotel only. She had to foot her own fare. Before she knew it, she'd dropped three grand. Stole her first credit card to pay for it. Cocktails looked like sunsets. Women wore dresses that dished up their boobs. Slots pinged all night, and she gave into her every want: money, dazzle, David Copperfield misting from a shock of dry ice.

The hotel was the Venetian. Just like Italy! That's what she envisions, a gondola shuttling guests from their rooms to activities, maximizing use of both sides of the property. Sweetheart packages might include monogrammed flutes and private massages. Imagine the possibilities! But it's not her job to dream.

Outside, an addict hugs his dog on the sidewalk. PROVE I EXIST, his cardboard sign dares, so she drops a quarter in his water bowl, picks up soup from the luncheonette, an unwise choice in the heat, the lid leaking, wetting her bag. At Hand's

Hardware she purchases a box of pencils and a roll of butcher paper. Once she starts drawing, her hotel rises like a wedding cake. Like designing her own dollhouse. Something she never had. Always on the outside looking into rooms that stood ajar for maid service. There's upholstery to consider, color palettes. Sea foam and heather. She maps out tennis courts and a dance pavilion, penciling fixtures, chandeliers strung with crystal tears.

When she looks up, it's almost closing. Misty Drake has switched off her desk lamp, eyes fixed on Noreen like she's keeping her. Noreen gathers her instruments. Tomorrow she'll return to tax laws, the dry-as-dust stuff. She'll type up her findings for Frank & Messina, consult Kole about staging. His place could use a thorough cleaning—the lake, a fresh name— but the promise is there. The only nut to crack is Ira. He's tricky but tricky's her specialty. Along the magazine rack, a disgraced pop star has reinvented herself as a best-selling cookbook author. *America, the beautiful. Land of infinite chances.* Noreen swipes the issue, rolls it like a periscope and slips it into the deep, oiled well of her handbag.

TZVI

On Friday afternoons, Route 17 becomes a used car lot. Honda Odyssey, Toyota Sienna. Silver, silver, blue. Dents on the fender, dents on the door. Somewhere in the throng is his father, heading to the same cottage, to his new family, returning on Sundays as always. On Shabbos, his father walks with the other fathers as though impermeable while visibly melting in the sun. Once upon a time he assured his son the discomfort was something he'd get used to. His father's posture, angled and determined, as if barreling into a storm. Occasionally, there is a nod of recognition beneath his *shtreimel*. Tzvi does not say *tate* in return.

Tzvi leaves the window and lies on his cot with his shoes on. His phone has been nonstop. Customers want their goods before Shabbos. He meets them by the Dollar General, behind a sugar maple. Occasionally there is a special request. Yonah Fine is in a pickle. Some trouble with business. They ask him to handle it, shmear the *mashgiach* to look the other way. Tzvi is not an intimidating presence but he does whatever is asked. He investigates loopholes and shortcuts. Every community needs someone like him. He serves a purpose he never asked to fill.

Had his father sought out a similar agent in matters regarding his mother? Tzvi's never been able to piece much together. Chaya was a child bride. She had her hands full. Four babies under six, her own parents in Jerusalem. Who wouldn't be overwhelmed? When is motherhood not overwhelming? If she'd been acting out—what would that even look like? Her body turned up on Tisha B'Av, the holiday of mourning, so no one drove out until the following day, the police already polluting the scene. His father hailed it as the work of Our Creator: How all grief points to the destruction of the Temple. His mother's drowning. The saddest day of the year.

When he closes his eyes he can see her: slipping wild flowers into a soda can. The smell of linden, of yeast in a bowl. Her *sheitels* perched on faceless heads, the good wig stored in a special place because it was 100 percent human hair. He remembers sitting on the edge of her bed shoving his tiny fist into her stocking, his *mame* frowning until his hand became a puppet, buzzing along her shorn scalp, and she burst out laughing. A laugh so rare he can still feel its echo. He scratches his elbows. He'd had eczema since birth, but his flareups worsened after her death, his skin cracking and bleeding. He scoops out two fingers of thick cream, so silky and slick it's hard not to rub on himself. He is weak. He prays. His patches turn a milky pink. He does not succumb to every temptation.

Last night, one of his housemates had an out-of-town guest. Male or female, he was not sure, only that seemed a narrow way of viewing them. Everyone was talking about paths. Off the *derech*. From here to where? In the fog of drink and smoke and heavy guitar riffs the guest thrust him a piece of paper, which Tzvi now unfurls. A phone number, a website. Before sundown, he punches the address into his phone. *Mitzrayim*, the homepage reads. *Out of the desert. Into your life.*

BETH

"You can't sit around all summer," Ira says, blocking her sun.

"Watch me." Insomnia has her strung out. Wallowing feels right and good. Hours bleed like a laundry mistake she can live with, everything's salty pink, everything is easy, easy. The light refracts off the lake like a jewel. Maybe this is how her mother felt about the red rocks of Sedona. She can all but stop thinking. "Ever wish you weren't an only child?"

"I'm just glad my folks took a night out of canasta to have me. You know, after the war many survivors aborted their firstborn."

Beth drains her Bloody Mary. "Does Zach need a sibling?"

"What your kid needs, sweetheart, is a friend."

He cigars his celery, plucks her glass from her hand. He's cleaned up, shaved his jaw save for a soul patch the size of a postage stamp, a tickler.

"And what you need is a road trip. Let's go. I've got *shpilkes*, ants in my pants."

"Maybe it's crabs."

"Kids need kids. In my day, we'd scram. Get lost for hours."

Lech and his bungalow tales. The man is always talking, which excuses her from conversation. She drifts in and out. Hard to know what to say in the heat. This much she's heard before: Even on rainy days they got out, overshoes and fireman slickers. Her sister, Amy, does this, too, talks and talks, and it's freeing, to disappear into someone else's memories. They'd catch salamanders or garter snakes or spy on Sy Tillman's older sister. The rain beat the roof like hooves pulling carriages in Central Park. His mother played cards. Ira played backgammon, sat through a skippy reel in the clubhouse. People laughed and ate. In the evening, they wore sweaters.

"When the sun came out, we'd dart off for every possible incarnation of hide and seek. Cops, robbers. Cowboys & Indians, we played Nazi & Jew. My mother never asked where I'd been. A deer tick camped behind my ear for nearly a week before I ended up in the infirmary. Ruth had her own world and people. She had her sloe gin fizz. Provided I washed my face before supper, I was free, and summer was mine, glorious, ripe for the picking. Don't you want that for your kid?"

"What you forget is one, the world was different then, and two, you were older than Zach. You weren't four. You were a real kid."

"I'm real."

"Of course you are, baby."

Zach dumps his Lego bucket. He is missing a part. Ira says it's important to improvise when you can't find exactly what you're looking for. Two pieces snap together and become one.

"Presto." Zach snuffles his arms around him. Sunspots float in Beth's line of vision, the Adirondack chair large as a throne.

"I'm stuck."

"Here." He offers his hand and she takes it.

Half-hour later, Ira's put on a clean shirt, short-sleeved like a math teacher. "Your chariot awaits."

"Zach needs a car seat."

"Bring yours."

"A person needs a degree in astrophysics to install these things."

Beth's traded her cut-offs for a sundress. She's got a good buzz going, warm and loose, hulas her keys.

"I'll drive."

"You're not driving. Hop in the back. We'll do it how we used to do it."

Beth pushes the leather front forward. The safety belt's a choker, so she stretches the strap behind Zach, and they are off, top down, she and Zach in the back seat, his legs on her legs, hair whipping her face.

"Where are we going?" she shouts. It is an appropriate thing to ask and she is trying to be appropriate.

"Just sit back and look pretty," Ira says.

"Faster!" Zach chants, bouncing on her bladder. Elbow out the window, Ira narrates as he goes, naming everything the way a toddler does (*Sky! Clouds! Power lines!*) pointing out landmarks, Sideways Pizza, but she's not really following. They pass a field of horses and Zach and Ira cry "Horses!" at the same time, leaning in like a single bullet, tires kicking dust, red clay, gray clay, cows and sheep, the occasional steeple. There goes a granary, a family of wild turkeys, a dizzying fringe of black-eyed Susans. Hold on, she hears, as he cuts left. She's been holding on for so long she's forgotten why she's holding. The sky is a preposterous blue. Stenciled Hebrew letters on warped wood, arrows indicate this and that camp, what Sullivan County's known for, Jews and camps and railroad bridges.

"I'll never remember where I am."

Ira floors it. "Guess you'll have to stick with me."

Camp options are limited. In Callicoon, facilities feel more like daycare. Large groups of runny noses cluster in a cramped room, hardly a window, with an occasional trip to the town pool. No one has a nut-free policy. The director steps back. Can she smell Beth's breath? Lady. Look. I've got thirty kids, another fifteen in diapers, half of them pack peanut butter sandwiches. You expect me to tell all those parents about the one kid from New York City who's going to ruin it for them? Beth storms out. That is, she kind of zigzags. Zach zigzags too, so Ira makes a game of it, zigzagging out to Kiamesha, with its dress code of black and white. Women shuffle by like geishas, gazes lowered, ankle-length skirts.

"We're not far from Max's."

By default, her mind goes to *Dirty Dancing*, which, Ira says, was not filmed here but down South. Even *Dirty Dancing* is a lie.

"Thought Max's was gone."

"Ghosts linger." He shuts the car, blows his nose. The man's a waterworks. Beth has seen Doug cry exactly once. Not at Ryan's memorial, not in the months and anniversaries or at any of the World Trade fundraisers where the stories were so wrenching you literally had to be a robot not to tear up. Doug is a problem-solver, rock solid, and she's both grateful and resentful of his solidity. It is nearly superhuman. Does the world need more heroes? He cried only when Zach was born, his son's tiny fist coiled around his finger.

"You'll see." Ira dabs his eyes. "This is what happens when most of life is behind you." In front of them: a dozen shacks, women in head coverings, a handful of minivans. A bleached out sign is staked to the ground: *Camp Shalom Yisroel. Open to the Public. All groups welcome. Inquire within.*

"Zach believes in Santa."

"By the appearance of things, I'd say Shalom Yisroel would be jazzed for any business."

"He just fell asleep. Let's come back."

"We're here. Don't be a tease."

"Don't be a prick."

"I am what I am." Ira starts the engine. "Who the heck are you?"

It lands like a slap. Because: true. She's lost all concept of who she is. Doug wanted Zach uncircumcised, and she agreed, she was agreeable, her hormones raged, the world was violent enough, the covenant a crock, all pacts meant to be broken. Sometimes she dreamed his penis was a finger wagging, a lollipop in a crystal dish at the bank. She eases Zach off her knees.

"Don't try so hard, kid." A tube of lotion sails over, a ball cap. "Sun's stronger than you think."

The hat smells unwashed. Beth puts it on anyway. Feelings are a trap. Either way she is guilty. "What if I'm a horrible, selfish person?"

"Say again? I'm a chauffeur up here."

Gingerly she climbs over the gearshift. His jaw ruddy from where he's nicked himself, a staple of dried blood in the cord of his neck.

"Everyone else seems so happy."

"You don't believe that."

"I don't know." She's been talking too much. The radio crackles. With one hand, Ira reaches for the glove, plops a leather CD binder into her lap. In high school, she'd have been mortified if anyone caught her listening to Bruce Springsteen. Ryan dug Springsteen. Beth stomached Anthrax, Butthole Surfers, Nine Inch Nails. The people she hung out with were angry but she was never angry enough. In college she hid Dave Matthews inside cases of Rage Against the Machine. Secretly she wanted hair metal. Loud guitars with gauzy scarves, leather and boots and waxed chests; she wanted all those cheesy beats thrumming through her but was too embarrassed to admit her secret lust for Girls, Girls, Girls and its one-note misogyny.

She hands over Leonard Cohen.

"How romantic."

Her cheeks burn. "Nick Drake?"

"Don't be so obvious."

She feeds an unmarked disc it into the slit. The first song Beth doesn't recognize, it's super folksy, but Ira dials it up. A crinkle in his eyes, he whips out a joint.

"I shouldn't," she says, grabbing it, the flimsy paper hissing into the flame. At first it's not working, it's bogus weed, then harsh toke, she is high, higher than she'd wanted, shivering, tittering, stroking her forearms to a Bob Seger tune.

"The girls made me this mix for my fiftieth."

Summertime, summertime. Ira's voice, nasally and wistful.

Beth says, "I thought I'd have lived more by now."

"Life has a way."

She waves off the joint. Her mouth is dry. There goes a lamb in the clouds.

"I'm just so tired."

"Kid, you don't know tired."

His hand on her leg, fatherly or flirty. He pulls into a single-pump gas station, returning with sodas and a sleeve of cookies, a pair of hot dogs that must've been turning on coils for days. She pokes the bruised flesh. Ira holds out the wrinkled tip. "Eat."

"Look," she says. It's been an hour or five hours. Ira has an out-of-state subscription, prescription, so back at the house they've kept at it, which has rendered her sharp in the heart and muzzy at the rim, like a photograph coming into focus. *Don't you see?* Beth can't see shit; it's night, everything is black, she's suspended in the vortex—*VORTEX!*—of time and space. There's no delineation of land or lake. *What is she saying?* Something about a circle. She's out of her head, all numb and nerve-endings, the strangest feeling. Words float up and out of reach. She's never seen so many stars. *Isn't it beautiful?*

"So. Much. Sky."

"I don't mind if I never see another skyscraper."

She holds the roach as if she's just remembered it, blows rings. Doug calls it nasty, but it fascinates her, what she can create with her breath, lungs and tongue.

"Where were you?"

Ira means 9/11, of course. *How'd they end up here?* Maybe everything was self-referential, even national tragedy. Maybe grief was performative. Maybe it's the pot.

"Around." She stubs out the joint. Somehow, she'd managed to tuck Zach into bed without a hitch and pick up right where they'd left off, as if she were childless. "Ever wonder what you life might look like if you weren't a parent?"

"My kids no longer want anything to do with me."

"It's different for men. You're not chained to them."

"I'm a cage-free, free-range bird."

"You never doubted yourself?"

"There's only ever doubt."

"What if I'm screwing him up?"

"It's camp, kid. You make it sound like war."

"Will I ever be forgiven?"

"You're a swell mother."

"Cross your heart?"

"Hope to die." He takes her hand, slashes an X through her chest.

IRA

Her rings come off, that's the first thing. And now she's gone and made lunch. Fiesta bowls, five different spreads. Hummus, red pepper, quinoa. Chutney and tapenade, each paired with its own baby spoon.

"You really bent over backwards."

"Didn't know what you'd like."

"What's not to like?"

"Zach's finicky. He'll love something one day and reject it the next."

"What about your husband?"

"What about him?"

Which is all she needs to say.

"You should be more communistic in your approach."

"How should I be?"

"Lunch." He pounds the table. "Lunch is for lunch. The problem with you is you're a people pleaser."

"That's my problem?"

"Don't sweat it, kid, we all have our share. Hot heaven, is this melt in your mouth. Let me feed you. Come here. What do you want?"

BETH

This, she wants this. The place has got her in its teeth. The air, crisp; ground, lush. Dusk, her favorite hour, Zach at her feet, knees turned out, building a marble run.

"Watch, Mommy."

"I'm watching," she says, absently rubbing the groove of her finger. She's removed her jewelry so she doesn't have to keep remembering with each swim. "I could live here. Square off a plot, run some deer fencing, harvest zucchini, ten kinds of lettuce. Launch a CSA!"

"Sounds like a governmental agency."

She laughs. With Ira, it's all laughs. "Learn how to pickle, preserve."

"I am preserved."

"Craft key chains from entombed pansies. A floral cash cow."

"Spoken like a true homesteader."

"You aren't even watching!"

"The air alone. Bottle it, and you know what a fortune we'd make?"

"The Chinese would be all over it."

The lake, blue, the day placid and clear, the kind of sun you're warned against staring into directly—there could be consequences, it is that bright. *Does it get any better?* She actually says it out loud. Beth tans. Her skin deepens from shrimp to toast, white stripes on her shoulders in stark contrast to this new golden life.

"Raise alpaca! Spin wool into yarn, become merry knitters! Fuck New Jersey."

"Mommy!"

"*Fart* New Jersey. *Fart* all of it."

"You know," Ira's voice deepens. "This actually could work."

Ira tips his chair toward hers. His brows go up, like cats on attack. There's a whole story in his face. Fun to imagine what it might be like. The attention is nice. Also: like staring at a screen for too long, she has to break away. Zach snaps his maze into pieces. The marble slips off the track.

"What's eating you, Rube Goldberg?"

"I want Daddy."

"OK, then. Say goodnight."

"It's still light."

"Northern latitudes, Einstein. Hop, one, two."

She peels him off the floor, his body a dead weight. The marble is safe, she assures him. They'll find it in the morning. He can speak to his father in the morning. Together, they'll build a better machine.

Inside, the house is dark. They feel their way through shadows to his room where Beth curls beside him, their skin grassy and warm as they read page for page doing all the voices and she remembers, how could she forget, her son, he is only a child.

"Leave the door open?"

"Always."

"It's not that I'm afraid of the dark. It's that it's hard to be alone."

"I know it is, baby."

PAIGE

At best, Tommy is unreliable. At worst, he's an asshole. Once upon a time she'd trail him with naloxone, chewing her wrist until it bruised, love bites of her own nervous doing, but those days are over. Now, when he goes she does not follow. Tommy may love her but he loves his garbage heroin more. She knows you can't save people. You can only save yourself, if you're lucky.

Paige doesn't even want to get high anymore. Last time they hung out she faked a palm of Demerol. Tommy was so far gone he didn't notice.

It's been four days. Tommy left one of his animal traps in her room, rusted jaws like a prehistoric fish, some creaky bottom feeder, so he'll be back, even if he did take his stupid exterminator can. The quiet is a relief. She drops her keys on the counter. Even when Tommy's in the picture they barely mess around anymore, he's either soft or has dope dick, and Paige is tired of the hair pulling and neck sucking, the sloppy insistence with which Tommy goes about things, as if his affection means something, as if all that touch could transform need into love.

In the bathroom she slides her bra through her sleeve like a magic trick. As the room steams, she inspects a fresh crop of pimples framing her hairline, squeezing one in the fog but it's not ready. All she wants is the shower, the hot slap, to wash away the stink of service: bacon hash, fried onions, syrup by the greedy pour.

In Tampa, Paige will find a sunny one-bedroom efficiency with a balcony, in-ground pool, galley kitchen. The complex, called something cheerful like El Flamingo or The Sandbar, will be a walk from the ocean, not so close as to be prohibitive, nor so far as to defeat the purpose. She likes to picture where she's headed as opposed to where she's been. Everything will be white on white, a hand opening out to reach her, the blinding glow of crossing over.

In bed, her hand floats between her legs. No man can come close. If they weren't all jerks she'd almost pity them. She lifts her hips, alternating her rhythm, teasing herself. As her flesh swells, her thighs tremble like they might give out, some kind of weak-kneed Bambi, her body dissolving into the mattress, and she is infinite.

With Kole, they'd play the dying game. She was five, he was twenty-five. Face down, Kole would say, breathing over her, and she'd do as told. Nose in the dust, she fought the urge to sneeze as he pulled her arms taut, poised for flight, before easing her limbs slowly to the ground, which felt like falling and deliverance in one, until the carpet roughed her cheek and she popped up, shouting, "Again, again!"

Today during the afternoon lull a stranger came in. Paige and Connie were doing dinner prep, mincing onions into vats of beef chuck, raw meat up to their elbows. Diane had gone home so there was no one to greet the tall stranger teetering on canvas wedges. Fresh off the topless bar on Route 17 is what Connie said, but to Paige, she was a different species. Ethereal.

"Quit staring," Connie hissed, but Paige couldn't stop. Mermaid hair, breasts to the neck, breasts big enough to be their own person. Circus tits. Floaters. Fit for the County Fair. How did she not topple over? Were they even real? Paige couldn't imagine anyone choosing to bear such a burden. The shelf she carried, an endangered coral reef.

When Connie said, "Can I help you?" the men at the counter swiveled. Walt the line cook stuck his head through the window and whistled. The person ordered a coffee to go, ducked into the restroom, then split. Under her breath Connie muttered, "Freak." Paige can't picture her face, only her figure, which fills Paige with envy and anguish, how others make up their minds about who you are and how your life should go before they even meet you.

She rolls onto her stomach and thumbs her phone for encouragement. Bicycle tires, mylar balloons, man-breasts puffed like pastry. She refines her search: girls; regular. She doesn't add the word nude but that's what she gets: full girls, round girls, girls with substance and curve, high swoops and heart-shaped points, girls filming themselves as if for her only and not some subterranean in Kansas with a hand in his pants. Black girls, brown girls, Asian girls, girls in nothing but a prayer shawl. Bony girls, too. Sharp angles, muscled like chicken wings, girls in knee socks and school kilts; bull's-eye nipples, nipples hard as Jujubes. Swipe, swipe, and click. She smells her fingers and licks. Girls stuff themselves with garden vegetables, vacuum parts, household items. Girls open themselves up for scrutiny, purple as newborn mice. Is this what her body looked like? Connie said, "You have the right to know your own intimacy," handing over her compact during break; Paige used it to sniff Ritalin rather than to examine her cooch. Connie has a sex toy the size of a giant lipstick, like what a two-year-old might tote around in a felt purse. The thing cost $39.99. Organs come in putty and steel, veiny strap-on or battery-powered. Some girls are plugged in both holes. All three. How do they breathe? What were these girls up to right now? Riding vibrators bendy as book lights, curved like a desktop mouse, but Paige isn't about to spend money on what she can do alone. For free. Watch her go.

She is almost there.

NOREEN

The mall is like a bad boyfriend. Noreen keeps going back, keeps riding the escalator for a mirrored glimpse of herself on the up-and-up. No one would recognize her since her last run-in. She's changed her hair, lost weight. Sears and Penny's remain at either end, but the smaller, interior chains of hair accessories and whimsical socks keep changing, keep turning over, keep baiting her like krill.

Noreen was seven the first time she shoplifted. She'd taken things before, but hotel guests were careless. Everything was just lying around. Lighters, cigarette cases. She was called to shiny objects the way a baby is to light. Patrick's single bullet on a steel-ball keychain.

In her mind, she was doing retail a favor, moving inventory that stores couldn't possibly take care of on their own, removing sensors with a collapsible screwdriver. At the height of it, Noreen strolled the entire concourse in stolen shoes. She was that bold.

Once she took Pat's paycheck and cashed it. Her brother kicked her out, but not without first bashing her face into a door handle while Paige looked on, soiling herself. Nineteen stitches it took, the scar a bolt through her brow.

Sugar pumps through the vents blasting frozen yogurt, soft pretzels. She squeaks her straw through her smoothie. Twice the cost of a meal so it damn well better fill her up. It's not stealing when you use your daughter's cash. She's paid for her purchases. Maybe she'll splurge on a new lipstick or satin sleep set. A pedicure with the little fish that nip away dead skin, mechanical fists kneading out the twists in her back.

Women in tracksuits loop the food court, piercing kiosk, virtual reality booth. A security go-cart is stationed outside The Great Vape Emporium, which used to be a Limited. Couples spill out of Forever 21. A child wobbles along the fountain rim in fairy wings. The grandmother snaps, *mind you don't fall*. It's been ages since Noreen came here with Paige, since they did anything together. Every day her daughter becomes more unreachable, like an earring dropped in the drain, where all attempts at retrieval only push it down more.

Noreen checks her phone. A man in a windbreaker looks on. Her sandal slips off her heel. Frank & Messina have not returned her calls. Maybe that's normal. Maybe there are a million reasons. She's used to dismissal. People think she doesn't notice but she does. It's not useful to get emotional. Noreen is practical. Persistence is key.

Water sells. Murmur Lake is manmade but clean, more substantial than a pond, and nothing like the puddles of scum that crop up like gopher holes, dug from a case of beer and a backhoe. No motorboats or jet skis allowed, unlike the reservoir, which makes it an ideal spot for a new hotel. Picture it: *Midnight Lake*. How charming is that? Say it five times fast. A good baptism makes amnesiacs out of everyone.

"This is Noreen Murphy with Sullivan Sales," she says on the third ring. Her plan is to lead with "exclusive offering," "private" and "secluded." The man in his windbreaker is playing pocket pinball, feeling himself, so she tosses her hair, not exactly encouraging but also not discouraging. Everyone has their urges. She's always been stirred toward the desperate side of people. He gives her a moon-lidded look beneath his cap as she gets the runaround. *Detained, how?* Her mind goes to jail. Phone to her ear, Noreen paces over to the fountain winking with wishes. She has only bills in her pocket, Paige's money, so she flings in a ten. It sails flagrantly around a trumpeting trio of cherubs until the little nymph fishes it out, and the grandmother swipes it, flapping the wet strip in front of her like a flag.

"That's not necessary," Noreen says. Across from her a headless mannequin sports a leopard print in a boutique window, fingers fused together at the hip. "I'll try back."

BETH

Ira inches so close she can smell him, witch-hazel, weed, the vegetal damp of his breath. His scent attracts and repels. There's got to be a third option. Everything's confusing. For a supposed recluse, the man sure is friendly. Wherever they go there are hugs, backslaps; for the hostess, a kiss on the cheek, his gestures personal yet removed, like he's milking it for some political photo opp.

"You're like the goddamn mayor."

"Curse of the small town."

He winks, a salesman's assumption that they're on the same page.

"Do you know your neighbors?"

"Who knows anyone? Trollers ran the seed mill before my time. Today they're a wisp of their former selves. Pissed it all, gave it up or lost it. Some people bumble along on blind luck while others are saddled by strife. Son takes care of his mother. There was a situation and—" He sparks a joint. "It's a prison, to be land poor."

The paper wet from his lips. She pulls on it. "You could help."

"Kole Troller would sooner chase me off with a sawed-off shotgun."

"You don't know that."

"There are those born with the river in their veins, who know every grouse, trout and shad, Holsteins from Jersey bulls. And then there are nudniks like me."

"You said yourself he's desperate."

"And I have nothing better to do than wipe drool from his mama's chinny-chin-chin?"

"That's cheap."

"Truth is free."

"It's not like we're doing anything."

"Yet." He angles into her side body, and a charge skitters through her. Yesterday she made herself come four times in a row, each ripple a little smaller yet deeper, but it didn't rid her of anything. Up at the house, her son is sleeping. Her head throbs. Maybe the lake holds the answer. Beth stumbles to stand, crosses her arms over her dress, and lifts.

The plunge shocks her system, prickling her limbs. Underwater she can be anyone. If there's no seeing out, no one can see in. She remembers something dimly: she's in high school, she has a mother, she has no mother; she becomes a mother. As a teen, she binged on afterschool talk shows, some iteration of good girl gone. Lost to cults, to some untamed wildness. Parents wailed: *How could this happen?* (Unsaid: to *us?*) Beth knows how. The pull is right there. Watch. See Beth drift. See Beth sink. As her lungs contract, she kicks toward the surface where the water's root-beer clear, the scythe of moon so low she could pull up on it, Mac the knife winking like aren't you something. Back at the dock, Ira is opening his belt.

"Wait for me."

"It's cold," she says. "I'm going home."

TZVI

He hunches over a bag of sunflower seeds. Sucks the salt, cracks the shell with his teeth. On their own, each lone nut is too small to satisfy. He keeps coming back to the image of an actual person on the other end, listening. *What would he say? Where to begin?* He eats and spits and eats and spits until his bag becomes a hill of hocked shells.

IRA

Rejection, boy, how it stings.

All morning Ira sulks on his porch in self-imposed exile, working out his frustration through his sketches. At *Man's World*, they paid illustrators good money but he was merely a hobbyist, envious and inferior, his work reminiscent of street drawings: big heads, mollusk feet, jaws of a donkey, like the caricatures sold on Canal. He boils people down to their essence. Noreen: hair and breasts. Beth: bones and teeth.

What went wrong? They'd been getting somewhere. He trades his pens for his tattered scrapbook whose pages he returns to when real loneliness calls. Hubris, to think he ever could have pieced together a whodunit. His title was aces—*Bait, Tackle, Fly*—but everything else was awful.

> *An autopsy has confirmed that Bloch was three*
> *months pregnant at the time, raising questions*
> *as to what this mother of four was doing...*

What was anyone doing? When his mother died, a volunteer from the Jewish burial society watched over her, as was custom. His girls sat a similar vigil on the dock that July morning, and he could only hope they offered a certain peace. Chaya meant life. In return, she gave his kids nightmares large as a whale. He tried to placate them. When a bird dirties your head it may be good luck, but there was no aphoristic equivalent for death.

He grabs his towel. Screw it, it's still his property.

"Ira!" He hears as he swims by the dock, kid flapping orange cuffs. "Can I come in with you?"

"Free country, kid."

The sight of Beth's tiny bikini erases some of his bad feeling.

"Floaties are a crutch." Ira conjures a detached cool. "They teach a false sense of security."

As she slides off Zach's water wings, he notices she has more tattoos, a bumblebee between the shoulders, a lunar eclipse along her ribs. Ira wonders what it feels like to surrender the body to such vandalism, to lie there as a needle punches in and out. Does it hurt like hell or feel good after a while? He went to sleep one night and awoke with the whole world inked in color he can't decode, a raucous teal etched across her lower back, more junk up and down her wrists. He doesn't wear glasses when he swims.

"That's it," Ira pants. "Now toss him in."

"You heard Uncle Ira."

Uncle Ira?

"I'm doing a flying leap!"

"Uncle Ira will catch you!"

Uncle Ira.

"Promise, Mommy?"

"Promise."

He's winded from treading, but motions for the kid anyway. Never been anyone's uncle. The kid jumps face-first and it's not pretty.

"Save some water for the rest of us."

The kid thrashes but Ira knows the benefits of healthy struggle, so he lets him flounder until Beth says, "What the hell's wrong with you?" diving in only to find the kid's figured it out, and lo, he's floating on his own.

"No wonder your own children don't speak to you!"

"You really think I'd let anything happen?"

"I really don't know!"

"I swimmed!"

"Swam," Ira says.

"Now you're all blue." She ghosts a towel around him.

"Someone did die here, you know."

"Very funny."

"Uncle Ryan died."

"See what you started."

"Drowned. It's hardly a secret."

Ira flips onto his back to rest his legs. He's more exhausted than ever. He spews a thin stream of water. "Oh, but it was ages ago."

"I'm not even answering you."

"Newspapers went to town."

"Why are you trying to scare us?"

"Who's scary? I'm only honest."

That night, he goes to the pub. If he stays home, he'll feel worse. From the outside, The Lion's Den looks almost abandoned, siding curled like a cat food can to reveal the pulp of its frame. Top-floor windows are taped up with shipping cardboard. A puddle oozes from the dumpster. The once-neon sign has blown: GOOD ATS.

Inside a dozen patrons are staring into their beers. A table of camp counselors slam quarters into cups, chanting *Chug it, pussy.* A couple with full-sleeve tattoos (again, with the tattoos) slides toward the jukebox, his arm around her waist, her arm through his, her head nuzzled into that spot in the neck, which always felt like a tricky, delicate thing, to move with any sort of grace while attached to another body, but they've got it, these two, his nose drops into her hair, breathing her up because what good fortune it is to have someone to lean on. Or else, the man's too drunk to walk straight.

"Well, if it isn't Ira Lecher!" Noreen calls from the bar. "Your ears must be ringing!"

"Always know how to charm an old fart." He tries sidling up beside her, but the stool has him feeling like an elephant attempting a circus stunt, so he angles against the bar instead. She peels a square of tissue he'd placed over a shaving nick.

"Saving this for someone special?" She blows the paper like a wish, her plum blouse dipping at the neckline.

"Only you." When she leans in, he can see the beige stripe where her make-up ends and her neck begins.

"Where have you been hiding?"

"Here and there."

"Mysterious."

With Noreen, he doesn't need to be clever. They can sit and drink or watch the game or not and have a night regardless. "Nice to see you taking a break from work."

"Funny you should say." Her lipstick is askew, or maybe it's her grin. Her tongue is practically in his ear. "Let's take it to a booth. I don't need the snitches up in my strut when I make you an offer you can't refuse."

"That so, Murphy." His zipper tightens at his groin and it's incredible, just like that, how heat rises, how young he becomes, what a little devotion can do.

BETH

Of course: Beth is sorry and Doug's disappointed. "I don't get it."

New Jersey, Fourth of July. Ryan was born on the Fourth of July. Every year there's a beach barbecue, Frisbees and leather spice, just the way Ryan would've wanted.

"Everyone's counting on you. Do I have to spell it out? We're a family."

For their island honeymoon, Doug had chosen an all-inclusive family resort where they ran into half his senior class who inconceivably already had kids. Doug was impatient, eager to catch up, to place himself at the altar of adulthood. It's not that he was unreasonable. They were just different. They had different visions of adulthood.

"Can I at least take Zach for the weekend?"

"It will feel so empty here."

"Should have thought about that beforehand."

She's quiet. That is what she thinks about. What if she never comes back?

Doug says, "What will I say?"

"Come up with something. You won't even miss me."

"Don't tell me what I'll miss."

Party plate of bun crusts, sandy relish. She almost feels bad.

"You'll have a great time."

"You promised." Doug's voice cracks, more pained than angry. Doesn't he know by now her promises mean nothing?

PAIGE

She tries the bar but it's wishful thinking. As if that Breakstone mermaid might burst from a cloud and whisk her off deus ex machina style, like that play she'd once read.

Memorable people don't stay in Sullivan County. Wouldn't be the first time Paige tried to replace fact with more palatable fiction. There's product in her pocket, fewer takers in town, but the bar trumps the river. Any place trumps the underpass. But then, with the bar comes her mother.

"There's my baby girl!" Noreen embarrasses her from across the room. Drunk already, holding court as usual. Nick, tending, hands her a lager and bag of chips. Crisps, he calls them, on account of a cousin who exports from overseas: bacon and cheese, beef and onion, snack and dinner in one.

"Don't mind my daughter. She's angry because she is always angry."

"Been here long?" Paige whispers. Nick shrugs, squeaks his towel through a pint. She starts to say sorry then stops, fed up with apologizing for the same things, for things outside of her control, for how it always goes.

Ira calls her over and that's another thing: she hates when men call her kid. Even when she was a kid she was no one's kid.

"Your mom and I were just talking about you."

What did her professor say in Am Civ? Great minds discuss ideas, mediocre minds discuss events, small minds discuss people. A president said it, actually a first lady, but the man took all the credit. Paige spits a sliver of nail.

"See what I have to deal with? For your information, Little Miss, we were saying how bright you are. My greatest accomplishment."

"Your mother thinks the world of you."

"Would it kill you to be grateful? Don't walk out, pigeon. Paige!"

She relents to avoid a scene.

"Remember when I used to do your hair? I could give you a fresh edge. Once the ends split like this they only keep curling onto themselves."

"Don't touch."

Her mom touches. "I told Ira how you and me are going to become real estate partners someday. Not always easy to divine God's plan—not that I'm cut from the most devout cloth—"

"I say the divine lies between people."

"YES!" Her mom clutches Ira's hands. "Who hasn't taken a bad turn? For all my detours...tell Ira, tell him, Paige. When opportunity arises, I'm ready to strike."

"If you say so."

"I know so. You have such a sweet face if you'd only let people see it. Ira, doesn't she have a sweet face?"

"You gals are like sisters."

"Stop it, go on." Her mom scoops up her hair, fans herself. When she drinks like this, she gets all blotchy. "I'm too old for flattery. Another round? Paige, be a doll and ask Nick for one on the house."

"He'd sooner cut you off."

"Kid has a point."

"Well, I need to use the ladies' anyhow."

They watch her go. Paige shreds a coaster. Ira takes her by the wrist.

"What do you make of all this?"

Her mom's backside curved like a heart, swaying. *Don't stop believin'.*

"Doesn't matter what I think."

"I no longer trust myself. See these hands? Shakes. Sometimes I wake up and don't know where I am. Or I do but I'm a child, a boychik in an army cot, only I've goddamn pissed myself. Honest to God. I'm out of sorts, I smell like wet socks. This is what you have to look forward to."

"You're not even that old."

"Kids these days, you all have something. I figured—"

A customer. She digs into her sweatshirt, fishes out her Tic Tac box. It's covered in smile stickers. She flips the lid, takes his palm and shakes.

"How can I repay you?"

"Be cool."

"I'm Joe Cool."

He smells like coleslaw, Russian dressing. Even the grossest concoctions, like ketchup and mayo, can be reinvented with branding. She stares at his ponytail, capillaries sprouted through the tip of his nose. He blinks, like he's trying to muffle a cry or a sneeze. She wants to say: It's alright. We all feel awful at times.

Instead she says, "Whatever, pops. You know where to find me."

"You two catching up?" Noreen says loudly. She has touched up her face and overdone it. "Did you talk about my offer? Imagine, with sale profits you can buy multiple homes, a condo in the Bahamas, a bonanza in Jackson Hole."

"How do I know you're not plotting to get rid of me?"

"Can't get enough of you, Ira. But you have to face facts. This is not ancient Egypt. Nothing goes in the grave along with you."

"Such a fatalist, your mother. A real philosopher."

"I'm trying to make you rich."

"Wealth comes from within."

"Only a filthy bastard would say that." Paige squeezes out of the booth.

"That's all we get?"

"What more do you want?"

"Don't be fresh, pigeon."

"You're a joke." If she could take it back she would but her mom's gone and thrust her sloppy self in Paige's face pushing Paige to the verge, unable to focus on her mom this close: lips swollen, pores pitted as rind, skin feathered in pleats. It's like looking in a time-warp mirror, something from *The Twilight Zone*, telegraphing how she'll end up if she's not careful. Paige raises her bottle, feints. Neither is a stranger to violence, but Noreen ducks to land a new cruelty: Her own mother's afraid of her.

"Ease up, you two." Ira says. "Love each other, would you? Warts and all."

Tommy returns just as he left, as if he'd always been there, riding her ass, trapping Paige in his headlights. He blows his horn, fender a snarl, the grill practically grazing the backs of her knees. Paige moves to the shoulder.

"Now you come around, fuck face?"

"Don't act cute," he says, pulling up. Paige cinches the strings of her sweatshirt, punches her pockets. "I'm talking to you." He is swerving, steering with his elbows.

"Get in."

And she does, because, duh, it's Tommy and it's been almost a week.

In the cab Paige kicks off her shoes, her feet unholy, puffy and red. A platypus's beak. Part reptile, part mammal. An animal caught between two things. He pushes off her hoodie, fumbles through her hair. She wipes her mouth. Glitter comes off on her wrist.

Tommy talks as he drives, eyes electric and speedy. He's been hearing things, he says. *What things?* The air is honeysuckle and trefoil until she starts smoking. Then the sweetness goes to shit. Tommy floods his high beams. Oncoming cars flash him to quit it but he doesn't take the hint. Or if he does, he doesn't do anything about it.

"You're a Jew-lover now."

"What are you even saying?"

"Don't play me. Petrillo's my boy. Here I am busting my balls, and you're going around behind my back."

"You and I don't work together."

"What I want to know is if you were ever going to tell me."

"A dime's a dime."

"Spoken like a true whore."

"Were you dropped on your head as a baby, Tommy Potts?"

"Answer me, woman."

"I don't owe you a damn thing."

The parking lot of the Bowl-A-Rama is deserted as a slasher flick, the dark sign looming like a giant Weeble.

"It's their Sabbath, Tommy. Give it a rest."

"Their Sabbath," he mimics. "I'm of half a mind—" This is one of Tommy's favorite phrases. "Half a mind to." He trails off. "Fine, be that way."

This is how he concedes defeat. Tommy braces his arm against the headrest as he spins out in reverse, the gesture so familiar it's nearly loving. Now they are back on the road, another road, the lane narrow as a collapsed vein. It opens up again as they approach the Galleria, hug the dividing line, dirty white, Tommy locking his jaw, Tommy on the dial, Tommy flying from idea to idea. He wants out of extermination, all this dying. She's not sure what he's on—he's jittery, a mix of things, but it's clear he's riding something other than dope because he's not nodding at the wheel. Every once in a while they pass a row of houses with holiday lights still strangling windows. Only takes one good idea, and tonight he's hit upon it, he is hyped on a plan, rattling off numbers, offering a cut, he says, but now, *in light of her behavior*, he raps on the wheel like a school principal, he's not so sure, he has half a mind to punish her, to keep it all to himself. Become a proper entrepreneur. He pronounces the word En-TROMP-a-NOR. Tommy and her mom are both suckers. Believing every scam is foolproof. Calling cards and phone chargers, headphones the size of plungers, a hot stash waiting for him in the back of BIG LOTS thanks to a friend of his cousin Silko who works the stockroom. Tommy's eyes wild, they pass a drive-through and Paige's stomach cries out for a Whopper, no pickles, a strawberry shake, but Tommy, when he's like this, food is the last thing, he slings into the next lane, plows through the mall's exit, nearly puncturing his tires on the spikes, kills the engine, shuts his lights.

"Can I trust you?"

"What are we doing here?"

He tells her to can it. He is bugging, drying his palms on his thighs, his gaze darting from the side to rearview like a mad dog. It makes her dizzy just watching.

"This is my plan, I invented it, no one else did. Got it? Understood?"

"Jesus, Tommy."

"Wait." He shushes her. Shuts the radio, flips the mirror. He hunches in his seat. It's like he's reenacting a sting operation from a bad movie, trying to remember his lines.

"Last chance. Float me three hundred and I'll triple it when I'm done."

"No freaking way."

At which point he grabs her purse. She grabs back. Contents spill out: lip gloss, tampons, half a Milky Way.

"Why are you always such a fuckhead?"

He picks up her smokes and crushes them.

When Paige opens the door, he backhands her in an attempt to block the exit, more of a brush than anything, Tommy can't hurt a fly, but she hugs herself as if stung, anyway.

"Paigebaby."

"You really are the worst, Tommy Potts." She pulls a plastic bag from her jeans and tosses it at him. "Here, go kill yourself."

"Paige! Come back. You'll be sorry! You're making a mistake!" He hollers, but she takes off through the parking lot, insects clinging to the fury of lights, and keeps going. Even when she hears the slam of his cab door, the stagger of feet, she does not turn. Eventually, he'll stop trying; he'll get back in; drive on. A blister is blooming on her left heel, so she plows ahead barefoot, swinging her shoes in her hand.

Soon enough it will be morning, but for now, the road, this night is hers.

TZVI

After Shabbos, he walks. His phone buzzes but business can wait. He wanders until he is beyond the perimeter, the thinly strung *eruv*, out of range. There is safety in shadow, in the cloak of night. Sometimes there are deer, a rumored bear. Always: his *mame*, whispering in the wind. When cars clip the shoulder, he presses himself against the bark of a tree. Roughness feels good. Feeling feels good. To imagine the path she took, if she'd not been taken, but exited the gate on her own two feet, if she'd been alone. She couldn't have covered the entire distance in one night. If she'd lay down to rest, somewhere in a field halfway between. Walking is what he does to draw her closer. He doesn't get far before he turns toward the bowling alley. Sticks out his thumb only to be passed. Honked at. Spit on. Egged. He wonders if she stuck out her thumb. If anyone slowed. If she got in. If she knew the driver, where she was going. *If.*

BETH

"I don't feel good," Zach says. He is carsick; nothing sits well. The roads are crummy. One missed turn and she doubles back, past the signs saying HUNT SAFELY. She plows over the remnants of a rodent already ground to smithereens. His mashed bean breakfast, swaddled in paper towel, smells like organic dog shit.

"Look out the window."

"How will that help?"

"It just helps."

"Did Uncle Ira tell you?" Her son lowers his voice. "He's not really my uncle."

They'd told Zach the bare minimum about Uncle Ryan—he was a brave man, a hero. He'd have loved you to pieces. They spoke in platitudes, Beth firing clichés that Doug took for earnest. Ryan was a horny teen, she got him off; she didn't fucking know him. This was Doug's territory: his brother, his livelihood, an industry that transcended loss. Zach was on a need-to-know basis. What did a four-year-old need to know? Life was a mammal of grief. There would be time for everything: buildings, planes, questions.

Two weeks in, and Beth is Zen as an ad for vaginal hygiene. Maybe the rest cure isn't complete Freudian bullshit. Mountain air mists her cheeks; the selvage down her nail beds has smoothed over, resuming its natural color, and even her hair, which grew in sprouts after years of nursing, is enjoying a hopeful bloom.

"Here we are," she practically sings. The familiar Shalom Yisroel sign flanked by ladybugs and faded suns. Zach unbuckles his seat.

"Wait for mommy!"

She has become a parent who refers to herself in third person, everything she'd swore she'd never be, porting around an arsenal of baby carrots and wipes. At the top of the hill stands a modular unit, like one of those auxiliary classrooms installed on city blacktops to accommodate public school overcrowding.

"Well, hello! Who have we here?" The director steps onto the porch, stylish wig fixed to her head, dark as liquid lead. Beth wants to touch it. Feel the weight. Try on a new hairstyle. Try something.

"This is Zachary. He's not circumcised, but he's Jewish, I mean, I'm non-practicing—" Heat floods her face, like she's auditioning for something. "Isn't it the mother that counts?"

"Mom."

"Beth."

"Welcome. I am Este Fein but you can call me Morah. Why don't we have a look around? Malkie!" A freckled girl—a counselor? no more than thirteen—pops out of the door, back brace bulging through her shirt like an exoskeleton.

They skip over to a jungle gym where a dozen or so children are climbing and hanging upside-down, side locks unraveling like fly paper, skirts flounced over their heads. There are regular kids, too. Not religious. Zach melds into the crowd—how easy it is for children to make friends. All they have to say is: *Do you want to play?*

"As you can see," Este says. A necklace of sweat bubbles at her collar. She wears a floor-length jean skirt and three-quarter sleeves; a lanyard strung with keys. "Your child's comfort is our number-one priority." Este moves with a surprising fluidity for someone this buttoned up. She seems so relaxed in her skin. So...sexy.

"At Camp Shalom, we offer nature, kick ball, gaga—that's like dodgeball. Flexibility is our rule of thumb. Day-to-day, week-to-week. No Fridays, no Sundays."

"My son has allergies."

"We're accustomed to dietary restrictions." Este opens the door onto a waft of yeast, apple juice. Crackers dust the carpet, but Zach can't have crackers. He can't have anything, she starts to list, but Este stops her. "Don't worry. We'll take care of it." Zach will be in good, better hands. Godly hands. This is what she wants, isn't it? To surrender? Why is separation suddenly so hard? Beth sifts her fingers through the sensory table, plucking a toothbrush from the trough of raw oats, a sparkly rubber ball.

Este relieves her of her tote bag of EpiPens, Benadryl, inhalers, gluten-free pretzels, and nut-free cookies, steers Beth toward the exit.

"It's for his sake as much as for yours, Mom." Este's voice is so calm Beth could melt into her. "At some point, we all must cut the cord."

IRA

Last night was a mistake. Ira pushes against the calf of Noreen, her body clammy but warm, like meat that has been left out and turned. It doesn't spring back. No overnight guests: perhaps his only policy. Ira is not one for rules—except maybe to break them—but with Noreen here, he feels like a beast in doll quarters. Like his head could bust through the roof. One pill makes you larger kind of thing, which is what happens when people overstay their welcome.

His blanket itches. Alcohol seeps from his pores, mingling with hers, stinking up the place—all four hundred square feet of it—his home a veal cage. A water glass by his bed tastes like breath. He's fresh out of the samples Paige gave him. He tries fixing his hair, but his hand is useless, as though he's slept on it funny. Ira makes a fist. Open, shut. He could go for another nifty pill.

"Rise and shine."

"What's the rush?"

The few times they'd gotten together he'd gone to Reenie's apartment. It was convenient. But ever since her daughter had come back from school, there were problems. Boyfriend problems. Other problems. Everyone had problems but Paige had problems in spades. Ira could see it in the girl's pinball eyes, swirly, hypnotic; the kind of eyes that blocked out the world before the world could destroy you. She'd strode into The Lion's Den without shoes, which by itself was nothing, maybe. The temperature was mild. Feet were feet. Combined with problems, however. They were playing gin rummy when Paige upset the game, sending Ira under the table to recoup the cards, Noreen steering Paige by that wishbone of an elbow. Her feet all cut up and blistered, like they'd been through it. The whole room heard them. Heartbreaking, the things people said to each other in the name of family.

So he bought the next round and the next and he and Reenie drank and played cards and he'd made an exception out of a twisted mix of empathy and pity, because if he knew anything he knew that distance made the heart fonder, rendered the intolerable tolerable, and Paige, he could tell, needed space from her mother. Poor mothers. They endured the brunt of everything. Noreen couldn't have been more than a girl herself when she had her.

He squared the deck on the table.

"You're a good man, Ira."

"Don't get any ideas about me."

"I only have one." Noreen reached for him by the jukebox. Noreen acted on instinct and Ira was grateful for it, so he took her home to let the good times roll, and roll they did, without shame or apology, like children. In truth, they fit. But the place, at the end of it, was his.

"Up and *Adam*."

"Would you like to freeze off my tits?"

Ira lives alone, sleeps alone. Another nudge, this time scraping Noreen with his toenails. She doesn't flinch. That's one of the things he likes about her. Reenie won't break. Only in Sullivan County could you find bones like these. Good bones. Shiksa bones. Push all he wants and still she holds—

"Where do you possibly have to be?"

Ira has exactly nowhere to be. He wonders if Beth's around, where she's been zipping off to in that go-cart of a car.

"Night's over, sleeping beauty."

"What about my grand tour of the property?"

A sliver of scalp peeks through her hair. Just like that, desire morphs into disgust.

"Not today, kid."

She smells like deli meat and booze. Ira has started smelling old. He noticed it recently, hints of his father. He is what they call well-preserved, he can swim laps around the pot-bellied Millennials hawking homemade yogurt at seasonal markets, he is unburdened by knee braces, virtually without complaint, complaints he has, but his father was dead at seventy. Simon Lecher remained a stranger, inscrutable to the grave. Undershirts and paisley trunks, socks threaded gold at the toe. Never took his son on a sales trip but carried his entire life with him for months at a clip. Once Simon brought him to the Playboy Club, flashed a members' key to open the gates of Gehenna. But the road to freedom wasn't all waxed legs and cars, either. His father had fled another life. Neither had much faith in monogamy. Impulse, they had in droves. Like father, like son. Intimacy was forever a stranger. Noreen is a lady friend. One of many ladies Ira knows or has known, all of them lady friends. The phrase depresses him. Still, she makes the spring in summer, the winters a little less wintry.

Ira sets the kettle on the stove.

"Later, then?" She sits up. "I'll bring over paperwork."

Viv would murder him if he sold the place without any consultation. That is, unless Noreen really made good on her numbers. Then Viv would murder him anyway, but with a designer knife.

"Call me old-fashioned, but let's take things slow."

"It's just a listing agreement." She cups her mug. "Many people your age downsize."

"Putting me out to pasture already?"

"You're going to thank me."

"I thank you already for the root and toot."

But there is a schedule to keep. It's time for his swim. Blame the German blood on his regimen. What a compliant soldier, a good fascist he'd have been, if only the end game hadn't been mass extermination.

The screen whips behind him as he heads down to the lake. Ira needs the water as others do prayer. Sometimes in the off season he doesn't bother with swim trunks. It is the beginning of July. He bothers with trunks. With a running start, Ira catapults cannonball-style and soars, the closest he gets to glory before his body crashes through the surface like a pinky ball through a tenement window, only instead of an angry smocked Fraulein shaking her fist, Murmur receives him, ripples out in embrace. This, to him, is love. Something brushes against him, a water snake, a leaf, small-mouthed bass, but it doesn't faze him. He frogs his legs. Whatever it is skitters away.

He swims a graceless freestyle through mysterious pockets of warm and cold until he nears the center where he treads in place for his heart. Sometimes, he performs a reverse dead man's float, belly up, sun kissing his lids. Other times, he paddles the entire length, five hundred meters. The Troller side festers with rusted machinery like the skeletal remains of the armored convoy he saw on the road to Jerusalem when he visited in '74. Ira has no idea how his neighbors live. How much can one get for a bale of hay? Nothing seems in working order. Slender cows wade, a goat defecates into the shallow end.

Today, Ira sinks to the bottom. Mud squishes through his toes. A person drowns in your waters and there goes your innocence. His daughters never got over it. *Who isn't haunted?* Take Beth. Something about her nervous energy, her hellish tattoos that enrage and arouse him. He can't put his finger on it. What's her story? Eventually, he runs out of air.

By the time he reaches the dock, he's spent, legs rubbery as a prop chicken. Lately, he's not been feeling himself. Who else might he feel like? Ira wears his towel like a prayer shawl on the slow walk home through moss and nettles, lacy discs of lichen the color of mint gum. Back at the cabin, Noreen is gone. So is his car.

PAIGE

Paige knows her mom can't help herself. Can't open a credit line from here to Ulster County, and couldn't tell you the number of nights she's spent in jail. (Three.) Her mom never believes she'll get caught, and when she does, she treats her sticky fingers as if they were a separate entity. Paige knows old habits don't die. But this is the first time she's ripped her off outright.

"The fuck, Mom?"

"Watch your mouth." Noreen lisps, bleach stickers taped to her teeth.

"It's one thing to short Peter to fund Paul, but last time I checked, I was still your actual daughter."

"Have you asked Tommy? The way he's been stumbling around like the living dead—"

Paige is not falling for it. Tommy with a rig in his arm is not crafty enough to find her tackle box. Tommy had a hard enough time with his flatbed of stolen goods, which he and Silko unloaded in midtown then blew in the gutter, scarcely making it home alive. It takes everything he's got to heed a house call for Animal & Pest. There are skunks in the attic, a raccoon in the shed, an army of carpenter ants to eradicate, there are more animals than ever, but Tommy is too busy ruining himself to mercy-kill another.

"Think I wouldn't notice?"

"So I went to the mall. You can't be mad."

"I can be however I want to be."

"Consider it an investment. Fake it till you make it. Remember *Let's Make a Deal*? What's a few bucks when a windfall is headed our way?"

A windfall is a tree struck by storm, sawed into logs and whisked to the lumberyard. A windfall has Puritan origins, circa eighteenth century. This is no windfall.

"How much are they paying you at The Breakstone, anyway?"

"I've been saving, klepto. Try it sometime."

"Live a little, honey." Her mother shakes out a blouse with a ruffled top. It belongs on a baby. "Isn't this cute?" She holds it to Paige's chest. "It would look cute on you, too."

Paige swipes away her hand.

"What is it with you? Sue me, Scrooge. I went to Dress Barn."

The glint in her mom's eye, like a schoolgirl with a crush, makes it hard to stay angry. Her mom's hair is a fresh crimson, darker at the ends. Ombre, it's called, though Paige can't tell if it's deliberate or a bad dye job. There is stain around the ears. Paige hopes her money didn't pay for that facial border.

"Want to see what else I got?"

"What *I* got."

Her mother opens each package slowly, as if it were alive. A periwinkle top with pearl buttons. A coral blouse looped in a bow at the neck. A taupe poly-blend suit. A pair of slides, open at the toe, make her feet look like hooves.

"What do you think?"

"Should have asked."

"I gave you life."

"Give me a break."

Paige pictures her mom diving beneath her mattress, heels cracked like a riverbed, for the tackle box Mark Troller once gave her to store acorns, seed pods on which she'd drawn faces, the box decorated with Sharpie and glitter glue. Although the bait shop closed before Paige was born, the leftover inventory sat gathering grime in the Troller basement. At one point, her mom tried selling hand-tied flies of bucktail and peacock on eBay.

"I don't keep secrets from you. What do you keep from me?"

All those times Kole Troller took her to the cellar, the smell of bleach and wet clay. Paige doesn't answer.

"You never would have spotted me had I asked."

"Not true." Yes, true.

"You don't even give me the time of day, pigeon."

Paige unfolds the receipts. "Where's the rest?"

"I ran into Kole and—"

"I knew it."

Paige storms out. In the kitchen she chugs a beer, lifts Noreen's keys from the decorative rack, GOD BLESS OUR HOME. The road unfurls before her. She wants to drive all night long and keep driving and not stop and never look back until the ocean laps at her feet. Leave before she forgets to want out. That's the real casualty of the county; once it's inside you, it's nearly impossible to shake. Every ounce of gravel she knows like a birthmark on her body. Stick around and she'll never get out from Kole, Tommy, from whoever comes next. This is what stirs her, engineering smiles wide enough to break her face when customers send back their eggs, or make her wait outside the bowling alley like a third-rate citizen. Destination: Florida. She can almost taste the citrus, coconut cream. She smokes and drives, pops the amber bottle tucked inside her jean jacket and sifts its contents onto her lap: one bar, two. It's a fine balance. To calm herself enough to get through the next few hours, but not beyond. She veers slightly to the left, then corrects.

It's dark at Kole's place. For someone so smart, her next move is stupid. She puts herself in situations. Asks for it, Tommy says. Kole is not her father but he's the only father she's known, which is why she's standing there after hours, pounding at his dark door.

A light flickers in the upstairs window. She smokes down to her fingers.

"Look what the cat drug in." Kole's hair sticking out the sides of his head like an electrocution.

"Where's my money, Kole."

"Howdy to you, peach."

"My mom had no right—"

He confuses a hand in his shorts. Paige blows past him. The hall is decorated in knick-knacks of sorry-ass pigs. Kole's mother was obsessed. Pig-shaped doorstops and pig-stitched needlepoint pillows. When she lived with them, Paige collected stickers of Piglet and Miss Piggy to add to the potholders, the dish towels that said ONE MAN'S PIG IS ANOTHER MAN'S BACON. Foolishly, she thought, the more figurines she pinched out of clay, the more she'd please the matron of the household, the kinder in turn Mrs. T. would treat her and her mom, the more she'd actually feel—

"We're family. You know that. What's mine is yours."

He cups her ass. Blood, it's not always thicker than water. Water can be plenty thick. Kole, lest she need reminding, knew her before she was born. Took her and her mom in like a pair of strays. Not many people would do that out of the goodness of their heart, as if goodness and hearts come without strings attached.

Her eyes tear at the spoors of dander, the thick scent of maple syrup. The TV beckons its blue glow from the den where Mark sits facing the window like a sentinel on night watch. Kole creeps behind her.

"Here I thought you've come to pay respects. This morning my mother wakes up dead, but no thanks for the sympathy."

Now, this shit? "Aw, Jeez." The guy loved his mother. "I'm sorry, Kole. I am. But you have to understand, that money wasn't to be given. I earned it; you need to give it back."

"We all got needs. Folks around here pitch in during times of need, or has that college coursing gone to your head?"

She knows what comes next. He takes her wrist and bends it, steering her toward the stairs. People are so predictable; she would laugh if it were someone else's life. Steps groan as she takes them. He is not gentle. From the top of the stairs, a dormer window stares back at her. As a child, she used to imagine flying through that porthole on the threads of Peter Pan, Tinker Bell, a godmother, a good witch. It was important to know the exits.

"Your mother understands the importance of a proper funeral. Noreen is a generous woman. Generosity would do you some good."

"My boyfriend will whale you."

"Tommy Potts couldn't find the Easter Eggs if he hid them himself."

When they reach the landing, he stops. The floor slopes like a funhouse. To the left is his room; to the right, the room Paige once shared with her mother.

"Heck, Paige. Tonight started on the wrong foot. Let's try this again. How about a proper hug for your pal Kole. Don't be rude, especially as you're the one dropping in so late."

She glances around. "Where's Kathy?"

"Why are you always trying to hurt me?"

His bed is unmade, sheets bunched to one side. She taps out another bar and takes it dry. Down the hall the toilet is running, as if it might actually go somewhere.

"Need to replace the valve," Paige hears herself saying as Kole peels off her jacket.

"Never miss a thing, do you."

His breath eggy, the pillow oiled beneath. Above her, the ceiling fan is broken, but she keeps this to herself. Where she's headed, there will be sequins and spiny fins, white dunes and salt waves. In Florida, there are entire amusement parks devoted to fairytales. Dolphins in captivity but happy endings, too. There are mermaids in tanks. How do mermaids keep their sparkle from washing away? *What was that thing about habits?* The heel of

Kole's hand grinds her forehead, his weight compressing her lungs. She drifts up and out from underneath him.

"Tell me," he grunts. "When have I ever kept what's not mine?"

The fan is a carousel, an asterisk, spokes on a wheel. As he drives into her she grips the blades. She spins and spins. By daybreak she'll have her four hundred dollars.

IRA

Ankles, tender, the size of his wrists. Knobs protruding like windup buttons. Boxed in his shower, Beth soaps and Ira listens to the sluice of suds wondering what's her pattern, does she wash from toe or head first, is she a scalp massager or scratcher, as she slides a loofah between her thighs, into the armpits then buttocks, cheeks slapped pink, a little extra in the fold, will she erupt into song? Youth is always so hard to resist. Her toe polish is chipped, Achilles shackled in a vine. Man alive, now he's stiff.

"Hello?"

A prattle of excuses, he's come to check a window, to read the gas meter, he's come because he can't not, it's been days. He waits for the froth to clear.

"Glad you're making use of the outdoor shower. Built it myself. No frills, but great pressure, right? Worth risking a splinter, if you ask me."

The flick of the latch. He busies himself with the stack of junk mail he's collected, circulars, catalogues, letters from Ayn Rand's fan club one of his girls joined years ago. Objectivism aside, Howard Roark was a dreamboat. *What's a hundred dollars for a lock of phony hair?*

Beth steps out in her towel. "Can I have a minute?"

"Take all the minutes. About last week—"

"Close the screen. There are ants."

"Goes with the territory."

"Well, I didn't invite them." Her bedroom door slams. He squishes one on the console, boots a toy to the wall, nearly skidding on a sticker book of emergency vehicles. In the kitchen he helps himself. A burly fly zooms from the mouth of the fridge.

"Beth, I came to say—"

"You're the landlord. Take care of it, please."

They take her car. His car's with Noreen but hers is a thimble.

"Where's the rest of it?"

"It's bigger than a Smart car."

"Can it do my taxes?"

"It can go 65."

"Does it come with a shoehorn?"

There's the smile, there he is, redeeming himself. Fitting into the seat is like stuffing a sleeping bag into those ridiculous sacks. His head grazes the roof, making him feel bigger than he is, clownish, but he could see how, like a Cabriolet, it could puff up a smaller person.

He feeds her a joint, which gets her talking. She won't shut up. Husband this and Jersey that, the same tiresome refrain. Always the pretty ones who think they have it worse.

"This is so not me." She says over and over, like she's trying to convince herself. They pick up the kid. Zach's in camp now. Thanks to Ira, he's got circle time, share time, snack time, play time, rest time, snack time, pack-up.

"What did you even do all day?"

"This and that. Grown up, boring stuff."

"Errands?"

"Hard to know where the time goes."

They roll past farms of stone and ochre. Ira stretches an arm across her headrest, not a come-on, but rather, he cannot fit in this goddamn car. It's like being trapped inside a woman's brain: snack wrappers, hair ties, sunglasses with a popped out lens.

She shakes a tin of mints toward him. He accepts her offering. The road dips, the sky blue, the fields rising and falling to meet it. Then, barf. One minute everything is grand, hunky dory, only Beth anticipates the turns as well as a student driver, her dinky car lacking shock absorption, so the next minute, the kid is fluming up a lung, there's vomit everywhere: pink and brown chunks, kernels of corn, regurgitated pulp the size of collector coins. It is foul. Ira has forgotten how disgusting it is, children, the smell of parmesan, which made Heather gag at a restaurant once when it was dusted over her meatballs and spaghetti, his sensitive daughter, so sensitive, sensitive to the slightest of things.

"Jesus H. Christ!"

"Who's the child here?" Pulling over, Beth sets to work. She scoops clumps from the upholstery, mops her son's cheeks, runs a wet nap through the valley of each finger.

"Don't worry, baby. These things happen."

"I am Mount Su-vi-us."

"Right-O, volcano. Sip." Water bottle snaps. "Tell me when you're hungry again."

"Are you a glutton for punishment?"

"He's too small to sacrifice meals." Beth eyes the rear view. "Sometimes you need to purge and start over, right buddy?" She pops in a playlist, patronizing and cloying, as if the singers have been sucking helium. Why there's an entire genre that panders to children when music is music, but he shuts up through "Aiken Drum," the muffin man, the one about the ducklings busting out into the world and ditching their mother.

Besides, she's still talking.

"Wait, I totally went to camp around here once, *oh my God*. How could I have blocked out that summer? Maple Ridge: all girls, reveille, I hated it."

"We don't hate."

"You tell her, kid."

"I ran away."

"Where did you run, Mommy?"

"I was like, 'You can't make me.' They made me. My dad and his new wife believed you had to try something three times before passing judgment, like frozen peas. Meanwhile, my sister Amy marched around in her uniform loving every minute. My stepmother waddled up on Visiting Day looking like a house boat, insisting there was no greater gift than a sibling, as if their, quote, 'baby-making efforts' were done for our benefit."

"Pop-pop poked his penis into Gramgie's angina and fertilized her with his semen."

"You're ready for *Jeopardy*, kid."

"Ivy was born three months later. My mom not dead a year."

"You never talk about your mother."

"One morning we had to make our own lunches. Her note said *Someday, you'll understand*. The woman drove west to remake herself as a potter. I never saw her again. She died a few months later."

"You miss her?"

"She abandoned us."

"I'd miss you, Mommy, if you were dead."

"Looking back I can see how we walked all over her."

After the drowning, he brought his girls to Wickham Waterpark, but Viv scolded him for their sunburns, which blistered and peeled. Whatever Ira did, he could not protect them. Today the park is smaller than he remembers, crouched behind a candle factory wheezing juniper and sea breeze. Beth wedges between minivans, a *Moshiach Now!* sticker.

At the ticket booth, Zach ducks under his mother's dress and Ira is awash with envy. No one ever sought refuge in a tent made of him. Inside the gate the kid straightens his spine against the barn animal yardstick, but he's too small to ride.

"You measure up—in my book."

"You don't count, Mommy."

Earlier, Ira had been waffling, board shorts? Ball busters? In Manhattan, he'd sit in the *shvitz* to the embarrassment of his girls, Heather with her freckles, and Hillary, thick limbs melding into ankles like the puffy extremities of drowning victims. *Why do dead bodies float?* Hillary wanted explanations, as if logic could explain the illogical, eventually turning to religion, to orthodoxy, while Heather dove deeper into marine science.

"I'll hold the fort." Ira touches his toes, waistband crunching. How many sixty-six-year-olds can do that? But no one's impressed; they're off and running into the waning light. Beth boosts Zach up the slide. They splash into the pool. Skip off to the twisty octopus, the lazy river whose float tubes are twice their size. His socks have cut into his calves like diaper elastic. Ira works over the ridges with his thumb.

"Hey, kid. Give you a buck to get Mom on the big Kahuna."

"That's not necessary," Beth says, and off she goes to the monster slide, returning breathless. "I've never felt so alive."

"Dopamine," Ira says. "Same as that allergy pen."

"I mean, wow."

"Wow is Mom upside-down."

"Hungry?" She drips onto her tote bag. The sadness of brown apples, bread scrabbled with paste. Her food offends him. *You think in Theresienstadt we cared about flavor?* his mother would say, dropping a withered frankfurter on his plate. Dumplings. Plop. Red cabbage, raisins fat as cockroaches. His mother boiled everything to a saltless pulp. Nevertheless, there was always dinner. Ira misses the women who fed him. Noreen could layer lasagna noodles into corning ware, but it wasn't the same, the smell of roast chicken and new potatoes. Nights when it is just him and his toaster, he loses his appetite. Anthropological, perhaps. There's no pleasure in eating alone.

"When he was first diagnosed," Beth says, breaking her sandwich with her fingers, "we didn't know what to do. Reactions weren't clear: eat a cheese stick, spring a rash. He was sick all the time until he all-out stopped growing, he was off the charts, so I took him to endocrinologists, gastroenterologists, psychiatrists. There's a term for it: failure to thrive. I started experimenting with elimination. Gluten, then dairy, the two in tandem. Nuts are different. Nuts permeate everything. Pretzels, ice cream. There's danger in proximity alone. At least, dairy and wheat won't kill him. Shellfish elicits hives."

"What did you eat in pregnancy?"

"How original, to blame the mother."

"When I was your age—"

"Here we go."

"Occasionally, you'd see a bee allergy bracelet."

"Bees are practically obsolete."

"The human race is practically obsolete."

"This is not some Munchausen fantasy."

Ira unwraps the kid's sandwich.

"Don't touch! One fatal handshake, one innocent kiss, one hug from a child who licked a peanut cup, and boom, his airway will shut down."

Beth squirts a round of sanitizer. Only so much you can control, Ira wants to say. What happens, happens, is going to happen. She happens to be shaking out a sack of fresh cherries. They dip into the wet bag together. Ira demonstrates how to eat one whole, like this, braced against the front teeth, pushing out the woody stem with his tongue. Zach swallows his pit.

"Now a tree will grow inside of you!"

The kid stops mid-chew. Ira spits the seed into his fist.

"Christ. Never trust a grown-up. Nine times out of ten we are full of it."

"Full of what?"

"Motor oil, concrete, cotton candy. You name it."

"Poop."

"Now you're talking, kid."

"Many children outgrow them, like a stutter. There's a researcher in California who introduces small doses of allergens with the intent of bulking up immunity."

"Slowly poisoning them?"

"Apparently, we can become desensitized to anything."

"Until we're all comfortably numb."

"That's the data. There's always more you can take."

"Well, you're the mother."

A low-flying plane cuts overheard. "The clouds are writing!"

"Chemtrails, kid. Nothing but smoke and exhaust."

Zach reads. "Break....Out...2014..."

"Color war." Ira lies on the blanket, head in his hands. "At fifteen grand a pop, campers ought to be parachuting in Mylar suits from that *farshtinkener* plane."

BETH

He had been handsome once. Not in a traditional sense, but he has that smart look, features bold and outsized, like a Yiddish puppet. She'd seen a show once on PBS during an abysmal stretch of mood when she'd drop Zach at preschool then crawl back to bed, to those marionettes with bushy eyebrows dense enough to hide a covetous lust for thy neighbor's wife. The way Ira is lying beside her, fading light on his cheekbones, he looks almost beautiful: a gentle, lazy bum. He has good hair, skin supple as a well-loved handbag. He smiles, suddenly cognizant of her attention, his teeth shiny but off, as though dipped in a glaze of soup.

Doug is attractive in a conventional way, iron arms, shaved chest, fuckable if not particularly solicitous. Rarely does he lift his eyes from his phone, and when he does, he levels them past her. He practices his speeches in the mirror and lifts weights in the mirror, pounding his chest like a baboon. Ira meets her gaze and winks. A group of religious women have entered, waterproof skirts and blouses clinging to them like wonton skins, their hair tucked in turbans, swim shoes webbed like duck feet.

"I wonder what it's like," Beth says. They look like Este Fein. The girls are all dressed the same. Only the boys are different. The little ones, younger than her son, toddle along the path, hair flying long and free. Ira says what a pity.

"It's a limited, sheltered life."

"It's admirable. No questions, no doubt. Everything in service to God."

"God is only called upon out of fear, to rationalize bad behavior, to deny individual freedom. Who do you think makes these laws?"

"I don't know, it's kind of romantic. Keeps the mystery alive. Doug takes a dump with the door open." She pops a cherry.

"Mystery is overrated. Holiness is a hoax. I know these people."

"These people? Aren't they your people? Mine? Aren't we all just people?"

"To them, we're heathens."

"Este Fein says everybody's welcome."

"She's Lubavitch."

"Love a witch?"

"You call yourself a New Yorker? There are sects. Bobov, Satmar. Lubavitch Hasidim may act inclusive, but their agenda is to recruit you back to the fold..."

"Everyone has an agenda."

"Ha Shem is here, Ha Shem is there, Ha Shem is everywhere," Zach pipes on cue.

"You're screwed."

"Oh, it's sweet."

"Would you call a fleet of ambulances barreling down 11th Avenue on *yontiv* escorting rabbis to high-priced call girls sweet?"

"What's a call girl?"

"Here, Zee." She hands over a pad, markers. The women fall into formation, a centipede of feet, coolers clocking against thighs, older children in charge of younger ones and so on down the line.

"Should I sign you up for their *mikveh* club? Oh, wait. They don't want you. You're not good enough. Why do you think they have so many kids? God will provide, they say, mouths open, hands out, taxing the planet. Flouting any secular law they don't like. Shocker, the world hates us."

"You're a self-loathing Jew, Ira Lecher."

"Face the music, Brenda Patimkin. Our tribe has a likability problem, and they don't help matters. Am I awful? Who isn't? No one notices the good apples. Religion, in general, is a raw deal— unless you're the man. For women, it's no way to live. I lost my own daughter to her faith. That what you want?"

LECH

Beth's cheeks steam as the women pass her by. There's something beautiful in the way they intuit what's required from each other without speaking. The sight of them—Sisters? Cousins? Friends?—confined by their clothing yet unfettered, indifferent to spectacle, fluid as a murmuration of starlings, fills her with longing. She thinks of Amy, Ivy. *Could they ever come together like this?*

"Of course, we're all hypocrites."

With that, Ira tags Zach—"You're it!"—and they're off to the ropes and swing bridges. Beth wraps up their leftovers. Zach's needs have turned her into a peddler of special meals. In this small way, she is one of them. A large bucket tips over Ira's head, sending Zach into stitches and Ira into mock outrage, high-kneed chase. She has to admit he's the best toy for her son.

She can't remember who said it, about male-female friendship. Amy likely cribbed it from a movie. Beth, short on friends, never gave it much thought. Niceness made her suspect, so she avoided it. Someone was always trying to get in the other's pants.

"My son can't get enough of you."

"Likewise." Ira, panting, plops down: nose pink, lashes wet. A fat bead of chlorine lands on her thigh.

"Spell me," Zach demands, sliding into the V of her legs. A game they play. Beth traces invisible letters on his back and he puts them together. L, O, V.

Ira scoots behind her in the chain.

"You're tight. You're all twisted." For a second she thinks she feels him harden, and pushes into it, daring him, but he's gone and receded, leaving nothing but a phantom pressure against her tailbone as the soft pads of his hands work her muscles, loosening her toughest knots.

"It's getting late," she says.

They get home after dark. Ira grabs her stuff from the car while she carries Zach up the drive, his sleeping body a lifeless weight. With a click, Ira closes the door behind them.

TZVI

The first time he's picked up, he accepts it as the will of G-d. The Torah teaches: Torah is the way. Torah steers the righteous, the simple, and wicked. Is he testing G-d or being tested? Whatever he gets he deserves. The car slows to a stop. The upholstery is unclean. There are more men in the back, snorting like rutting beasts. At first, he looks out the window as darkly the world goes by. Is he more alone in banishment or belonging? Who can choose? Drugs. Money. What's wanted is his body. The second time, he will not spill seed. The third, he submits to a hierarchy of violence. To the rape of his *payos* by pocket knife. His side curls, shorn, look like a pig's tail. He does not fight or scream. The fourth time, he asks: What kind of G-d? He can no longer breathe through his mouth. He does not want. He chokes down tears. *Where is G-d now?* Infinite, everywhere. Trembling on the fifth, he swallows.

NOREEN

At Ira's place, everything feels used up, yet temporary. A mirror tilts off a sticky hook, curtains tacked with pushpins. There's a bathmat for a rug, sofa since the birth of Jesus.

Naked, Noreen renders hospital corners as her mother taught her; her mother, who made a life of cleaning up after strangers, knew more from their mess than they knew of themselves. Her breasts judder as she tucks, areolae like poker chips, but what's one more ache. She's come this far. Nothing happens on its own. Her mother called laziness the devil's business. Noreen may have entertained plenty of devil in her day, but those days are over.

Next she dusts every surface of his cabin, casting particles into the air before directing attention to herself, cupping and lifting, hooking the eye of her bra. Edged in lace, her undergarments are mismatched, but no longer the size of the American flag. She pats herself with her whole hand. A point of pride: how hard she's worked. So long Miracle Whip, hello salad sack. Deprivation pays off. Her body has always served her, but her new body has whistles and bells.

In all her life she's never seen this side of Murmur. Sometimes Noreen would prop her daughter in the Troller window, Mark palming Paige's young back so she could look out without falling. That was the most he could give. Kole would say, *Get a load of them.* What he meant was summer people, namely Jews. A hundred shades of them, all of them trouble. The hatted ones down by Monroe created an uproar over the water supply, something about microscopic shrimp; froze out farmers by importing their own butchers and eggs. "Who died and made them king?" Kole said. At 17, he was indignant. "We need to take care of our own."

I need to care of myself, Noreen decided years ago. It was a Saturday, because that late-night variety show was on, where celebrities mock people in front of a live studio audience. The host known for her signature hairstyle as much as her sitcom, only now it was teased in a perm and mussed with a clip. In the skit, she wore a check-out vest, cracked jokes about patio furniture in the living room.

"They think they're clever, but isn't it mean?"

Mark faced away from her. She called it his electric chair pose. It was his only pose. Noreen shut the TV.

Upstairs, she attacked her hair with Kole's scissors. Sawed the length then shaped the dull, mousy tufts that clung to her ears like a poodle. Pieces fell in the sink.

Down the hall Paige slept balled up in their shared bed. As Noreen snipped, her hands shook. Rage was a wasted emotion. Summer people lined up outside the Dairy Barn, flapping $50s as they barked for milkshakes and extra toppings, you'd think they could buy themselves courtesy. Now, thanks to her craftsmanship, she looked just like them.

Before she'd left, Noreen lay herself out on Mark's boots, arms looped through his calves, knuckling his unused flesh. There was so much she wanted to say: *please* and *thank you* and *I'm sorry. Everyone hurts.* He raked his fingers idly through her new hair, but it was only reflex.

"Don't be a stranger," Kole said. After she moved out, he continued to ask for Paige, treating her to birthday dinners as if she were kin: unlimited breadsticks and ice cream and cake sparklers, *go on, make a wish,* the whole restaurant clapping just for her.

Kole could be decent like that.

She steps onto the porch. Movement ripples through the high grass. Rabbits. Always, rabbits. (Once Paige found one with a runt in its teeth. "She's eating him!" At the time, Noreen didn't know how to explain: mothers do this. They devour the weak;

they desert their young. Instead she snatched the cottontail by the ears and quickly dispatched it, handing it off to Kole to skin.)

And deer. Their quiet omnipresence melds into the landscape, but buyers consider wildlife exotic. When Noreen takes out her phone, the doe does not glance up, such is the singularity of her focus: how animals eat to live.

Now a pair of fawns peeks out from the brush because of course, that's family. Motherhood may have been thrust upon her, but it's what's kept Noreen going, kept her from the worst of herself. Paige scratching on the door. *Can I come in?* Sitting side-by-side pinching rose gardens on the undersides of their forearms, digging for seed, pounding for thunder, pedaling their fingers for rain. Becoming a mother ruined her as it saved her. With this sale, finally! Noreen will have something of her own.

Mountains surround, soft at the edges. *Blue*, she remembers from elementary school. Everyone assumes the hills are brown or gray, but they're wrong. Look closely. Draw what you see. Blue means distance, the color of longing.

Her instincts are correct. Although the Troller side sags beneath the tree line, the lake is still the lake. Together, they make a helluva property. Too precious to be parceled off, too fertile to pimp out to frackers across state lines. Not in her town. Not after that Susquehanna family was electrocuted by the water from their own damn tap.

The meadow rises like a golden egg. In the clearing stands the house. It's in that style—what's its name—that's meant to blend in with nature, but sticks out instead, a hodgepodge of odds and ends. Later she'll return with surveying tools, but already she can tell that the wall of pines will need to be leveled to accommodate a golf course. There'll be a pool, of course, two pools, saltwater is classy, that's what the Sagamore has up in Lake George, she's read, scrolled through pictures, lights for night swimming, and here, right where she's standing, would be just the spot to break ground for the new hotel. The existing structure, of course, would have to go.

In town, the line weaves around the block.

"What, are we giving houses away?"

Sundays in Sullivan County. City people, people with money, with ideas about quaint cottages and second homes. They snatch real estate fliers from The Breakstone. They come from New York, Pennsylvania, Delaware. They're coming more and more.

Noreen chugs two paper cones from the water cooler. Sally and Chris must be out on calls already. In her cubicle, she rolls out the script:

"What can I do you for?"

Couples lean back, sunglasses crowning their heads. If they've brought children, Noreen jangles her candy dish. Lately, there's a survivalist angle.

"Can't rule out the possibility of real and certain catastrophe," the wife says.

"Sloane," the husband says.

"If you think I'm living through a second Sandy, you have another think coming."

Noreen pulls out placards, dealing one for the husband, two for the wife.

"I can give you a great price for this geodesic dome, if you like personality—"

"We have enough personality."

"We want to be prepared for whatever's coming. Ask her, Hank. Just *ask*."

"Ask me what?"

"Do you have anything for sustainability, going off-grid?"

The wife can't contain herself. "You know, for the *anthropocene*?"

"Anthropocene?" The word sounds like a killer bug. Noreen dabs her neck. Many of her listings are on again, off again, owners waiting for the right price. Everyone has their number. She bypasses the dated and dilapidated, homes that need too much TLC, as this couple already seems short on love. Changing the scenery won't fix them.

All day she indulges other people's fantasies. She does this, for free. It is the stink of the business. Buyers are out there, it only takes one, but you have to be patient, and play the odds to win.

IRA

When their lips touch, the war is won. He is no longer a boy and she's not some girl, they are matinee idols, of one heart and mind, outside history and color reel, on set of *The Long, Hot Summer* at the Monticello drive-in where classics flap on canvassed sheets and everyone's striving for skin. They are Paul Newman and Joanne Woodward; they are hustling the take. He does not ask, no need, he merely pulls her in and she answers; pure summer, they are salt and grass and limb, they feast on plump cherries throughout the day, and the kiss, this full midnight kiss, *can you feel it?* Look at them. Kids. They're everything that's right in the world.

BETH

One kiss is all it is, and not even. Beth is no hugger, but after Zach's gone to bed, Ira stands around puppy-eyed, like he wants a biscuit. Firm in the chest, broad across the shoulders, he smells like petroleum jelly or maybe it's Band-Aids, so she returns the hug to be polite, and they go on like the dearly departed, like they're seeing each other for the first or last time; and it's nice, nice enough, his face right there, sandpaper chin, to spit some meager life into each other. *Goodnight, sleep tight.* It's hardly even cheating.

She is lying, of course. It starts long before that. Before their shadows creep along the wall to her room where he watches her undress, damp suit gliding down one thigh then the other, over the ring of each foot. Her skin shivers its plea: *Notice me.* In the stitching of her incision line, the curve of her abdomen. Look, see, but don't touch. That's the whole kink. In the strip of lamplight, he gets it. She feels him feeling her, and oh what a thrill. Only now the punishment begins.

The smell is mellow at first, like day-old garbage. Beth assumes it's coming off the compost bin, which would be apt. Can't even get shit to rot properly. She shuts the windows, but the odor only intensifies, dank and foreboding, confirming that the problem lies within. She throws off his sheets, digs along the couch, inhales pillows, she lights up the house with candles. All the vanilla in the world can't mask it.

"Do you smell that?"

"Smell what?" Zach's finger up his nose.

"Not sure." She inhales his scalp. "Help me?"

They turn it into a game. On hands and knees they become the sniffing, snarling household pets they'll never own. Zach slithers into hard-to-reach places where Beth cannot fit: under the sofa, behind the stove.

"What are we looking for?"

"We'll know it when we find it."

Ira arrives at dusk. He's wearing a bolo tie, hair in a bun. It looks like a tumor. She tells him he looks nice. The effort's what kills her, the anticipation knotted into his belt and Hawaiian shirt. His pant leg is caught in his sock.

"Are you going like that?"

"Like what?" She's in Doug's chambray, thin at the elbows, tied at the navel, hair in braids. She looks like the part of country bumpkin in a local theater troupe.

"May get nippy."

"I'm not changing, if that's what you want."

She frowns. He beams. She's in no mood to go out, no mood for the Fourth of July, but Zach's raring to go in his rain boots, pajamas with patriotic stripes.

"It wasn't here a few days ago."

"Sinuses are shot." Ira's nostrils flare. "I can't smell a thing."

Already there's a decent gathering at the park. But it's no Jersey beach, and it sure isn't the city, where everyone crushes together in an inebriated blob for a measly slice of East River. Ira shakes out a baja blanket. Beth removes her shoes. The overcast sky means less sunset, more convective haze. Music tinkles from the gazebo, a folk duo covering The Beatles in skimmer hats. The crowd—families, retirees—hunches over buckets of fried chicken and tubs of potato salad. Zach has eaten already but Beth's brought dessert. The wine is twist-off. She pours. They clink. Grape popsicle streams down Zach's wrist. Kids wave hand sizzlers, throw cherry salutes that make her jump, like a gun going off.

"Aren't you glad you came?"

It's beginning to wear on her, his constant checking in, like she needs looking after. A couple is shamelessly going at it against a nearby tree.

"People! Get a room."

"Summer lovin'."

Who said anything about love? The pinned woman can't break free, not that she seems to want to, her lust on his throat, hips, ass. Beth feels it in her thighs.

"There are children here."

"Quinn!" Zach wiggles off toward a child, and she is only too happy to follow, to be excused from it all, to be a mother at the playground again.

"Hi, I'm Beth. Zach's mom?"

As if there's doubt. This is how it is with mothers: her unease returns. The dumbest stuff spills from her mouth. In slouchy pants and a ribbed tank, the other mother radiates the casual confidence of someone who's been popular her whole life, who never had to work for friends, for anything. If Beth wore that outfit, she'd look like a genie. But here's a woman who wears clothes and a baby well. Beth stares at the baldy slung like a pageant banner across the woman's chest.

"Who's the cutie patootie?"

"Matilda," the other mother says with a bounce. *Australian or affected?* "Unplanned, despicable timing, but I just couldn't stomach the alternative. Wouldn't have been able to live with myself, you know?"

Beth says she knows.

"I mean, I'm all for choice—but I chose this misery instead."

"Our boys seem to be pals."

"Mine's a hellion."

"Aren't they all," Beth trills, although truth: Zach is almost annoyingly angelic. The mother's not listening, anyway; she's dipped into her carrier, shifting, rotating, opening flaps, pinching a nipple, finding a mouth. Her shoulders slacken with relief.

"Zach was a boob man, too."

The newborn sucks.

"Camp's been a lifesaver," Beth tries again.

"Oh god, that place. But beggars can't be choosers."

She catches herself nodding like a bobblehead even though she feels defensive about Camp Shalom Yisroel. "Zach's happy as a clam. A *kosher* clam."

The other mother smiles with her eyes, as if she's fighting a bad taste. Charms dangle from her neck like dog tags, engraved with letters: M, Q. She calls herself Ailene.

"First summer in Sullivan?"

"That obvious?" The wine bubbles up: grapefruit.

"Not too many of us without feathered hair. Tell me you brought help."

"Help?"

Her vision goes black. His musk a giveaway. Beth slips from Ira's hands. He tucks a flyaway behind her ear.

"We're not—it's not—"

But Ailene seems to have lost interest, redirecting her attention to the baby. The band strikes up the Star Spangled Banner.

"Fun's about to start," Ira says.

"Care to join us?"

Ailene calls her cute, like she's seven.

"I'm waiting for someone, too. You don't think I'm crazy enough to do this alone?"

I am alone, Beth wants to say.

"Well, see you at the Fair!"

"The Fair?"

"Stop. Shut up." Ailene scrapes Beth's arm with her armory of rings. "The Sullivan County Fair is only the single best event of the season. You've not lived until you've experienced the annual racing of pigs."

"Maybe we could go together?"

"Ping me," Ailene waves. "I'm in the camp directory."

A rocket whooshes across the sky. Fireworks give Beth that corkscrew feeling, a gathering twist, sprawled in the overgrowth behind her parents' house, the feathery thrust of cheese curl tongues. Her mother in off-white linen, smooth as a taper, glowing like a paper lantern. How beautiful she was, when summers held wonder. This is the sound of remembering. Hiss, pop, oh. That memory—maybe it's a photograph.

"Ever feel like you're 15 and 115?"

"All the time." Ira stretches out like an odalisque. Gold melts into pink, white yields to blue. Another firework launches, then the next, hushed torpedo bursting into a medusa of color. Zach muffles his ears. He doesn't know whether to love it or to fear it, so he buries his eyes in Beth's stomach, scissors his fingers cautiously.

"Mommy's here."

"It's only chemistry, kid."

Nothing is only one thing. A thousand feet in the air, the explosions feel close, somehow closer than in past years, when they'd watch strings of neon from the rooftops of Margate City, and people would ahhhh and Doug would lift her at the waist like a sacrifice to the midnight gods as he invoked his brother's spirit and Beth would play along like a good wife. And they'd hold up beers and toast to Ryan, *God bless his soul.* Then they'd tumble home.

Tonight feels personal, as if each blast carried a warning, tendrils like tea leaves she cannot decipher. She tilts her face toward the grand finale, a deafening, dizzying display of flash and collision, as the climax builds, then keeps going, past its peak, the show eternal, it will never end. Ira licks the slope of her neck.

"Down, Fido!" She elbows and he cowers, mumbling about the wine; the moment, at last, is over.

"Don't be mad."

"Are you four?"

"Admit it, you liked it."

She admits nothing. What a colossal waste. Happy birthday, America. Fuck the birds. Scare the dogs. Enjoy your noxious gas.

"Is that it?" Zach pops up.

People are folding chairs, blankets. Beth carries Zach to their car, his chin bumping her shoulder, legs belted around her waist. Ira's hand inches down the curve of her back. She can smell his saliva on her skin, the fog of gunpowder.

"Was that great, or what?"

Zach says, "I wish it started with the end."

In the morning there are flies.

A black cyst in bloom, a thickening hum, and soon, the insects are everywhere: giant as jellybeans left in an Easter bag of assorted. She tapes flypaper to the beams. Within hours the paper is a garland of dark tinsel; there is no keeping up.

She calls Doug. "You remembered."

Ryan's birthday. He would have been 40. She forgot.

"Of course."

"Mom just made Ry-dog's favorite breakfast."

"Egg in a hole."

"You know it. We're all here. Mom, Pop, Walsh, Smitty. Listen, I don't want to keep doing this. Ryan wouldn't like it. Can't we kiss and make up?"

"Ok," she says, like it's simple. She has a fly problem. He suggests a swatter. "These suckers could bench press a swatter. It's *literally* out of this world."

"Call an exterminator. I don't know what else to tell you. Yo! Speak later? Kelly and Tim just walked in."

That October, Beth had not wanted to go to Kelly and Tim's.

"It's not like the sky would fall if we bailed."

"But their Halloween party is the best party besides their Christmas party."

"Tell them we're sick."

"I was with the guys last night."

"The sitter canceled?"

"They'd have us drop Zach at my parents'."

"What if the sitter cancelled and Zach is sick?"

Beth twisted a Q-tip in her ear, one towel a turban, another a tube dress.

"You look like soft serve. Enough with the ear sex and let me have at you. Everyone's going. It will be fun."

Doug possessed enough positivity in his pinky finger to last Beth a lifetime. Businesses paid for his "authenticity," hard-won through the heartbreak of Ryan's death. On stage, microphone hinged to his face, Doug radiated a magnetism that stirred the crowd; he was relatable and half the booking cost of Tony Robbins. More, he was a real person, lacking the tanned waxy finish of others in his field, their noses long and thin as a ball peen hammer. Doug looked like a lacrosse player who'd downed an extra pint: his jaw square, his waist wide, an athlete who'd become a father, a lover not a thinker; for Beth, he was an uncomplicated relief.

Doug was the first one sweaty and drunk (but good drunk); the one to make fin eyes and obvious jokes and suck lamb chops off her plate. He looked out for her. Like a child safety device, Doug kept her from self-harm, sharp objects and live wires. Now all he wanted was a night in New Jersey. *Was that so much to ask?*

There was a certain comfort in expecting the expected— sex, drugs, just enough to feel bright and sunny, to weather the moms in leather and heels. Tonight they'd be simply costumed versions of their normal selves: go-go dancers and slutty hippies, sexy cats and high-tailed bunnies. In high school these were the girls who'd played sports purely for the uniforms. Those whose looks had suffered could opt for clever. Kelly Borden—her house, her party—could afford to be neither. In her cupcake regalia, sprinkled with chips and cherries, she could pull off both sexless and dumb.

Doug lit a joint. Beth cracked a window. The babysitter came early so that they could pre-game in their bedroom, towel snaked along the door. She crawled onto Doug. Many of the fathers in Zach's preschool had let themselves go—to baldness, beer guts—so it pleased her how well Doug kept himself. He was human, but preserved.

Tonight, however, with Doug between her legs Beth couldn't stop thinking about New Jersey. What would become of them—of *her*? She had spent her whole life plotting her escape; to end up right where she'd started felt like certain defeat.

"There are good people everywhere," Doug loved to tell her, as if she were joining a book club or knitting circle. Beth studied the ceiling as he grimaced, a drop of his sweat landing on her like a third eye. Maybe he was right. The only good thing about their apartment was the *en suite* bathroom. She loved saying the word, as if she were French. How many bathrooms could they swing in New Jersey?

"Thanks, babe." Doug softened and slipped out. A pearly tear glistened on her thigh. She plugged herself with tissue and crabbed off to the toilet. When she returned to the bed, he was cutting lines of coke.

Cocaine they reserved for special occasions, like tonight when they were expected to last past two in the morning. How else would she get through it? By coke standards their habit was tame. Recently, she declined an invitation from a PTA mom to some uptown blowout right out of the 80s, which just went to show: you can never know a person. The mom wore chinos and squeezed Beth's knee. At the playground, she overheard rowdy recaps from Vicodin massage parties. Relatively speaking, Beth was a prude.

She hunched over the mirror on her nightstand, bitter dripping down her throat. Doug wrestled her to the comforter once more. He was big. She was small.

"I vant to suck your blood." His teeth would leave a mark, but it was Halloween. She lay there. Eventually, he'd have his fill.

Doug passed her the bill, but she lacked the drive, so he hosed her share, squeaking his finger along his gums. She didn't want to stay up all night and pay for it tomorrow. She didn't feel like it, any of it, the store-bought getup, plunging her chin in an icy trough of apples. Above all, she dreaded the inevitable wife swap part of the evening, where she'd wait around like a duster on a used car lot. It was the same, year after year. Everyone wanted an upgrade.

"We could stay in."

"Time-honored tradition." His bare ass, pale in contrast to his leftover tan, partitioned his body like a Colorform she could peel and paste in a Cubist rearrangement.

Carefully, he laid out paint tubes, makeup pencil, hunk of Styrofoam, switchblade. His plan: to glue an elaborate injury to his head and paint it porno red.

Doug waved a sheet of latex. "Touch."

Doug traced his wound from his jaw over his ear, like a kidney. It resembled the pasty flank of toy vomit sold in gag stores. Her nurse costume sat suffocating in a bag, counterpoint to his trauma victim.

"Quick," he said, "Hand me the blood, would you?"

Her eyes filled, nose leaked. She was high. Crying, her breasts shook. Never large—once they'd been pert, proud handfuls, but now they stretched low and thin, diving for the floor like yo-yos. Silly, to be this sensitive. She twisted a corner of tissue and screwed the tornado up her nostril. Here was her life, this was her husband. As soon as she sobered up a little they'd have a reasonable time together.

Beth brushed her teeth, getting lost in the rhythm, until Doug shouted, "Did you fall in?" At which point she spit. Returned to her face. Two lines bracketed her mouth, as if whatever might come out of it would be better kept off stage. Applying makeup had become a strategic nightmare. Foundation always seemed to crack. Beth reached for her brushes. She drew her eyes big to offset her crow's feet. Flipped open her lash box of drama housing her falsies in a row, like a display of dead butterflies, opting against a full lash for a few single sprays, to look natural. The lashes stuck. Delicately, she separated them with a doll-sized comb.

Next came the souped-up bra Doug bought her on Valentine's Day. Hot pink and rhinestone, it pressed her like a panini. Cleavage rose to her chin. She sprinkled it in powder. The nurse dress was vinyl, sticky and hot, with plastic snaps, like a child's raincoat. They'd ordered it online one night along with feather ticklers and whips. Fishnets came next. Every Halloween she wore them, and every year she was newly surprised to find the hosiery made of open netting. Tonight was no different. She kept poking her toe through the holes. When she bent down to zip her boots, Doug goosed her. It would happen all night. In fact, she'd feel worse if such a desperate outfit did not elicit this kind of attention.

"So?" Doug said, dripping in gore. "Do I look sufficiently fucked?" He dusted his hand. She sniffed his fist like a stray.

By the time they arrived, New Jersey was in full swing. An inflatable pumpkin wobbled in the wind from its pitch on the front lawn. Disembodied wails seeped out from speakers disguised as gravestones.

A mummy opened the door. Within minutes they were swept apart. Parties like these quickly became a segregated affair. Some of the women had been in that Winnebago on prom night. To them, Beth would forever be Ryan's girl. They stroked her arm. *How have you been?* They meant well. These were mothers who chaired fundraisers and completed runs for leukemia in diamond studs the size of subway tiles, women who swapped paperbacks and hairdressers, who all but held hands in the bathroom. Betsy Frank, Maris Messina. Women unlike her, and yet how was she different? Men gestured wildly at the flat screen. Typical, to be groped by one who thought, or at least pretended to think, he was groping his own wife. And that was on regular nights.

She popped a pumpkin cheese ball, bummed a cigarette from Captain America. On the patio cold shot through her. The sky filled with tiny stars.

Eventually, the swap went into effect. Doug and Beth had a pact: *When in Rome.* Sometimes they got wasted and found it, if not appealing, then at least, not worth the protest, but other times, during this part of the night they slunk off to the home theater in the basement and watched *The Rocky Horror Picture Show.* This was when she loved Doug the most.

Tonight, when Doug disappeared upstairs with a woman in gauze (belly dancer? slutty refugee?) Beth was relieved. He could go get his fix; she could be left alone. Couples paired off in Ark formation. She slid down the seagrass wall.

"Trick or treat."

The voice familiar, she hadn't heard in years. Matt Donovan, above her like a shield. She rubbed her eyes. A lash came off in her hand. "What are you doing here?"

"Last people on earth, huh?" He was dressed like Kurt Cobain, hair shaggy and pink. Beth was not sure it was a costume. "I lost my person."

"She's probably with my husband."

He joined her on the floor. She held up her cup to toast. He shook a keychain of sobriety tags.

"Nurse, that stuff could kill me."

In high school she and Matt hung out in the art room and mocked this very crowd. Matt had been a pimply kid with too much hair and too many expendable inches. Once Beth gave him a hand job in the back of the bus, after which he carved her initials into his wrist. It was the nicest thing anyone had ever done. She teased him viciously. Matt dropped out. Later, she'd heard he'd enrolled in art school. Rehab, apparently.

"I'm sorry." Beth plucked the bobby pins from her Red Cross cap. "Who is she?"

Kelly's stepsister. He'd met her on the train. She was visiting her parents; he'd been installing one of his sculptures outside the station's ticket office. Matt made art out of repurposed machinery, metal from the dump. There was charcoal in his nails. She was twenty-eight.

"Never been so happy. Strange as it sounds. You read about it, but I didn't think it was for me, that I'd ever find it." His voice caught. "Love. What a beautiful absolute mess."

She felt suddenly responsible, like Doug was stealing Matt's one special thing, taking a spin on his new bike only to ram it into a pole, this romance of three months. He stroked her hair until she grew sleepy.

When she awoke people were leaving but Matt was still there, their legs outstretched, heads slumped together like forgotten puppets.

"Whatever happens," she said, "don't let it get the best of you."

By afternoon, the situation is biblical. Flies mob the ceiling, worship their florescent gods Jedi long and flickering. Beth shuts the bathroom door. A fucker lands on her.

Ira is not home.

She goes in anyway.

His cabin smells like mildew. She empties her bladder standing so as not to touch the seat. Maybe it was seeing Matt, or maybe it'd been the party itself, but that Halloween night set off something inside her. All she wanted was to hurt, fuck, feel. Beth would drop Zach at preschool, then plunge into the maw of the city like a secret agent, staking out subway stations, leafy parks and bodegas. She never had to go far to find someone to rail her: the man in the Town Car idling on the crosswalk each morning, the dad from her pre-K chat whose wife was dying of cancer; the soft-spoken Music-in-Motion teacher stroking his nino cabasa; the bartender with Popeye arms who called himself a poet at heart. The problem was their hearts. She wanted nothing to do with them.

Doug acted differently, too. Men pick up on the scent of others, but he never mentioned it. To name it would be to acknowledge all the ways they'd failed each other. Instead, her infidelity only fueled his attraction, strummed his competitive spirit, when it rained it poured, and so for a period of weeks she carried on in a frenetic fashion, as if her body were separate from the rest of her. For Beth, it was all or nothing. She fucked strangers in coffee shops. Or she was celibate in the woods.

Months later, she was pregnant. Doug's—despite every-thing. It was basic math. It was a sign. *Change your life*, the sign said, flashing with arrows and lights. Would she even be here, right now, if they hadn't gone to Kelly and Tim's?

Never did Beth ask how Ira ended up in Sullivan County. Paint decades thick, cot thin as a diving board. *What had he left behind?* Of course, he'd had a whole other life. She drags over a musty crate and there's Ira Lecher on the masthead of *Man's World* magazine, a third from the top. Had he been good at his job? What kind of father was he? She hadn't asked about his daughters, his first love. One sepia frame on the wall: an unsmiling couple in serious wool and laced boots. His parents, she assumes.

The ceiling fan teeters, like it might break for her head. Looseleaf scatters: a caricature wrecked with tattoos, big head, labial in the mouth, obvious. A spiral notebook on the table catches her eye.

Bait, Tackle, Fly by I.M. Lecher

The body turned up on July 31, 1990, the day my mother died.

Facts fixed as a flesh pit of stone fruit: The body belonged to a woman. A mother. Daughter. Sister. Wife. Jew. End of story. Don't know what car she drove, if she drove a car, what her favorite color was, how many siblings she had, whether she favored white meat or dark, a juicy thigh or leg, Yiddish over English. Face-down, how they found her. Naked as a newborn. Bun hot, as they say. At least, that's the murmur, but murmurs don't make facts, and a spitball of facts can't solidify into immutable truth.

H+H boycotted their grandmother's funeral.

They've seen enough, Viv said. Won't you lay off? I could not. Who survives a holocaust only to be forgotten? I went apeshit. Grief can do regrettable things. I may never be forgiven, but my God do I miss my girls.

Did I know her? I did not. Had I seen her? A Hasidic bride pushing a stroller? Maybe I saw

her. Like crows without wings. They are a dime
a dozen down on Route 17. But here, away from
the flock, would I've noticed? Like the back page
of Highlights for Children: Who are we to say
what doesn't belong? Night shadows could be
anyone, fingers hovering on buttons, collarbones
an illicit conduit to the coming light.

    As for the culprit? It's always the people you
know. The ones who're supposed to protect you.
An inside job. In the kitchen, with a rope. But
then, my daughters could tell you, I'm lousy at
Clue.

    Why does anyone do what they do? Maybe
that's the question. Instead of the blame game.
What happens to the life we're given when it fails
to align with the one we want?

The "book" rambles on a bit more before petering out to blank pages, a drawing of a Semitic Sherlock Holmes. Hat, pipe. Tired jokes in talk bubbles. *I almost had sex every day this week! Almost Monday, Almost Tuesday, Almost Wednesday. Doc says good news! You have twenty-four hours to live. Bad news is, I should've told you yesterday.*

Clippings spill from the spine. *Sullivan County Monitor.* August 1, 1990.

Body Found in Private Pond

    The body of a naked woman was found
yesterday in Murmur Lake, a privately owned
residential pond off route 191, Sheriff Jeff
Johnson said. Investigators are working to
identify the body, discovered early Tuesday
morning by the 8-year-old daughters of local

*property owner, Ira Lecher. The woman
appeared to be of child-bearing age and the body
not to have been in the water for long.*

Beth rocks back on her heels. The next clip is dated August
3, edges yellow and insect-thin. ***Woman Identified in Lake Death.***
Grainy image, veil lifted, eyes hollow, wedding lace rising to her
chin.

> *Bloch, a member of the Satmar Hasidic
> community, lived in Brooklyn but spent summers
> in Monticello, some 33 miles from where she was
> found. "We're treating it as a suspicious death,"
> Sheriff Jeff Johnson said, without further
> elaboration. Bloch had gone missing after
> sundown on the evening of Monday, July 30,
> which marked the beginning of Tisha B'Av, a
> Jewish fast day. A mother of four, she is survived
> by her parents and siblings, her young children,
> and husband.*

> ***August 5, 1990***
> ***Autopsy Requested in Death of Religious
> Woman***

> *Local authorities have requested an autopsy
> report in the suspected drowning death of a
> Brooklyn woman. Coroner Louis Potts said that
> based on preliminary findings, and the fact that
> the body was unclothed, she may have been
> performing the ritual bath, a monthly religious
> custom tied to a woman's menstrual cycle.*
> *Meanwhile, the owner of the property where
> the body was found had been away at the time.
> "What am I, the grim reaper?" said Ira Lecher,*

42, whose daughters discovered the body Tuesday morning. Lecher attributed his distress to his own mother's recent death. "Forgive me," he sniffed. Lecher claims not to have been acquainted with the victim and is cooperating with the investigation. Authorities say they are asking the tight-knit Satmar community to please do the same.

The next one is missing a date.

Police suspect foul play in the drowning death of Chaya Bloch, found last month in the privately owned pond of Murmur Lake. An autopsy revealing cerebral edema has confirmed drowning as the cause of death for Ms. Bloch. The report also found that Bloch was three months pregnant with what would have been her fifth child.

Satmar leaders have threatened legal action against law enforcement officials who obtained the autopsy without clearance from the rabbinic court, citing Jewish law, which forbids the despoliation of a body once it is deceased. Rabbi Yehuda Friedman also disputed the suggestion that the woman may have been engaging in ritual bathing, claiming pregnancy as an exemption, explaining that bathing is forbidden by Jewish law during the observance of Tisha B'Av. He informed The Monitor that the community is conducting their own internal investigation, starting with why the young mother was so far from home on the eve of lamentations.

Bloch's family members were unavailable for comment. No arrests have been made.

Beth bites a cuticle, dotting the newsprint with a speck of blood.

September 7, 1990
Local Law Enforcement Clashes with Religious Group

Temperatures have been rising between the Satmar community and local Sullivan county authorities since the body of a young religious woman was found thirty miles from the bungalow village of Kiroyat Balk last month. The Satmar Hasidic community is a closed, religious sect with its own ruling body.

Authorities have clashed in the past as members habitually walk in the road on Saturdays, to the scorn and near-accident of drivers. "This is Route 17, not the back roads of Minsk!" shouted one County man who wished not to be identified. "Why should they get special treatment? Know what would be special? If they go back where they came from."

In June, a tribunal of rabbis gathered to discuss potential action against the Orange County Water board for what they allege to be a compromised water supply. "Water is a basic right," said Rabbi Yehuda Friedman, who has requested that extensive filtering systems be installed in the four Satmar bungalow villages along Route 17 in Monroe. Microscopic crustaceans known as copepods are harmless, and impossible to see with the naked eye. But they are in the same family as shrimp, lobster, and other shellfish forbidden by Jewish law. Although New York is one of few states that does not have mandatory filter laws, Satmar leaders have threatened to close down reservoirs if these costly systems are not implemented.

Tension drew to a head last week when Sullivan County Sheriff Jeff Johnson arrived at the insular Kiroyat Balk community, where Chaya Bloch had been spending the summer.

"We come to ask a few questions and are met with fists and stones," said officer Ray Gonzales. "This is the twentieth century. No one is above the law."

"It is an affront and a disgrace, to come charging through here, rounding up members for interrogation. I will not permit this pogrom. I will not abide the sacrilege, the accusations of wrongdoing. We who make life do not take life. Suicide is a sin, halevei, verboten by Jewish law." Rabbi Friedman refused further questions. Requests to speak with widower Menachem Bloch and other family members have been denied.

"Please," Rabbi Friedman said. "Honor our privacy as we mourn this grave loss."

October 17, 1990
Person of Interest

Inquiries into the drowning death of a woman found in Murmur Lake this summer have led law enforcement to name Mark Troller a lead person of interest. Troller, 25, son of Mark Sr. (deceased) and Mary Troller, is a resident of the adjacent property on which Chaya Bloch, 26, was found on the morning of Tuesday, July 31.

*His relationship to the victim remains unclear, as
he has declined questioning. Troller runs the bait
shop on County Road. Kole Troller, 17, said of his
brother, "He's taking it like a girl. All's I'm saying,
when Pop died, he was dry-eyed."*

That does it for Murmur. The rest is random: local history collaged onto the notebook, poorly copied, ads for orchards, crystal caves. *See where Rip Van Winkle took his epic snooze! Relive the catastrophic paper mill factory fire of 1888!* There's an invitation to the opening art exhibit from the Concord Hotel: Memories & Memorabilia. One last article, from 1996, folded into a square.

Century-old Crime Solved

*When they purchased their charming
Victorian home, the Rushton Family of East
Rutherford, NJ was not expecting to be involved
in solving a 123-year-old murder case. Imagine
their surprise when renovation contractors
uncovered human remains from the ground-
floor walls. Local historian Grace Watkins
believes they belong to Catherine Walter Blue,
who she said was the mistress of nineteenth-
century owner Winston Wolf. "I think she must
have lived in the carved-out space," Watkins
said. "He must have marched her out and
returned her at whim, like a closet plaything
from Dr. Caligari's Cabinet."*

And a letter in taco shell stationery.

*Dad, consider this from both of us. Camp
sucks the food sucks don't get me started on the*

people. Heather thinks we should have written
back on toilet paper, taste of the old medicine,
but she can hop off her heinie and write herself
(P.S. she made the swim team) so I'll give you
points for funny.

Whoever's renting the house better not be
wetting my bed. It rains nonstop, I still have bad
dreams, suppose I always will, only now I can fall
off my bunk. If I break my arm you'll have to
come get me. Bring Pringles. Love Hil.

The screen clangs. Beth whips around, but it's only the wind. She hurries the notebook into her shirt and flies out of the door, chest wheeling, blood coursing, a deafening pulse in her ears. She runs like hell for the house. The letter sails to the floor.

IRA

Maybe he's transgressed, but Ira's always transgressing. Can't a grown man feel how he feels? What's the world coming to? *Jeez Louise.* It was one lousy lick.

Today it's not even Beth that's got him all whipped up. Today his pain is physical. He feels like a wool sweater caught on a nail, unraveling at the cuff. Maybe it's the flu. Maybe Lyme. He inspects his body for a bull's eye, an explanation, but all he finds are a few new moles. If only he had someone to check his hard-to-reach places.

In the shower he tugs at himself, conjuring Beth in her bathing suit, thighs parabolic in their pelvic socket, palms running down his chest and back, his hair, she strokes, he glides, she tickles his balls, he pumps faster, there's nothing wrong with him, he is firing just fine. Beth's hip bones jut like a steering wheel at the kitchen sink where she's braced over her jars of mustard and artichoke hearts, slurping slippery stalks of canned pale palm, my god, he spatters clear beads like salmon roe, arriving at his unceremonious end.

PAIGE

Most men don't even knock. Ira just takes up the living room.

"Mom home?"

"You're blocking my view." Paige waves him off the TV. Ira steps beside the couch, props a foot on the armrest.

"What are we watching?"

"Like you care." It's a travel program on the restoration of sight to Himalayan villagers whose vision had been lost to sun-induced cataracts. He slides into the cushions, depriving the room of its oxygen, as if they were all perched on a mountainous cliff.

"You're following this?"

"Shhhh." She shuffles over, tearing up as the patients tear. Even Paige is defenseless to this moment, an outpouring of gratitude, however performative—*I can see!*—and Ira's not about to ruin it.

When he scoops her feet into his lap, she boots him.

"You have a fetish or something?"

"I could use a refill."

Her tube socks are thready with tobacco, gray in the soles, plucked from the hamper. "Fuck you if you're using her."

"Who's using who?" Noreen comes out in a clog of perfume.

Ira coughs. "Sending me to the gas chambers?"

"You reek, Mom."

"I'll never understand why women try to cover up the best part of themselves."

"The best part?"

"I like you *au natural.*"

"It will fade." Her mom noses her wrist. "Ready?"

"Thought we'd stay in," he says, patting the couch. "I've been kind of pooped."

Paige gets up.

"Not again, pigeon?"

"Yes, again."

"Don't roll your eyes."

"Not rolling."

"Looks to me like you're rolling."

"I can't change my face."

"Your mom just wants to spend time with you," Ira calls down the hall after her, like they're the goddamn Cosby family. And look what happened to them.

Her bedroom walls are thin. "We've been at each other for so long, I don't remember how it started."

"Let me talk to her."

She can hear his approach. Ira is a mouth breather. He sounds like a ventilator prescribed to the lost souls of SCCH. Once on the vent, there's no getting off.

The deal is quick, a few of this and that.

He grabs her flat soda to wash it all down.

IRA

It's cool, he takes it slow, like a tortoise cursed by life's carriage. Paige is a blur, scurrying past, kissing her mother's forehead, saying please don't wait up.

Reenie knows nothing. "What's your secret, man?"

Ira is CIA. KGB. He's the goddamn Mossad. "I told her be a lover not a fighter."

That gets the lashes going. "Good, 'cause you're going to love this."

Watiting for the goods to kick in, he watches her punch her calculator with the head of her pencil and it's sweet, lips moving, color bitten off, like she's the first person to have the bright idea of selling his home.

He's got an idea, too. He strokes her arm.

"You know how to make a man smile, Noreen Murphy."

"Sign on the line and I'll make you happy, too."

"You'll have to fertilize the hills with my ashes first."

"Ira Lecher!"

"Don't Lech me. Time's a wasting."

"All the more reason, then, to let go."

The next day goes like this. Ira can't be imagining. Visions have never felt this real:

He picks Beth up, as he does, as he's been doing, kid's at camp, out of the picture, but something's off, she is stingy in her affection, glowering like a teen. He picks her up because he's the honoree of the Chosen Yarmulke Club, they're having a luncheon at one of the old hotels, and would she be his date, no, escort, his smorgasbord companion for gravlax, caviar, a kosher spread, would she humor him for the ride?

After all, they're besties, partners in crime, they are in this life together. Maybe he's groggy, he's been having symptoms, everything's symptomatic of something else, lightheadedness, muscle soreness, an intermittent tingling in his legs, sometimes he forgets to eat, never can he forget death, that dark horse, galloping round the bend, but he does not wish to dwell on it. Not today, mortality. Today he drives like they're the last people on earth past Max's, which is gone, which is now Camp Shalom Yisroel, toward the outer ridge of the county, home to the Concord (Brown's? Grossinger's?) only the car is not his car and the hotel—whose kitchen staff once trained him to "serve at the left; clear from the right," to fold napkins big as Playtex brassieres—is not his hotel. Which is when the confusion socks in.

God, the place is a dump.

Cordoned off like a murder site, the place is a ghost of its former self, given over to graffiti and weeds. There's a backhoe on the lot, jaw raised in threat. *Must be some mistake, I could have sworn,* Ira attempts a joke—*must have been the brown acid*—but memory, that trusted wheel, has failed him again.

Whatever, Beth says. Nothing is ever as good as your idea of it. We're here. Might as well look around.

They trespass through the criminal tangle of abandonment, a rusted band of wire, syringe, bottle, and excrement, animal or human he can't be sure, got to watch where you walk, the grass so tall it scaffolds his knees, scything their way through the rotted grandeur and up the everlasting hill. The pool is an Olympic grave of chairs and vellum, oceanic drapes, pillows bursting at the seams. Stencils of NO DIVING NO JUMPING NO RUNNING have been tagged over with swastikas and anarchy signs, YOUR MAMA sprayed in bubble letters. It's like staring into a memorial pit, until Beth latches on to his elbow, like his parents steered him to shul on the rare Shabbos his father was not on the road, careful not to get their heels caught in the concrete, cobblers do not come cheap, my son.

She leads him past the basketball court whose nets are bunched like eager panties, dandelions rioting along fault lines, the tennis shack heaped with broken rackets like Auschwitz artifacts. She squeezes his hand, pumping out a rhythm of affection toward the main hotel, whose edifice is crumbling, stripped to bone, tattooed with more swastikas and SUCK ME and WHAT WOULD JESUS DO in Day-Glo paint. This is no yarmulke luncheon. There are no chosen yarmulkes, who ever heard of such an organization, for Chrissake. Instead there are junkies, an opioid throng of squatters sleepwalking the historic halls, infiltrating the Borscht Belt in all its former glory. Look. There is a gathering of spoons by his feet, snakes in the grass, no, tourniquets, rubber tubing, vials, cigarette butts, Narcan, nasal and injectable, needle caps hopeful and bright as oversized ear plugs. In the window he watches. No one makes eye contact. One droops like a flower in a dress with moon stripes and sailor buttons, the kind a child might wear. She, too, is practically a child, undone by ritual, powerless to the snare of habit, if ever he did dream it.

Let me see, Beth says, mounting an upturned bucket the color of an Elmer's tit. Her waist narrow enough to snap in his grip. The carpet has been rolled off to one side like a cigar rimmed with gold and maroon. Water has eroded the plaster.

I've been here before.

We've all been here.

You don't understand.

Let me guess: a lifetime ago. Do you know how many lifetimes are lived in a life?

What will become of the place?

They'll raze it. Fill the land with something new.

He knocks the stool out from under her, pressing her to the filthy glass like he'd press his own girls to 5th Avenue Christmas windows, for a view of the ballroom, banquet hall raided by raccoon, the chandelier shattering, his nose sandwiched in her tush, toppled divans, more floral upholstery, more torn stuffing, more rugs ravaged by time and neglect and rodent and blood. *Put me down, perv*; her body scraping the façade, he catches her, spins her—takes one to know one—and flattens her against the rough wall.

It is a moment of before and after. If this were a movie all action would grind to a halt. Beth arrows a knee to his balls, and he jukes, he could wring her skinny neck. *How could you choose this place?* You came, didn't you, he says, grasping, gasping after her through the wreckage as she stomps off, the ragweed rising to meet her and the goldenrod lashing out like a tide, lapping at her ankles.

Now it is raining, a hot, insistent summer rain, the ground swelling, out of pace, which is why they call it a flash flood, because it comes on like a shock, the rate of absorption slower than the speed of release, every clomp through the earth spewing shit puddles because it serves him right. The shit. He stumbles after her, but she's too far ahead, blazing off in his car, leaving Ira drenched and alone among roadside detritus.

Well, crud.

Ira rubs his eyes. It may not be the first time he's passed out on a walk, defenseless to the soporific effects of the sun, but to sleep a dead man's sleep through a soaking July storm marks a new low. His shirt sticks to his ribs, the grass pressed flat from the heaviness of his body.

Hours later Ira remains disoriented, dizzy, wracked by chills. Last time he saw her, Beth bitched about flies, so he dropped off flypaper. *Welcome to the country, kid.* She tore through moods like Viv did outfits. Impossible to know what women want when they're constantly changing their minds. Pig, his girls would say. All he ever did was love them as if they were a part of him. Maybe he was too territorial. Maybe there was a better way to go about loving. He's only played the parts expected of him. Deadbeat dad. Philandering husband, yearning son, idiosyncratic hermit, irreverent Jew. Name your archetype. *Daddy issues?* Lech is your man.

A loose letter on the rug. From Hillary, years ago. There are hearts in her "i"s and now he is crying. Ludicrous, to think someone like Beth might stay through winter. They always leave. His own daughters are never coming back.

Viv is at the gym when he reaches her. "I've been thinking."

"Don't hurt yourself."

"Who's going to take care of me when I die?"

"You'll be dead."

"That's good, Viv."

"There's nothing wrong with you, aside from everything that's wrong with you." He can hear her scaling the treadmill. "You're too healthy. You have too much time on your hands. If you spent more time around people instead of trees you'd know age is just a number, but do what you want, Ira. Get yourself checked out, book your blood work and anal probes and joyful colonoscopies."

He tries explaining: I'm like a lone sock in the dryer. *Aren't you frightened?* Sometimes, at night, he lies in bed overcome with urgency but unable to move, as if locked in an iron lung of his own torpor. He's started buying those drugstore diapers.

"I'm a big baby," he says into the phone.

PAIGE

If she's stuck on a gerbil wheel, then Tommy's flailing from it. Down by the river, Tommy's had a tough night, so she stays with him through morning, mulling over her budget, allocating for gas, food, lodging. Her wisdom tooth is killing her, throbbing at the root. The sun hangs over her like a webbing. She takes something for pain, breaking her daytime rule but she doesn't have to be at work for hours. Work is hardly neurosurgery. She skims another, crunches a third.

Sooner or later her mom will figure out she didn't register for fall semester, hasn't filed transfers to Cortland or Purchase, either. Noreen will demand a conversation.

"What's the point," she says aloud.

"Huh," Tommy says, coming around.

Even with Paige's scholarship, school gobbled her money. Faculty spoke off-speed, administering open-book tests, as if they couldn't imagine their students actually studying or showing up prepared. Failure was their only expectation. Besides, she's learned more about vital signs and bedside manners at SCCH than in any of her nursing classes.

The effort of leaving weighs against the ease of staying. Maybe she's kidding herself, maybe this is all there is. Provided she takes orders, cashes out the register, no one makes any demands of her. She could go through life barely using any of herself.

Paige runs her tongue over her molars, feeling along the gum line, her mouth tacky with sleep. The topography fascinates her, especially when high. The inside of her cheek bumpy from chewing it, from something she ate, salt and vinegar chips, just gross enough to be addictive, abrasive to the flesh. In Intro to Bio, they'd scraped toothpicks for a cell sample, drop of iodine, made a slip slide for the microscope. They'd done the same experiment in high school but it still unsettled her, to see herself up close like that: papery blue circles, cells misshapen, barely touching one another. Paige cups her jaw. A two-inch scar runs along the bone line. Supposedly, she'd crashed into a mirror at her mother's brother's. That was the story. She was a toddler. Patrick had big dogs. Sometimes he chained them; sometimes they broke loose. There were teeth marks, gnashing, shattered glass. Dogs coming for her. Noreen said it was no place for a child.

That's how they wound up at Kole's.

Her scars are a map of scrapes and survival. She likes them. The slash across her left buttock, for example, she can't see without a mirror but feels it, the raised, knitted tissue. Granulomas hard as peas, proof of all she's lived through.

Tommy's phone rings and rings, it's been ringing since dawn. *Animal & Pest?* He mumbles. There's a nickel-sized burn in the isthmus between his forefinger and thumb. His egg sandwich rolls off his thighs, cold and uneaten.

"Business," he mouths, slinking away.

The Neversink rifts blue to green, coins of light speckling the surface, rippling in the wind. When it isn't ugly, this place sure is beautiful. Tommy paces the embankment.

"You name it, I'll take care of it."

"Let me drive."

He covers the phone. "Do you mind?"

"I mean it."

He pinches her wrist but it doesn't hurt. Tommy's rangy, hollow as air. Like a chocolate foil mold sold at the checkout that looks solid until you bite in. His boss put him on notice because he's no good at killing living things.

"See what you made me do?" His breath is metal. She shoves him, digs around for his keys.

"You're not going alone."

"Walk, then."

He's left a pizza box in the cab, and the heat's gotten to it. Tommy takes the back roads around the farm to the other side of Murder where the grounds are trim and smooth. She calls it Murder because everyone does, because names and reputations stick. (Paige's theory: the girl drowned simply because she did not know to swim.) Kole Troller handled pestilence himself. The only people who hired actual exterminators were tourists.

The house at Murder looks too big for a single family, let alone for one person. She's heard her mother brag about Ira's assets: his car, his house, his fountain pen. Like she's ever been inside. Like someday her mom might lay claim to any of it. Like he's really her boyfriend and not another guy, one of those seedy older dudes who wears their hair long as a string. Paige sells him the occasional Vicodin, Xanax, she overcharges and he doesn't know the difference. Whenever Paige goes online she has twenty requests from men like him, from all over. It's nuts. Her picture is hot, chin down, low in the chest, and it gives her a sense of power to imagine them jerking it to her avatar, filling her inbox with emojis. *Don't be cruel to a heart that's true.* (A heartless fool is how she always hears it.) They are divorced or dying, they've a new lease on life after a harrowing transplant or thirty years of military service. From their couches, they can be anyone, but if they they want her, they have to pay. She is no complimentary side dish. Soon as she gets a bank account she'll link her profile to it for direct deposit, in exchange for services rendered: photo, voice, video. At least Ira understands the market economy. He's courteous, says please. At The Breakstone, he eats well, tips generously. Her mother could do a lot worse.

As they pull up, Tommy almost crushes the small car in the driveway.

"Watch it!"

"I saw."

"Remember to wipe your feet."

"I'm not an animal."

Which makes her nervous for him. He needs this job. She thumbs the scruff on his chin.

"Cash only. Don't settle for less than two hundred."

He stands there for a minute, as if he's forgotten what he's come to do. Paige holds out her hot Coke like he's a child. Mothering was thankless, but this is their cycle. Tommy and Silko drove all that swag into New York City, only to have the contents confiscated before they could unload them in Times Square. Booked on misdemeanors so Paige had to wire him, and now, between paying fines and her mother's nonsense, she's back in the hole.

Math, that's what she was doing before the distractions. Numbers. Tommy apologized, said he'd learned his lesson, which is horseshit. Tommy with his big ideas and even bigger habit. He takes and takes. She prods her tooth with her tongue. In Florida, she'll get it pulled. In Florida, she'll get braces, the clear kind, like a sports guard that snaps in and out.

"Don't go anywhere," he says.

"Where am I going?"

He twists the key from the ignition and pockets it anyway. She tilts the seat back and lengthens her legs on the dash, windshield cooking up a noonday fire as Paige stares into the sun's blistery center, blinking and blinking until she sees stars.

NOREEN

A means to an end is what it is. Sixth of July and too muggy for nylons but Noreen knee bends into a pair anyway, pliés the seat to her crotch. She feels like a stuffed sausage. When her parents died, they were buried without wake or ceremony. Patrick wanted cremation, but she prevailed. Even if it was cheaper, Noreen couldn't justify an oven. Burning. It just wasn't Christian.

She borrows her daughter's dress, the one Paige wore on the college circuit, securing full rides to Scranton and Wilkes-Barre before selling herself short on community. Such a smart cookie, but Paige doesn't want to hear it. The fabric is forgiving. She zaps lint with masking tape. Dark clothing hides nothing, but she can't exactly walk into a funeral dressed like a frosted peach.

Mary Troller outlived her few friends. The chapel is awash in a buttery glow; Noreen has a filter in her phone just like it, to show every interior in the best light. At the podium, Kole is mid-eulogy. Pulpit is the church word, not that Noreen is churchgoing. Kole looks out of place as well, as if he's forgotten lines in a school play, his hair a hardened swoosh.

"These last months were no cakewalk, but at least Ma was out of it. That's mercy. I hope to God I kick before losing my faculties."

He blows into a handkerchief. Noreen folds in a stick of gum.

"She could be blunt. In her mind, my Pa had too much passion, and me and Mark, not nearly enough, but she had no patience for complaining. Kathy, well, Kathy and me—" He scans the pews like she might turn up. "Wish we could've given her grandkids. Land, family, country. That's who we are."

Guests bow their heads. Mark holds himself stiff, Western shirt strained at the yoke. The pastor stands. "Now let us pray."

Kole greets mourners by the casket like it's a receiving line at his wedding; the bloodless woman luxuriating on a bed of satin fancier than anything she'd laid on alive. Noreen ditches the cemetery. This, too, feels like a sham, stones like bad teeth cluttering perfectly good land. How people spend all their money honoring the dead while ignoring the living.

In town she picks up a roast and potatoes, a twelve-pack, a clutch of daisies. Milk and eggs, a drum of oatmeal, a pound of coffee in a red metal tin.

"Twenty cents a bag." The checkout girl wears a crown of barrettes, plastic barnyard animals, like Paige wore as a baby.

"When on earth?"

"Our earth, exactly." Her hair is dipped in alternating purple and pink, like a unicorn. "How many you want?"

"Just give me what I need."

Noreen feels the girl's eyes, like Noreen ought to know better. Reluctantly, she shakes out a brown bag and punches it open.

"Oh, for crying out loud." Noreen snaps it from her, bags her groceries herself.

On Main Street she spots Ira through the window of the General Store. "Ira, tiger! When are you getting a phone?"

He looks up from the table of trinkets. "I have a phone."

"A cell."

"It's not for me, Reenie."

"It doesn't have to be *for* anything. It's just a phone. How do you expect people to get a hold of you?"

"I don't expect."

"You want your car, I suppose. Been meaning to return it."

"I got a lift." He nods to a white-and-blue runt of a thing the size of a roller skate.

"Where's the rest of it?"

"That's what I said."

"I'm good for it, you know."

"I know you're good." He holds up a flight of honey. "Does this make a nice gift?"

"Don't know who'd cough up $30 on a 4-pack sampler smaller than a teacup." *Ira would, of course. Summer people.* "Anyway, Kole Troller buried his mother today, the old hag. I'm headed out your way. Join us for supper."

"I don't think so." He clenches the table, upsetting the souvenirs.

"You okay?"

"Misplaced my sea legs."

"We're two hundred miles from sea, mister. I don't like your color."

"What color should I be?"

She touches his ear. Tiny hairs cluster in the drum like a small animal.

"Shall I swing by after?"

"I'm not up for company."

"But it's me."

"Even you." He turns, jeans sagging. In the next aisle, Noreen overhears a mother to her child, "Look with your eyes, not your hands."

Frank & Messina are on vacation. Their answering service uses "summer" as a verb.

"With whom am I speaking?"

"Murmur Lake!"

"Can you spell it?"

"They wanted *me!*"

"Frank & Messina explore many properties."

"Your men don't know what they're missing."

"Would you like to leave a call-back number?"

"Tell them, their satisfaction is my guarantee."

The Troller place could use a good smell. Fastening an apron splashed in pigs, Noreen sets to work, peeling carrots, puzzling meat and onions into a charred dish. It's a wonder the kitchen hasn't disappeared from disuse. Overhead, a bulb hums, clotted with dead moths. Noreen turns on the radio. A baseball game. Voices are company. There is a kinetic thrill to the commentators, an infectious hope, like even with the Yankees trailing, the outcome is up for grabs. It could go either way.

Noreen never told Paige about Mark. She wouldn't believe it. *My father? He's practically catatonic!* It wouldn't change anything. Wouldn't make Paige rich or give her any kind of leg up. To Paige, Noreen is trash. She's said as much. The fights coming so fast lately, like rolling contractions, Noreen hasn't had a chance to correct the story: she was nineteen, bartending, it could've been any number of men.

Patrick called her a whore.

A spiteful streak ran through him when he was drinking, which was most of the time. His trailer tight, tighter with guys from the lumber plant stinking it up, tightest when he brought girls home. The portacrib blocked passage to the bathroom, causing accidents, Noreen throttled to the wall, mirror crashing, shards piercing her skin. Before she left, she bagged empties of Genesee and carted them off for exchange. Maybe Kole stared at her for too long without blinking but he never raised a finger, and he bought her daughter shoes, sneakers that lit up the sides. He always had an extra pencil, a quarter for milk. That night in The Lion's Den she could hear Kole breathing heavy through the back screen. Everyone courted their strange. For a while, they conducted themselves like family.

Easy to picture how the place once looked, shiny with promise. The Trollers possessed a proud legacy. Once upon a time fireplaces worked, chimneys blew a proud smoke. Kole's great-grandparents came in flushed from the harvest to warm up in the crackle and heat. The seed mill was up and running and corn production was good. Now the only thing flourishing was the gulf between what was and what now. Faces change. Hand crews were transient. Hard to keep anyone around. Her parents had been immigrants, too, from County Clare, but people are quick to forget we all come from somewhere. Noreen sweeps a trail of mouse droppings, sets the table, cracks a beer.

Of course he is home: Mark in the parlor window, handsome as ever. Mark had played football, his hair slick as a seabird, hands deft as a surgeon's to string lines or hook bait. Even now, he emits an unspoken knowing.

"Too bad about your mom," Noreen says.

If her voice registers, he gives no indication. She goes to him anyway, tucking her heels beneath her. It is here, before Mark, that she knows her true self, the scent of snow in winter, of blueberries in July. The difference between sex and love. Drink from drunk. In his presence she can practically taste the *kreplach* and *kasha*, burnt slabs of brisket, fish molded into pucks, the hotel leftovers her own mother brought home in silver foil. Of the old hotel, her father said, *that place will turn us Jew yet*, but he accepted the candelabras given to him each winter hardened in a rainbow of wax.

"May she rest in peace."

When Paige was young, Noreen used to make up bedtime stories. Once upon a time. A beautiful maiden lived in a faraway village with a strict, punishing father. He laid out rules. Do this, don't do that. Fetch, roll over, obey. Marriage was set by fathers who sold daughters like meat, so the girl married and bore many children. One day she strayed from town. Flour, she was supposed to buy, eggs. The sun was setting, her children at home, when a car pulled alongside her and asked if he could help.

Who was he? Paige asked.

Love at first sight, she'd whisper as they slept, legs braided together. This man took one look at the maiden and saw through those heavy layers of clothes. A friendship formed, forbidden, of course. *What is friendship, if not love?* There'd be no happy ending. He was an outsider. She was married. What choice did they have? Light reaches only so far in the tunnel of despair. To this day, the man watches over her. In this way, they're never alone.

An alternative version, on nights Noreen came home hammered: the husband caught wind of her running around. What a hussy, this mother of four. All hell broke. Rage and shame and the midnight hunting of men through back woods where they stripped her down—her people, her family—and held her underwater until her eyes bulged and her face blued, bubbles dissolving at the surface, while her lover, this stranger, was tied to his chair, captive to her gruesome fate.

And then what? Her daughter wanted to know. The bad guys—Were they locked up? And what could Noreen say? There are bad guys everywhere.

What she took from Mark she never could return. When men forced themselves, there was a name for it. That night in The Lion's Den, she'd felt emboldened, irresistible, entitled even, steel in the toe and snug in her jeans, as if her want was large enough for the both of them. From this want came Paige, and from Paige a lifelong task: to reconcile the violence inside her with the stabbing persistence of love.

Light moves off the lake. On the other side, Tommy's truck pulls out, Hollywood blue, crowned with a claw of antlers.

The front door creaks.

"Kathy, that you?"

"Sorry to disappoint, Kole. Figured you could use a hot meal."

"Thought I was seeing things." Kole staggers, drunk. His chair scuffs the floor. He rubs his jowls, eyes sinking like raisins in dough. Hard to believe they're the same age.

"What's the good word?"

"These things take time."

"Bank's already calling."

"Buyers will be here by month's end."

A lie, although it is her intention, and dreams follow intention. Kole has a thread of beef on his chin. Noreen touches her own mouth. She picked this up on the Internet. People are like monkeys, mimicking the behavior they see.

"Kole," she points, wiping again.

"What's with the hot rod out front? Did you five-finger a bank, Noreen Murphy?"

She scoops potatoes. "Call in your brother."

"What for?"

"To join us, like civilized people."

Kole puts down his fork. When she brings his beer, he seizes her hand. Fizz slops over the top. "How's Paige doing, anyhow?"

"Honestly, I can't tell if she's coming or going."

"Tell her I asked for her, would you?"

The way he says it makes Noreen uneasy. "Go lie down," she says, as if he'd gone from the graveyard to the field instead of straight to the bar. "Thought maybe you'd paint the place."

"Why would I pay for paint?"

"Spruce things up a bit."

"Slap a coat of varnish on the village idiot while you're at it."

"Kole. Where's Mark gonna go in the event of a sale?"

"What do you mean, *in the event of*? Mark's a grown boy, aren't you, brother? Don't let his wounded act fool you. The man can fend for himself."

Paige is on the couch when Noreen gets home.

"Thought you had work, pigeon."

"Thought wrong."

Her daughter is peeling a roll of SweeTarts, popping discs like antacid, her face pinched and sour. Noreen drops her purse on the table.

"Don't you want to let some air in?"

On TV is a show on the housebound obese. The camera cuts to the complicated hoisting equipment, to the buffet of beef patties and soda, the family members who feed and mourn their loved ones in vicious cycle. Cut to the operating room, where lumps of marbled flesh excised from the abdomen ooze on the table like sacrificial lambs.

"How can you watch that?"

"Watch me."

Perched on the arm of the sofa, Noreen finds herself oddly transfixed. The body, pasted in identity-protecting black strips. It feels both removed and intimate.

"Mean old Mary died."

"Technicality."

"Would it have killed you to come to the funeral, after all they've done for us?"

Her daughter jacks up her knees. "I know what they've done."

A commercial for depression comes on.

"Come on, pigeon. Why can't we talk?"

"Can't I watch?"

"You do whatever you please anyway." Noreen knocks an ice tray against the counter. "Tommy Potts was over at Murmur today."

"I'm not his keeper."

Noreen waits for more but gets nothing. They used to be best friends. On Sundays they'd make chicken in the pot, which wasn't always chicken, but whatever they had, and as it simmered they'd play War on the rug, Paige wedging cards between her long toes for Noreen to draw, the game breaking into footsie, then laughter.

She carries her glass into the bedroom. Unzips herself, weighing each breast in her hands. Credit agencies can't collect on surgery. Someday maybe she'll spring for a tuck and a lift. She ties a red kimono around her, dragon splashed on the back.

In the bathroom she takes out a box.

Last week she'd splurged on highlights at the Salon but the stylist got zealous. All she wants is a little color around the face, lick of flames, to cheer her up. She loves doing hair, from peroxide to perms. Perhaps she should've gone into beauty. Her hands are so steady she once took a straight blade to Pat's neck and shaved him clean while he was sleeping.

In the mirror she inspects her part. Snaps on gloves, combines her little tubes, ammonia singeing her nostrils. She no longer remembers her original color. Her eyebrows are out of control but so is her tweezing, two lines plucked thin as villains. She frowns. But she can fix it. Nothing is beyond repair. The rest of her is fine, more than fine, she thinks, painting herself from tip to root, securing the shower cap to her head, then lowering herself on the lid of the toilet where she waits, head in hands, for all that brightness to soak in.

BETH

Beth laces up her shoes and runs. Always running *from*: boys, cops, Dick, Angie, in the low belly of dawn, when she couldn't think straight or couldn't stop thinking. One way or another she's been running her whole life, as if it might set her free. She's no athlete, but it's easier to run from than deal with, footfalls hard and heavy, she runs because she doesn't know what else to do.

Immediately, she's hurting. How quickly the body forgets its own capability. There's a stitch in her side. Crick in her knee. Gnats on her skin. If she stays on the road it will loop, but it's not the other half the property nor distance she's after, only escape: from the lake, this haunted place, the ceaseless pounding in head, heart, heels.

Try as she does, she can't shake the image of the drowned woman from the newspaper, barely a woman, still a girl, cheeks deflated, eyes skyward toward some invisible hope. Leave it to Beth to rent out a death trap. Brava, Barkman. Of course, now she wants all the gory details. She will ask Ira and yet she can't just say *hey, I was snooping around*. Already she feels him everywhere, lurking in corners, through the breaks in conifer and pine.

Plus, now—the flies.

Today the exterminator took a look around and said, "Where's the body?" Stood there scratching his jaw, like he didn't know where to begin. When a black cloud came for him, he threw up his clipboard and ducked.

"Watch yourself." Beth heard herself say, as if she were in any position to comfort. But he looked so tentative she had to remind him of his spray can. As he hosed the baseboards, she made a mask of her shirt. He called the chemicals organic. "Not to worry," he said. "Been breathing the stuff for years."

Beth yields to an oncoming car whose muffler looks like it might drop out the bottom. Counts the seconds until it fades from view, counts the occasions Ira has sneaked up on her: in the shower, down by the dock, night after night on the patio, his face in her window with a fifth of Kahlua, something she'd have stolen from her father's liquor cabinet along with a pint of crème de menthe. How often she'd said, "You startled me."

"I don't work miracles," the exterminator said. He had bad skin, vowels that knocked around like a rack of ice cubes as he rattled off the stages of decomposition. In situations like this, unless the source is located, flies will keep hatching until the cycle is complete.

"Sure it's a dead animal?"

"Something's rotten."

"What am I supposed to do?"

"Give it a week."

Her thighs burn. The hill at the end is like scaling a fifty-story building. As she rounds the final turn the house emerges, gambrel roof, Ira, a dot on the lawn, bowlegged, shaking a pair of plastic bags.

"What are you doing here?" Bile rises, sour in her throat.

"I come bearing gifts. Something old, something new. I'm your blue." He offers a frilly jar of honey. "Local specialty."

Beth hocks and spits.

"May I interest you in carrot tops, this old lime?"

She wipes the sheen from her forehead. "Scraps I'll take."

"Didn't know you were a runner! I put down the miles in my day." He swings his arms, cartoonish.

She snatches his bag.

"Your problem is you think life should be easy."

"*My problem*—" She wheezes. "My problem is I need to go get my kid."

That night, she tries pitching their plight as an adventure.

"Let's sleep under the stars!"

"We don't have a tent, Mommy."

"We have blankets."

"Can you build a fire?"

"We have flashlights."

"Batteries?"

"Check."

"Bear spray?"

"There are no bears."

"How do you even know?"

"I'm your mom, aren't I?"

Beth has no clue—*what if there are bears?*—but her answer seems to satisfy. They drag their bedding onto the lawn, build forts with comforters and pillows.

"Everything inside is outside."

"Kind of neat, right?"

Zach pulses his light. On, off, on. On. "That's our SOS."

Beth copies him, sending out a cone of light. They synchronize beats until their arms ache, and Zach chins his flashlight so he's lit up from below like a Jack o' lantern.

"Is Uncle Ira right?"

"Never. Why?"

"Quinn calls it murder, murder, murder lake."

"That's not nice."

"Why would he say it?"

"People can be so dishonest."

"What becomes of your bones when you're dead?"

"What do you think, buddy?"

"Daddy says Uncle Ryan is a star in the sky but I think he's dead in the ground."

"Ryan is wherever you want him to be."

"Tell me a spooky story."

Everything is spooky. What was that? She aims her light toward the woods. They are so isolated out here, in the dark, who would even pick up their signal? Her stomach growls. She can't remember the last time she ate; clearly, she will never sleep again, never enter that horrid house, not with the flies sprung from dead, rotting things, like that child's slapping game: bottom hand top hand bottom and so on, faster and faster until the tower collapses. Like that, with bodies. The exterminator said it's common. Animals find their way into tight spaces all the time, then can't escape.

"Let's think happy thoughts instead."

In the morning, their blankets are sodden with dew.

Things she does not say to her husband: *help.* The grass is my chamber pot; I'm shitting in McDonald's, scrubbing myself raw in the outdoor stall. She does not speak her fears. Of this place, of herself, of what's next. Come back, he'd say. See? I told you so.

Instead she says: "How about that weekend with Zach?"

"Thought you'd never ask," Doug gushes, which makes her cry. Once she starts she can't stop, salt on the tongue, down her hot throat as she unpacks Zach's damp swimsuit and rinses his lunchbox in the fly-infested sink. Her son busts through the door, triumphant.

"I found bear poop!"

"Put the stick down, honey." Arrangements are set with her husband for a Thursday trade-off, with the promise of a Sunday return.

TZVI

Safety comes first. Through the Mitzrayim website, he can send a note privately or dial a toll-free number. Anything he says will be kept confidential. He clicks the link, which opens a fresh window with a form to fill out. Name, please, paired with the reassurance that this is for administration purposes only. Again, it's a matter of faith. He scratches his arm. Stares at the cursor, watches it dance.

NOREEN

Ira is fast asleep when she pulls up to his cabin. How feeble he seems in this light, nothing but pie hole, alone in his rocker, as if the air has gone out of him.

"Sorry to interrupt the fly-catching."

He wipes his mouth. "Dreaming of you, Reenie." She catches him under the armpit.

"Easy there, partner."

"You make the knees weak. Want a beer?"

"How about a chair?"

"I said, I'm not one for company."

"I'm offering a new lease on life."

"I have a life."

"What life?"

"I'm thinking about raising llamas. All the kids are doing it."

"Here's another thought: Sell your house, see the world."

"I haven't seen my daughters in three years."

"That's the spirit."

"But I'd miss these colors."

"There are sunsets everywhere."

"How's the car treating you?"

"Like a kitten."

"Keep her already."

"Oh, no you don't. Ira, it's a Mustang."

He cups her knee. "A car is a car. She suits you. Go on, you deserve it. Use her in good health."

PAIGE

"Dude, I've got it. We'll go door to door. I'll be a homeless teen; I can be knocked up." They've been up all night and it's been a good night, a rare good night, so even though Paige is jittery and half-kidding she doesn't want the good nights to end. Her eyes feel like they've been propped with toothpicks. They're talking money, what else, only half-serious but who gives a fuck. She spikes her lighter against her jeans. "Hit up all the summer people."

"That's tight, Paigebaby." This is Tommy, gentle, open, Tommy in the eyes and jaw, this is the best he'll ever be, so she skips work to bum around with him in her mom's Toyota, shitty brakes but he's driving, her feet out the window, his elbow on the wheel, like he's her pimp and they're selling the world something. "You're real smart when you want to be."

"And you're not always a dickweed."

The Times Square debacle set Paige back two grand, which she's already recovered, not that she's told him. Tommy is hopeless around money. A new tattoo has cropped up over his jugular, gangster script, smeared in Vaseline and cling-wrapped, another thing she's paid for. Can't read what it says but wouldn't be surprised if it's his own damn name. Otherwise, the dummy might forget.

If she can teach him a thing about saving she'll feel better about leaving. Tommy and Silko are still facing a court date, but Paige will be gone by then so he'll have to wipe his own ass. Tommy flashes his exterminator badge at the gatehouse of the development community called Eagle's Nest. The guard waves them through. Houses come in alternating styles: ranch, Swiss Miss, contemporary.

"Remember," he says, "this is your idea."

Just like that they've slipped into character. Clutching Tommy's work clipboard, her pitch is rushed and thin. A scarfed woman answers the door, a million kids behind her, barefoot, banging pots. Diapers at their knees. Jelly on their faces like they've gored each other. Paige is a good faker, but even her best performance won't siphon off more than ten bucks.

"Bring me the *pushke*," one summer mother says to her daughter. The daughter has a baby on her hip and a large sauce stain, returns with a blue box the color of Tommy's truck and shakes out a few quarters. Another family asks for change for a five.

"Well, that blew chunks."

"Let's try Murder Lake."

"Let's not and say we did."

"This client, I bet she pays just to talk. Feeds you, too. She's kind of extra, you know, sad schoolteacher, but she reminds me of you."

"You're a prince."

He twirls a rabbit's foot. "I love you, too."

The drive over is nice, like they're a healthy couple in a car for a minute. They smoke butts and welcome the wind, Tommy's hair lashing gold in the summer light.

"Who should I say I'm with?"

"Save the Children."

"Does that still exist?"

"Fracking, then. They hate that shit."

"Fracking's already illegal."

"But it's the *idea* of it!"

"You don't have to shout."

"Who's shouting?" Tommy shouts.

Paige wipes the smog of pencil from her eyes, squeaks her finger over her gums.

"How do I look?"

She is wearing a HUGS NOT DRUGS shirt from clearance.

"Like Joan of fucking Arc."

He kisses her deep, metal and ash, drops her off at the bottom of the hill. The climb to Murmur Lake is a face-melting, sand-in-the-throat, half-mile doozy, the house set back from the road. Through the window she can see a lime bikini pushing a broom. Paige isn't sure whether to knock or ring so she does both, flattens her nose to the glass.

Finally, the door opens.

"Good afternoon, did you know that every year more and more species face global extinction?"

It's a good one. Who can deprive the blue-footed boobies? The giant pandas?

This coldhearted bitch. Looks her dead in the face. Freckles stipple her nose, neck rashed in poison ivy or bug bites or sunburn, Paige can't tell, only that the woman hasn't been careful.

"I'm just the babysitter. Do you have a sheet or something? I'll pass it along—" Already the woman's closing the door.

"Every cent helps. We suggest a dollar a day, which can be issued in a tax-deductible lump sum. Surely, there's loose coin lying around. In 2012, the African elephant was added to the endangered list. Can you imagine a world without elephants?"

"Like I said, I can't help you."

Just then a child pokes his head through the woman's legs, prying her wide as prison bars. "Who is it, Mommy?"

IRA

Help, he needs help. Ira shivers in a membrane of sweat, unsure of the time, dusk or dawn; the light muzzy, the sound belonging to aliens or apparitions or great horned owls. *Who, who, who.* Nothing feels right. He should go to the doctor, he needs a doctor, but even in this state, he knows better than to climb behind the wheel, much less at this hour, whatever hour it is. Time is a slippery fuck. He pulls on pants. His sandals are sponges. There's his Japanese maple.

Hello, tree. He has no car.

It takes a hundred years to arrive at the house. "Go away. I told you no one's home."

But the door is unlocked and there's Beth in a bikini, holding a spatula, a fly swatter. The room buzzes, saffron paper coiling from the beams like party streamers.

"Jesus Christ, Ira, you don't just barge in on people."

Help, he thinks. What he says is: "Hubba."

"I could've been buck naked."

"You've got flies."

"No shit, Sherlock."

He goes to her and the floor buckles. "Beth," he says, his speech foreign, slurry. Distance pulls like taffy between them. For each step he takes she stretches away, farther and smaller until she's out of reach. A pill, he wants, a little blue pill, that'll restore him, a red, pink, three whites, the whole rainbow of pharmaceutical magic. He fumbles in his pocket to show her what he needs, unzipping, feeling around.

"What on earth are you doing," he hears as his liquid warmth leaves him, dribbles onto his hand, down his leg, pooling into his shoes.

PAIGE

Already it's been a hectic night at SCCH. Fletcher Samuels coded during Atticus Finch's closing argument just as Paige was reading, "there is not one person in this courtroom who has never made a mistake;" and now, beneath the glow of the nurse's station, while ordering the death certificate, she spies Ira Lecher's name scrawled on the intake board. Room 216.

"Welcome to SCCH! Hope you are enjoying the accommodations."

"Food's top-notch." His tray, a hardened slab of salisbury steak, tapioca skin.

"As you can see, we take real pride in the decor." She draws the curtain, scattered in seasonal leaves.

He chokes on a laugh, so she props him up, his grizzled hair now less revolutionary than Revolution-era, blousy smock completing the look of a banged-up Ben Franklin.

"How did I get here?"

Paige lifts his chart. "Someone named Barkman signed you in. Will you be staying with us long, Mr. Lecher?"

"Lech. What are the perks?"

His gown hangs off him, exposing a beam of clavicle, blossom of veins at the knee. Like that documentary on veterans, heroes coming home from war only to wither away on oxygen bags, garrison caps sad as paper boats. She draws the blanket over him.

"How about a magazine?"

"I was thinking more medicinally."

"For all I know that's what got you here, and I sure as shit don't need the hassle of you dead. Besides, they're pumping you with plenty of good stuff as it is."

"Dial your mom, then. Have her bring round those papers she's been harping about. Whatever she wants. Winner, winner, chicken dinner."

NOREEN

Noreen is back at the library with a renewed mission. "Where would I find old news?"

Misty Drake slips a bookmark between her pages. "Year?"

"1990."

Misty's ass is a pancake in those slacks. Sitting is the new cancer, Noreen's read, so she flexes her glutes as she follows, tightens her bladder muscles. She found this blog called "Kegel for Jesus," with Christ doubling as a bare-chested Fabio, so each time she squeezes it's a little like fucking—and prayer.

"Years go by of nothing, then bam, three people scour the archives in a day."

"Three people?"

"Let's see. First one was a Jewish. Ball cap ain't much of a disguise. Then another summer person, poky looking thing."

The microfilm is kept in a custodial closet. Misty flicks on the viewer. It clicks and whirs, emitting an inky odor. "Starvation never seems to go out of style."

"I'll take it from here."

"Holler if you need me."

An entire year of *The Sullivan County Monitor* fits onto a single reel. Noreen removes the roll, holds the negative to the light. Last thing she wants is to be caught off guard. The more she knows, the better equipped she'll be to field questions about Murmur, if Frank & Messina somehow got ahold of its history, and that's what's stalling them. She hooks the spool to the spinner, slides the strip under the light box, and twists the knob. *Residents Gather for the Easter Parade.* Carefully, she zips back, easing the film forward inch by inch. *Vandalism on the Rise. Congratulations Sullivan High Seniors.* July, August, September. *Arrest Made in*

Drowning Death. Mark Troller, 25, son of Mark Sr. (deceased) and Mary Troller, has been arrested in...

She runs her finger over Mark's mugshot, his features erased, as though his pupils had been pecked over by crows. There's got to be some kind of explanation. A man doesn't just flip on a switch. To be of the world, one minute, tying lures with dexterity, waxed threads and hackle, only to give it all up the next, retreating to a life of silence and devotion, like a monk, minus the robes. His oath: to the Lake, that night in August, the woman who went down in his waters only to rise again dead.

Close-knit community requests privacy, shuns reporters, smashes cameras. "Leave us alone!"

Back then you'd have to cut out Kole's tongue to quiet his ranting. Those Jews this and that. Kole's theory was the situation had been framed to look like a hate crime, with Mark as the scapegoat, but not even Mark subscribed to Kole's story.

"We're not ruling out the possibility of suicide," Jeff Johnson, Sullivan County police chief said.

The tape ends, rippling out hot. Noreen trades it for the following year, scanning for reports of formal charges, jury selection, a trial, but nothing materializes. There are no other suspects. No sentencing. The investigation neither ongoing nor closed. Mark is released after questioning, pat on the shoulder: son. Go home. Get on with your life.

Other reports crop up on the blotter. Rick Boyd's seven consecutive DUIs: one with heavy machinery, another resulting in a collision with Moe Leary's barn. The space heater fire that took Betsy Harrison's ex-husband's trailer along with his sister and kids, the closing of the meat processing facility, Victor Hines shooting himself in the face, but missing his brain, a blessing or a curse. There is no more news of Murmur. Mark went away. Mark returned. That's all she knew. Whatever actually transpired that summer all but fell away. She flicks off the machine, gathers her belongings.

Misty calls after her, "Got what you came for, I suppose?"

BETH

Beth fucks the exterminator while her son's in New Jersey. It is the fourth time he's come, jeans slipping off the hooks of his sunken hips, wielding his nozzle. For all Beth knows the can is a prop, filled with nothing but water, but for the smell: birch beer, sweet as a soda float. She pays him then overpays him, tipping 35 percent because she's at his mercy and the flies keep on coming. He warned her there'd be no easy fix. They are tenacious mothers. He comes back the next day, and two days after that, hands her his card. *Animal & Pest.* "Buzz me anytime." He picks his face. He takes her money. He calls her "lady," and it's marginally deferential. There's a name embroidered on his shirt but he does not look like an Ernest and she does not ask.

Sometimes he takes hours. She sits on the step and waits, anxiety flapping its wing across her breastbone, but no one hears her. No one sees her tears.

The exterminator is erratic, but ultimately, he shows, with his oiler and far away eyes, administering squirts beneath the kitchen sink, lowly puffs along the caulking in the connected bathroom. At first, Beth reflexively cupped Zach's mouth and nose, his breath misting her palm. Anything could set off an attack. Then she dropped Zach off with his dad.

From there, she tucked herself into a diner to binge on gluten and dairy. She'd forgotten how hungry she was, forking through the vinegary dish of pickles, waiting on her milk and pie. As a child, her mother would sometimes take them to diners as a reprieve from cooking. A kid's menu named after zoo animals: Elephant was a flatiron steak, bloody and pink; Giraffe, a chicken parm; the Rooster, a BLT. She devoured grilled cheese the size of her face, thick slice of tomato, seeds streaming down her wrist. In high school, she'd stab cigarette butts into puddles of condiments, bring the lit ends down on her wrists. She was sorry for so many things.

By the third visit, she stepped aside. The exterminator's boots scuffed the floor. He left his paperwork in the truck along with a girl, sunglasses, feet on the dash, his sister, maybe, his girlfriend, his wife. Beth wondered if they'd make babies with extra fingers or stubby limbs on account of all the chemical exposure.

Reasonably priced, compared to the city's Cockroach Coaches and Lice-No-More-Ladies (*now those were ladies*) who combed through Zach's curls; the exterminator is her saving grace. He is maybe twenty-five. She dials, he comes. He listens, unlike Ira, Ira Lecher who up and pissed on her floor, so she gives him extra in cash, then pulls him toward the bed.

"Lady," he says, backing up.

The exterminator is so hick it's almost a deal breaker, but he's young, she's drunk, there is a dimple in his chin like Prince Charming, the whole scene straight out of Uptown Girl with her playing Christie Brinkley to his Billy Joel. She grew up on MTV, so it takes little convincing. If she squints he almost looks like a young Matt Donovan, her old friend.

"Should I get the door?"

A ridiculous request—she's never been more alone—though his politeness charms her. He must have a mother who raised him right. She barely steps out of her shorts before he's gap-toothed and grinning.

"What?"

"Only I've never seen a hedge trimmed quite like it."

"A landing strip."

"Never seen one of those, neither."

She looks down. What she sees is her birth scar, a crooked ridge.

"Well, now you have."

If she is assertive, he needs it. This is no time to be coy. In dreams, Beth is visited by that dead woman, bloated in white, an ultra-Orthodox Ophelia. Beth sifts through boxes in dreams, packing and unpacking, what belongs to her, what never was hers to begin with. Ira's face in Joker paint beams from atop a milk crate. She grips the edges of his flesh and lifts, rubbery cheeks and cleft chin, only behind his face lies a stack of other faces. Beth secures every mask. Her own reflection stares up at her from inside the box.

But this is no dream. The exterminator smells like a fist of change left in her pocket for too long. He keeps his boots on, long-sleeves. She opens his belt, cracked leather. He is mealy and sour. She breathes through her nose, guiding his hand to thumb around inside her until she is ready.

Only he's not. He's nowhere close. She gives him a moment, pretends not to notice, but it's like coaxing a kitten down from a tree, he's stuck, frightened, her luck, surely this is a referendum on her, so she gets on all fours and starts rocking, cajoling, almost begging, *come on, Ernest, you can do it, that a boy, pony up and stick it in.* She feels predatory, like a man, like a creep, *you know you want it*, she says, she doesn't know anything, not a damn thing, every inkling collapsing onto itself, like the frame of a burning building, she is on fire, all but consumed, but for those children in Plexiglas looped to this guy's belt, matching reindeer sweaters, fake snow, the kind of photos done at the mall, are they his kids or siblings, nieces and nephews? My God, how sweet. His keychain swings.

Head to the wall. Now that's more like it. He thumps halfheartedly. She shuts her eyes, and the vision of rot returns. Maggots crawl through rice, skin warps like desert clocks, a film strip clicks; she's in health class, junior high, angel dust is not for angels. *Go Ask Alice* flits from locker to locker. It's taking forever. At this rate she'll be dead before he comes.

"Hold up," he says, and just like that, he's out and zipped. "Lady. You got an attic in this place?"

She waves in the general direction. While she collects herself—*was that it?*—he snaps on blue gloves like the kind Zach's counselors wear on bathroom duty. A few minutes later, he climbs down from the dark.

"Found your problem!" He jangles a rusted cage.

Bit of bird, mange of squirrel, possibly a rabbit, all but ossified. He found nothing. The trap is old. The exterminator did not set it, but Beth plays along, *my hero*, she says, going to him fresh. He peels her from his tattooed neck. *Lady.* Light's splinting through the rafters. Might want to see to those holes. Cracks can be systemic in a house this old. He knows a guy for that but she says, *No need, thank you, we're only renting.*

By the seventh day, it's over. Larvae stop hatching, flies start dying. Beth locates a dustpan. On her knees, like Doug proposing marriage at Ground Zero, she sweeps the fallen bodies into a small, black hill. Her father, always a little angry; her mother defiant in a caftan despite his requests to wear something more flattering. In the twilight, her mother turned up the music and reached for her daughter. *Dance with me.* Beth called her weird and walked off. Her mother in a station wagon smelling of skunk, twisting mood rings, her mother weeping behind sunglasses at the kitchen table, her mother piloting that carpool car out to Arizona only to blow her ambition to bits. Her father shaking his head. The fire was secondary. "Motherhood is what did her in. You should've seen what a heartbreaker she'd been."

Beth dumps the carnage, takes a bottle to the deck. Zach won't be home until Sunday; finally, she's accountable to no one, and it is unbearable. Even the crickets herald a dangerous sort of quiet. *IS THERE ANYBODY OUT THERE?* She wails into the night, but there is no echo.

What there is, is rice, their comfort food. Jasmine, brown, wild, enriched, fast-cooking, short grain, long grain, all grains gluten-free. One a little nutty, one more viscous but otherwise the same indistinct mash. She pushes around her spoon. Library research proved lacking. Had it been an accident? Crime? A third possibility: Chaya Bloch had taken her own life. How would Beth do it? Pills, probably. Always: the path of least resistance.

An ant is trapped in her rice bowl. Beth watches it struggle. It scales and slides. She does not rescue it. On her second bottle she dials Ailene.

"Your kid's a little shit."

"Welcome to my life." A baby erupts in the background.

"As if I can't tell murder from murmur. As if we've haven't had enough violence in our lives."

"*Claire!*" Pots clang. "Sorry, what were you saying?"

She hangs up. Amy is a last resort. As kids, Beth doused her hair in lemon juice to look more like her sister but they looked nothing alike. Her older sister went through things (got her period, shaved her legs) which gave her status, then left; her mother left, and Beth apparently only appreciates people once they're gone. Now that Zach's away she wants him back desperately, she sniffs one of his shirts, but his absence gnaws at her, swirling with the sour of wine. She makes quick work of a box of crackers, but the serotonin barely takes the edge off. She even misses Doug, the way you miss something you never fully have.

Amy seems unaware of how long it's been. To Amy, they could've talked yesterday. Her voice bounces along emptily, as if she already assumes no one's listening. Beth puts down the phone and wanders off for a can of beans, rinsing and eating them cold like popcorn. Had they not been related Amy would've been one of those girls who teased Beth in the halls, girls with big hair, riding shotgun in fast cars, girls in black tank tops (you could never have too many) chalked with deodorant stripes, powder fresh, after P.E.

She stands in the window. In the city everyone stares into everyone's homes but here she feels like a target. Shame washes over her. Every sound is a judgment.

"Hello? Hello? Hello? Beth? Are you still there?"

"I'm here."

Her sister is talking about rosé as if she just discovered it, a spunky new instant fridge that will chill a bottle in minutes, like that ice plunge therapy—what's it called? There was an article in *People*. When you pay gobs of money to freeze off your fat?

"You know what I mean." As if Amy might be misunderstood. Now Beth is crying, her whole body quaking, tears mixing with snot, a sweet cream. Her nose leaks, and she swallows herself. The new bottle already half-empty.

"Amy?"

"Listen, Beth, got to go, I've a zillion things, but it's been great, so great to catch up with you."

PAIGE

Every time she goes to the river Paige tells herself it's the last time. She tells herself this as July flumps into August, the air an aggravation of no-see-ums, as she scrambles beneath the hull of the underpass. The three spanned bridge makes a viaduct, as if the Delaware were a waterway through ancient Greece. Someday, she'll travel; she owes herself that much: to see beyond here, with half of Neversink stupid and strung out. The river is what keeps her straight even when it runs contrary to her particular hunger. Everything is relative. She is relatively sober tonight.

When they first got together, Tommy called her a narc. Who goes to the river just to watch? But she was fascinated by the dip and dab, the zombie stare, syringes jammed with blood, eyes an ungodly white. Paige has a nervous habit of laughing instead of crying. Seeing her classmates slumped in nods, heads heavy as iron balls, Brittany and Regina and Peter Ruxton, almost makes her roar.

She kicks a shoe. "Tommy."

His high-top twitches, but it's only reflex. Tommy, chasing weightlessness, is a heap of dead weight. Up on the cliffs, Silko and his boys are out of their minds. They've taken over a deserted hotel not far from Liberty and now have all these notions about living. Like a commune, straight from the sixties, Silko acts like a drug-crazed Jesus, only minus the smarts, charisma, or any organized leadership. Paige watches them totter, their voices carrying across the narrows, here is New York, there is Pennsylvania, but no one's listening. They are close to the tree line, that's how high they are, Paige the only person alive for miles. Silko sways like a pogo stick, boxers half-out of his pants. They all look the same from this distance. A feral, interchangeable pack.

The cliffs rise in a series of carved-out tiers, celebrated in high fives and wagers. Boys don't do anything without bets, but with bets they'll do just about anything. Paige has watched Tommy snort dental floss, snort spaghetti, flossing through the roof of his mouth for a dime bag. She has seen them play chicken on a one-lane bridge. Usually they are too fried to do much harm, but tonight Silko's keyed up. He beats his chest. Holds a licked thumb to the wind. Shoves a fist in an armpit, an imitation of something.

"Get up, pussy!" he hollers, his jaw pocked in acne scars.

"Tommy, don't."

"Let me see you fly!"

The cliff must be forty feet high. Tommy wobbles to his feet.

"Sit your ass down. You don't jump because some moron says jump."

"Chillax." He drawls, removing his shoes. Tommy's toes translucent in the moonlight. "I can clear it in my sleep," and true, this is what they do, what they've done for hundreds of years, this is the fire that burns through his blood, but tonight, she can feel it, will not end well. Even at the deepest part of the river, people have wound up paralyzed, spines busted on a rusted fridge, you can't see the bottom. Silko goes over first, a running jump, but the rocks are slick and he slips, scraping his back, *Jesus! Mary! Joseph!* His body falling like a sudden tragedy, crashing into the deep.

"Wait for me!"

"Don't!" Her voice cracks, but Tommy's fine, invincible, assholes are always invincible, his jump so clean there's hardly a splash, only he forgets to remove his hat, trucker foam bobbing like a buoy downstream.

"Halle-fucking-lujah," he bellows.

When he climbs ashore, Paige peels off his wet things and unzips her sweatshirt, his clammy fingers feeling clumsily under her shirt. Her nipple is a stone.

"What am I going to do with you, Tommy?"

He passes her a beer, but Silko won't leave them alone. "I'm bored. Let's go rustle up some fun. Paige, where are all your Jew friends tonight?"

"Not friends." Paige scrapes the foil off her bottle.

God's Country is what they call the clusterfuck off Route 17. Thursday night so people are out, hitching rides, dancing their odd dances. Silko says let's shake a few bucks from their stockings and pilgrim shoes. A bad idea from the get but she can't police every idea, and someone has to chaperone. Paige can barely reach the pedals of Tommy's truck, rather, his brother's truck. Tommy's brother is in Iraq. Afghanistan? He's some place. Or was, last she'd heard.

They drive through Kiamesha—the town sign says WE MEAN CLEAN WATER—and pull into the Bowl-A-Rama. Black hats turn on asphalt, and immediately, Paige regrets coming. One foot in Florida if she can keep it together; she is this close to gone. People stop talking and stare. Like ants at a picnic, there's strength in numbers. Paige shuts the radio. Women and children stand to one side of the parking lot in matching checked dresses. It's late. *Doesn't anyone sleep?*

The men huddle up, talk with their hands. The women look old from far away but up close they are young, younger than Paige, teenage brides, heavy wigs hiding their faces. This one—pregnant, with a double stroller and two girls beside her—stares at Paige as if she were an aid worker on convoy to a refugee camp. As if Paige might save her.

"Who's the connect?" Silko says.

"I'm the connect."

"Shut up, Murphy. Which one is he?"

"He's not here."

She clicks the column into reverse but a crowd has gathered, preventing her from backing out. Tzvi stands slightly apart, cupping an elbow with one hand and twisting the short growth of his beard with the other.

Tommy stumbles out, ragged from the river. The black sea parts. If she intervenes, what good will it do? Everything is a hairpin from anarchy. Never should have mentioned the cash in Tzvi's pocket. A van careens into the lot, and out pour Silko's entourage, junkies fleeing a clown car, flannel shirts flailing behind them like capes. It's a rumble out of *West Side Story*, only it isn't, it's a wasted fantasy. Paige shuts her headlights. Tzvi steps forward as if to announce himself—*Here I am*—shoulders back, chest square and unafraid. Tommy slams him against an electrical pole. Silko waves a switchblade like he'll slice any beard but it's empty bluster. Black hats backpedal, punch flip phones. Within minutes, sirens move in.

Tommy turns toward the disco of red, white, blue, and suffers a hook to the chin. He topples easily. The crowd is cheering, jeering at Silko who's flapping around like an untamed hose. Tommy rolls to his side and spits. Paige flings open the cab door.

"Why must you ruin everything?" She kicks Tommy in the ribs. God, it feels good. He is helpless and weak. She kicks again. Once her rage is unleashed, there's no stopping it. Tommy writhes like a slug. He takes it. He doesn't even try to get up. His body is a Beanie Baby, a bag of buckwheat, punctured seed, she kicks and kicks, he spills, she is just getting started, kicking him long after he's bruised and bleeding, crying out for mercy, until the cops twist her wrists and pull her off of him.

NOREEEN

The theft is unplanned. Noreen has not come for the laptop or portable speakers or pair of designer shades, even though they're out in the open. She's come looking for Ira. Her sole intent is information. It's the car talk that worries her. Who walks away from a vintage sports car? Only someone who has somehow given up.

Noreen finds herself thinking about the old coot more than she'd like, his silly stash of pumice stones, rough on one side, smooth on the other, cradled in a shallow dish. But his cabin is empty and unmade, reeking of urine; it's not like him to leave things this way.

The tenant's car sits outside the main house like a buttoned accordion, cute for a doll but ridiculous for a person, a rich person, which sends Noreen hollering *helloooooooo* across the meadow, then out to the lake, the dock deserted, water steely and undisturbed.

She's not sorry. The renter is not home. One push and the door gives. Inside, everything's been cleared off the floor, chairs atop tables, hassocks on the couch, rugs rolled and pushed into corners. A couple of flies the size of watermelon seeds hover heavily on last wings. Broom on the wall, dustpan full as a mass grave. Spoiled, is what. The kind of people who assume others will pick up after them. Noreen lifts a towel off a chair.

That's when the pair of rings catches her eye, gleaming on the shelf, diamond big as a tooth, wedding band of brushed platinum. And that's when she sees the wallet, long as an Italian hero, on the table. Noreen jots down the driver's license info, just in case, then slips out a credit card for her rainy day fund. Her fraud days are over, but you can't rule out emergencies. The wallet is bursting at the seams. Those who carry this much cash are asking for it. Noreen skims off the top, helps herself to a bottle of wine, and is gone.

With it, the joy. She takes—there's always something to take—but her heart's no longer in it. The more she tries to hold onto her daughter, the more elusive Paige becomes. She barely sleeps at home anymore, staying out all night, and Noreen doesn't want to think about it, how little a mother knows. Paige who scrapes the cream from her Oreo with her front teeth first, who wears down her shoes from the inner sole out. Whose loose hairs on the shower wall are all Noreen has for clues. *Who is she?* Everyone says not my child, but no one is immune. Every moment feels closer, more urgent, like she can map every pore, and also, impossibly out of reach. Noreen holds the engagement ring up to the sun where it radiates a prism of color. She cups a flame to her lips and sucks. The orange tip flares.

IRA

For three days, Ira stays in SCCH. He's had some sort of malfunction. The doctor says it like Ira's a robot that's misfired, warranting a recall. They monitor him; perform tests, fasten nodes to his chest and scalp. Every wire has a beep. Can't remember the last time his prostate, or any other part of him, has received such attention, which is kind of nice. It's like they're genuinely curious. How he ticks. Periodically, he goes off, sounding into the night, so it's hard to settle into a sustained sleep or to know what time it its. Hours deplete. There are more hours. *How much time does he have?* Like jumping to the last page of a book, would knowing his own end spoil or improve his hourly existence?

"Level with me. How bad is it?"

The nurses laugh. They call him Mister.

"Ira."

"Mr. Ira."

"In another life, they called me Lech."

"Why would anyone call you that?"

Much as he likes being waited on, lying around makes him stir crazy. The ceiling is an iceberg, an avalanche, a spread of potted cheese, a galaxy of stars. He gets up, hospital Johnny breezing shamelessly at his back, but forgets he's tethered to an IV pole. Iodine has painted him with jaundice; his skin, after repeated prodding, quick to purple and welt. Results are inconclusive. Perhaps there is a problem with his heart, that crotchety—overused? underserved?—organ. Too hard on the outside, too gooey within, like movie house candy. Possibly, the other way around. These doctors haven't an idea. He can hear Viv saying: That's why you see a specialist in the city.

A nurse comes in for vitals.

"What has a heart but no other organs?" The device beeps. "A deck of cards!"

Every August Ira takes his stand-up to a side stage of the Sullivan County Fair. LOVE IT OR LECH IT. LIFE'S A LECH. The tagline changes but he remains a fixture, the weeklong gig his spotlight of the year.

"Doc says, 'Sir, hate to break it to you, but it's your heart. Broken, kaput. We have to do a transplant.' Patient asks: 'But where will my love go?'"

The nurse gives him a puzzled look, clicks her pen. "Know why I hate pencils? They're pointless!"

"Get some rest." The nurse dims the overhead, hands him the remote to the black and white bolted to the wall. It's all reruns. *M.A.S.H.*, *Three's Company*.

The only person to break up the ice chips and pudding cups is Noreen's girl. Paige comes by twice, dressed like a barbershop pole. Twists the evening blinds, leans over him in her pinafore to adjust his pillow.

"Great get-up."

"Haven't they bathed you?" She lifts his chart.

"Well, Doc? Am I terminal?"

"A lost cause. But you're due for a sponge tomorrow."

She plants herself beside Ira's legs, which are strapped into blood pressure cuffs that work on a timer to keep him from throwing a clot. They watch John Ritter trip over himself. Paige opens a bag of chips. Their hands go in at once. Time passes the length of a show, into another. Paige licks the flavor salt from her fingers.

"You probably have bedpans to empty, scripts to fill, candies to stripe."

She digs into her bib and drops a handful of amber bottles into his bedside drawer.

"Watch these, OK?"

"Now that's what I call candy."

"Don't be an idiot or I'll fucking kill you."

When Paige doesn't show on Thursday and then zippo on Friday, Ira's had enough.

"When can I break out of this gulag?"

The nurse unplugs his calf massagers. "Can't keep a patient against his will."

Out he goes in the same dungarees he came in with. The sun feels good on his face as he makes his way down hospital hill, around the discount sprawl of the cigarette mart, WHO ASHED YOU?, the second-hand clothing and exotic fish store, the outfitter emporium going-out-of business, looping around the main drag where his convertible stands parked in front of the police station basking in the sun.

"What's the problem, officer?"

Noreen turns. He can see in her eyes how he must look. His hand flies to his hair.

"Ira!"

She catches herself, face brightening, because that's Reenie Murphy, she has a way of making you feel like you're the only thing that matters, even if it's all an act.

"These wingnuts are holding Paige custody and I have somewhere to be."

"Watch who you're calling a wingnut, Murphy." The officer looks from one to the other. "Where'd you find this turkey, anyway?"

"I've got it, Reenie. Consider it done."

"You're a doll."

The officer clucks. "Word of advice, pal: Don't let your old lady play you. We could wallpaper a cell in Noreen Murphy's rap sheet."

"Sounds like a makeover."

"Worth knowing who you're in bed with," the officer shrugs.

Paige's charges: Disorderly conduct, public brawling, the incitement of a riot. *What kind of riot could one possibly incite in Sullivan County?*

When they bring her out, Ira says, "Checking out so soon? How was your stay?"

"Why aren't you at SCCH?"

"I'm on the lam, kid."

"This doesn't make you some kind of guardian angel."

"Lord knows, but I'm famished. I could eat a small child."

"I have work."

"Then let's get you to work."

Before he can back out of The Breakstone, Paige comes out canned. No two weeks, no nothing. She chews her thumb.

"Don't eat yourself."

"Screw off."

"Want to tell me what happened."

To his surprise, she does. About the river and Tommy and some scumbag named Silko and the Bowl-A-Rama and a prank gone wrong. How cliff fuckers and religious freaks share the same belief system, only there is no higher power. No one's holding a safety net. Jump, and it's not faith that saves you, but knowing how to fall. Break the water before it breaks you. Ira's lost what she's talking about.

"You do know I'm Jewish."

"But you're not a Jew Jew."

"Good enough for Hitler."

"I was trying to stop it."

He pulls into the Bowl-A-Rama. "You still have to apologize."

"Can I at least go home first and shower?"

"Nice try. Look at me, honeybee. I'm a natural disaster."

At the Bowl-A-Rama, the front-of-the-house guy is playing scratch numbers. The room is set for glow bowling. In the corner lane men congregate like they're davening, bowing forward, rocking back. They don't look wasted but you can't always tell. His parents would roll in their graves. The mere notion of Haredi on drugs? Goes against every stitch of their moral fiber. Simon and Ruth cursed the papers whenever their people were raked through the news. They said it like that: *Our people.* David Berkowitz, Leopold and Loeb, Jack Ruby. Born Rubenstein! There was no room for error. The tribal mentality: You could not be good or merely human; you had to be better. Everyone was watching. At *Man's World*, Ira ran an exposé of an Amish cocaine ring in Lancaster County. The reporter won an award for his thesis: Righteousness and separatism, beards and hats, can't mask the fact that we're all humans, reaching and ruined in similar ways. It wasn't groundbreaking, but it hit home. Stare into the abyss and it stares back at you, etc. Drugs offered a ready escape, and who wouldn't want to escape some of that scrutiny?

"Almost closing," the guy in the booth says.

"It's two o'clock."

"Summer hours."

"You have my stuff?" Paige looks past Ira's shoulder.

He hands over Percocet, Vicodin, Demerol. Xanax. She uncaps a canister.

"They'll lock you up for this."

"You messed up my count."

"At least spare a few for good behavior."

"That's it, grandpa. I'm cutting you off. It's for your own good."

"No one's ever taken such care of me. No one's even cared."

"Cry me a river."

"Where's this Tzvi, anyway?"

The man in front buzzes someone who buzzes someone. Paige crosses to the men's section as if she's invading enemy lines. Tzvi's carrot coloring makes him look more Irish than Jewish. The only females here are a band of sisters in staticky, ankle-length black. Klezmer music pumps to an electronic beat. Lasers bounce off the walls in beads of yellow and blue. The air smells like tennis balls. Ira is hungry and scattered. Hard not to insert Chaya Bloch into a scene like this, to imagine kids hanging off her like coats on a rack. Husband in his own fervent world. Paige steps so close to Tzvi they are practically touching. And now they are holding hands.

A few patrons tsk their disapproval but Tzvi ignores the outcry. Lined up, the pins glow like skull teeth. Balls clunk through the conveyor belt. Ira grabs one, glittered and pink. His fingers are so swollen they barely fit in the holes. The ball is heavy, his knees ache, he's too tired to throw. Go easy, was the discharge order, as if there was any other way to go. Two gutters and it is Paige's turn. Ira clears out whatever's left at the kosher café: one dried-out pretzel and three cold franks, polishing off the first in two salty bites, then loading up the second and handing it over.

"Pops like a foreskin."

"Do you mind? I'm eating."

Overhead lights come on. The carpet, an explosion of zigzags and stars, could use a vacuum.

Outside, the parking lot is a smog of heat. If only Ira had an ice-cold celery soda, that'd be a real trip to the glands. There is a bud of ketchup on Paige's lip. Her shirt rides up, toddler-tight. *God, she must be what.* Country girls were like freshly poured cement, begging for his imprint. He could sink his fists into her honest shape, built from economy as opposed to laziness, from working too many jobs, unlike women like Viv, sculpted by trainers and fitness fads. She is made like her mother, only springier. Her shorts could cut off her circulation. As a boy, Ira loved a bungalow kitten so hard he snapped its delicate neck.

Paige drives them out to Murmur as if they're coming home.

"Let me straighten up."

By the time he's washed his hands she's passed out in his bed, her nest of hair, dark magenta, like a berry gum, spread out on his pillow. Quietly, Ira curls beside her. He used to love tucking in his own girls at night, singing Fire & Rain, kissing their shampooed heads. They were his; then they weren't. How fast it was. How quickly children become people, separate and apart. He is not sorry for loving, or how he loved, without boundaries. Smothering, maybe. His own parents were dreadfully cold. He slides closer, Paige's breath a rustle of trees, and he is sleeping.

When he wakes, Paige is poking through his fridge.

"Make yourself at home."

"You've got nothing."

"I've been indisposed, kid."

She inspects a tub of coleslaw.

"Everything is spoiled."

"How about french toast? I make a mean french toast."

"What kind of ogre doesn't have eggs?" She scrapes the burnt discs of cheese that have hardened along the bottom of the toaster oven.

"My kids used to love my toast."

"These are the best," she says placing the blackened flats on her tongue. "At the grocery they sell parmesan crisps for seven bucks a bag."

"I've got a tin of anchovies."

"I'll pass."

"Puts hair on the chest."

"Are you in some kind of witness protection?"

"I'm a man of few needs."

The field stirs, alive with rabbits. They sit on the step and watch the light go from green to gray, the sky a haze of pink.

"The days are getting shorter already."

"In Florida, there's this mermaid park where people come from all over, Tokyo, Copenhagen, to watch girls underwater perform like Esther Williams."

"I know that place! We almost went there but chose Orlando."

"Figures. People like you always want bigger and better."

"Human nature, kid. We never stop wanting."

"All I want is out."

"Same difference."

"The only people in Neversink are young or old."

"I'm here," he says, leaning against her, as if there's another way to say lonely. "People like you keep a man like me young."

"You can't keep people." She gets up, brushes her seat.

"Go, then. Scram already." He clears his throat. "What are you waiting for?"

NOREEN

Paige is eating cereal in the dark. "Where were you?"

"Now you're the mother?" Noreen drops her bag. "What a day, pigeon. Shocking, how people live. You should see the slob staying at Ira's. A real piggy." She dumps the mud from the coffee pot. "What the heck happened last night?"

Paige crunches.

"I'm waiting."

Her spoon clinks. "Do you even have a buyer?"

"Me first."

"You talk to Ira, lately?"

"Of course." Actually, Noreen only saw him for that one second at the station. "I don't want to hear about any more trouble, Paige."

"You won't hear."

"How about after the closing you and me take a trip? Europe, the Taj Mahal!"

"That's Asia."

Paige puts down her bowl, a sludge of colored sugar.

"What, what is it?"

"Nothing."

"You're knocked up."

"Mom. No."

"What then?"

"I love you."

"I love you, too, pigeon."

"In case I haven't said it, you know...thanks." With that her daughter barrels into her, nearly knocking Noreen off her feet.

LECH

The hug—alarming, absolute—replaces all language. Noreen puts down her drink and pats.

BETH

Sunday night and the setup is sketchy: behind the mall, in the far far lot, known for its dealings in parked cars, as if Beth has come for sex or drugs and not to retrieve her son. Doug is delayed so she waits in the back of an Olive Garden feeling like a perp, watching waiters serenade diners from table to table. Somehow it is always everyone's birthday.

"How was it?"

"Awesome." They are of the generation when awesome is earnest, absent of irony. Beth says awesome, too. "Zach was the life of the party."

She cups her hand to the car window. Inside, Zach is asleep, mouth moving like a fish. Does Zach ever grate on Doug's nerves, she wonders, or does he save up the best parts of himself for Doug and stiff her with poop?

"So," she says, "What's new?"

He mentions the podcast they're launching, a host of user-friendly affirmative apps: for breath work and networking. He talks about conquering the new frontier as if success were a spice colony.

"You look good," she says, but he's on to happiness *factor* (snappier than *quotient*, don't you think?) the corporate interface of faith and fitness, *an ideal marriage*, arms curling, he is all arms, playground bars on which she could scuttle up and flip herself over. It always comes back to his body.

"I missed you, buddy!" She squeezes and kisses Zach as if he's both weapon and prize. Who can love him more? Doug stands beside her. Together, they made this child. She rests her head on Doug's chest. His lips graze her hair.

"You really know how to confuse things."

She wants to tell him everything. She wants to call him baby. She wants to take him to the side door of the restaurant, down the arctic hall framed in posters of forked pasta and vine tomatoes, into the bathroom, to bend her over the hand vacs while the hostess occupies Zach with song and crayon. She wants that to be her confession.

And she wants him to say: There's nothing you can do I won't forgive.

"Tell Mommy what a blast we had! Frank and Messina were there, Kelly and Tim. They all asked for you. Everyone wants to know how you're doing."

"What did you say?"

"I don't know, Beth. How are you doing?"

"I don't share your hard-on for New Jersey, if that's what you mean."

"Ryder says Tracy was like you until she found her people. None of the women are just sitting around. Mitch's wife is now a nutritionist. Don't you think it would be fun to set up a little web site? You could tutor. Make personalized placards and mugs. Tracy does real estate staging, accessorizes with pillows. Maybe that's something to consider?"

"I could also drink a bottle of Drano."

"Why can't you be easier?"

"I'm cold, Mommy."

"We should go."

"Hang on." Doug pulls a stuffed football from the car. "Take this. And this." He ambushes her with two envelopes. "You know, I'm a person, too."

Her lip twitches. Has it really come to this?

"Well, I've got an early symposium." Doug folds his arms, as if to say, this is her doing. She can't have it both ways.

"Right." She flings the envelopes onto her seat.

"Hey." His face in her window, the brim of his cap squished. There's the smile, the sparkle, the gap in his teeth. "Remember, it's only life, Beth."

TZVI

Slowly, the talking begins. Every word chokes him up so he keeps starting over. Take your time, they say. He takes it. What matters is he is not alone. There are people, many people like him, scattered all over. For his mother, there was no such thing. No whisper network. No underground resource. She had no one waiting in the wings. If she suffered, she suffered silently, but it doesn't have to be like that for him. It's not up to G-d to provide. They will provide clothes, food, they will locate housing. Connect him with counselors. He can attend school, legit school, if he likes. He has questions and more questions. One at a time, they say. They call themselves a family. They will help him choose a new name but he's keeping Tzvi. Like Herschel it means deer, his only constant. Good, they say, it suits you.

BETH

At pick-up she asks, "Where's your friend?" Snot bubbles from Zach's nostril like a bullfrog's wattle. "Blow."

"They're all my friend."

"I mean, the one from the Fourth of July."

Zach indicates a kid on the porch, dusty knees, skater hair. He shakes his wrist like he's shooting dice, sand sifting through his fingers.

"Why are you all alone, pumpkin? Wouldn't you like to come over and swim in our lake?" She hisses into his ear. "*Murder* Lake."

His eyes bulge and she feels like a monster.

"Ready to roll, Eskimo?"

Quinn leaps into a young woman's arms.

"I'm Claire. The Bowman au pair." White shorts and cloth belt and ballet flats.

"Where are you from?"

"Belgium."

"Lovely." Beth doesn't know the first thing about Belgium. "I'd love to set up a play date for the boys." This is what normal moms do: sip wine and say things are lovely.

"Do you have a card? Ailene likes to keep a record."

"There are business cards for mothers?"

"You're a summer person, aren't you? This is how it works."

Beth watches them walk off swinging hands. Her eyes sting. "Okay, Captain Zach. Give me what you've got."

He saddles her with his backpack, water bottle, sun hat.

"I had a good day, Mommy."

"Really? Tell me about it." She straps him in, holds his face, their noses touch. She swallows the mountain in her throat. "Tell me all the good things."

NOREEN

They meet at The Float, the best restaurant in town, known for its high-concept farm-to-table. Noreen couldn't have gotten better weather if she'd ordered it herself. In the back patio she secures a table overlooking the river, breeze on her arms, the second half of her sweater set hinged neatly over a chair. Purple: the color of royalty, good fortune. A lone monarch butterfly settles on the ledge. Late, this time of the year. Poor thing won't make it to Mexico. While she waits she sips a cranberry and vodka through her stirrer, checks her face in her phone. Lipstick's in place, hair more or less behaving, and here they are, in the flesh: Ed Frank and Steve Messina. Or is it the other way? Steve Frank? Ed Messina?

"Finally!" She claps like it's an accomplishment, a baby taking an assured step. They pull her in, pass her back and forth. Noreen likes them already. They are gregarious, good-humored men, even though she's not sure what the joke is. A round is ordered, and it's funny, how people hew to expectation. They are short and tan in ill-fitting suits. One is heavy, the other is thin; both damp at the collar. Knuckles swell around wedding rings, one sports a crest on the pinky. She lowers her eyes as she smiles, lashes going, chin tucked at a flattering tilt.

An eagle swoops into the valley.

"Would you look at that." She can see now it's a hawk but men get hot for bald eagles. "We don't often get a sighting around here. Must be your lucky day."

"We love lucky."

She was born for this game. Catches the strap slipping off her shoulder, relieved to be wearing her nice bra. She can charm the pants off a tree stump, but she is no floozy.

"Shall we get this party started?" She leans into their splashy aftershave, spiced fruit of an odor tree; hitting her stride, she deals documents and laminate, pushing her selling points while sounding spontaneous, as if the heart of her pitch is all just occurring to her. Frank and Messina say they like what they see.

When they order a third round she switches to a spritzer. When they flag the waiter for sauce on the side, she demurs as well. Make that three, with sensible sauce on the side. Napkins in laps. Elbows off the table. Enthusiasm unleashed. Noreen flushes with success. It's practically post-coital. Cream pie, fruit tart.

She slaps down a credit card. "Allow me."

It's nearly four when they head over to Murmur. She takes them to the Troller side first. A real estate trick: start with the lesser of the two. They make a comment about the curves of her county and she realizes they've had more to drink than she thought.

"As you can see, the potential is unlimited." A thorn of barbed wire, hens nipping at their feet. The neglect is of little consequence. If anything, it reflects seller eagerness. Toss out a number, any number, she says, as you can see these people are not holding onto much. A pair of broken threshers, a volcano of tires. The house is a teardown, but the ground is fertile, soil tested, it's the land that's for keeps.

From there, she takes them to Ira's. Messina wedges into her back seat, Frank runs a hand along the dash. "What's the horsepower?" He knows a thing or two about Mustangs. Thinks he's Steve McQueen. Sweet, in a way, when men volunteer trivia. As if she gives a rat's ass. Her bartending shifts were full of this: how to patch a roof, rig up a lumber belt, repair a carburetor. She'd touch the flats of their wrists. *You don't say, sugar.* Her one oversight—the tenant. Noreen hadn't factored in this variable, and here she is, a loose cannon booming through the fields. With the top down, there's no mishearing it.

"I am not your shit house!"

"Nice to see you, too," Ira says, cresting the hill.

"You can't just waltz over here anymore. I have a child, sicko."

"I know I'm sick, if you'd only calm down."

"DON'T TELL ME TO CALM DOWN!"

"Relax, kid. It's me."

"I can't believe I thought we were friends." She is sloshed, walking like she'd spun herself dizzy on a relay bat. Her swim suit snakes up her bottom. Here comes the flick.

"I ought to sic the police on you."

Noreen throws her car in reverse. "Let's come back later."

"Are you kidding? Who needs Broadway with theater this good."

Noreen opens her mouth but Messina muzzles her.

"I just came to thank you. Apologize for my leaky pipes, if you will. You saved my life, kid, like it or not. If it weren't you, I'd be standing here dead."

She lunges with a toy shovel. "Why won't you leave me alone?"

"Now don't get hysterical."

"HYSTERICAL?!" Jousting, she trips over herself, which would be amusing maybe, this lampoon of a woman at her worst, if Noreen weren't trying to clinch a sale. How in the summer thunder could this be happening?

"Death seeps through my walls, and you think I'm just some dumb girl who can't find her head from her ass. But don't think I don't know what I know!"

What does she know? Noreen hugs the wheel.

"I know," Ira sighs. "It's got to mean something, right? I thought so, too, kid, but all I've managed to come up with is anyway you slice it, life's gonna break you."

With that, bikini girl crumbles in a patch of buttercup, lump of shoulder and bone, and here come the tears: loud and ugly. Ira crouches beside her, working her back like he's trying to remove a tough stain. Noreen doesn't realize she's been holding her breath until Frank tests the horn and their faces turn, like animals roused from their natural habitat.

"Great balls. That's Doug Chase's wife."

BETH

Her rings are missing, a credit card gone, she could've sworn there was something else. Who would steal from her? Ira? He has no material interests. Surely, it's her fault, she's misplaced her wedding band like she's misplaced other items by not paying attention. Irresponsible, all this losing, as if one can ever recoup loss, as if objects might regenerate, or limbs. *Why can't she hold onto anything?* See also: marriage. She is a bad wife unfit mother absent sister lost daughter terrible friend and now her identity is compromised. Who would want to be her? She can't even remember how much cash she had. Had there been a bottle or three on the rack? She'd stopped keeping count.

Exhausted, she goes for a run. Counterintuitive, maybe, but once she starts Beth cannot stop. Doug warned her. It wasn't good—it was unhealthy—to spend a summer alone. One can lose perspective, come undone. He predicted this outcome because he knows her better than she knows herself. Now she's a scandal. Let the rumor mill churn. Salt pills at her temples as her muscles knit a daisy chain, such a fragile balance, everything always coming together or falling apart.

With Zach at camp, she has hours. Nothing to do but kill them. Back in the city, she'd weave a sidewalk apology (for Zach's fishtailing scooter, for the stroller, for her very existence) but here she takes up space, running straight down the center of the country road.

The key is to move past the part where she wants to annihilate herself with a tub of ice cream, so she can get to the state she's now in, an admirable efficiency of legs, lungs, feet. She powers through a stretch of fallen pine, turning where the dirt becomes asphalt. She turns again. Now there's a fork. She makes a choice. Doug had no ill intent. He merely wished she'd picked the

Berkshires, a more populated part of the Catskills, Woodstock, say, Saugerties, where she might know someone—*socialize a bit!* What if the road does not circle back? The creek, formerly lazing along one side, now lazes along the other. She should return, only she can't retrace her steps. All those bends. Why didn't she bring her phone? Never has she run this long.

Suddenly, her stomach seizes as if she's been punched in the ribs. Beth doubles over. Palms on knees, she pants, here comes a spasm, she could birth a baby right there, the force is wrenching, demanding its way out of her. It requires everything she's got just to breathe. To contain herself. But it's a losing battle. She runs off the road, and there's no stopping it, she shoves down her shorts, pops a squat and deposits herself into the woods.

Awful and humiliating and yet, it is pure. She is a cow, a bear; she is just another animal shitting in the woods.

Beth cleans off with a fistful of leaves.

On her way back she passes a trailer beside a murky pond, a puddle of scum, really, the well pump housed in a barrel. Door swings open, decrepit thing, and out steps the exterminator. Her exterminator. Ripped jeans and boots. Behind him is the frame of a woman, a baby on an arm. A baby in the belly. A third child, sucking a tube of flavor ice.

House call? Personal call? What was the difference? He didn't rid her of anything. As his truck peels away it dawns on her she should have sucked up her pride and flagged him down for a lift. Her feet swell and burn. She removes her sneaker, tapping the sole as if she's burping it. Out pops a pebble.

By now, the sun has shifted. Camp must be ending. She's half-jogging now, but it's like that dream she has where she can't cross the river to reach her son. No matter how hard she thrashes, the current only carries her farther away. What then? Doug would remarry in a nanosecond. Like her father, Doug would get himself a replacement wife and Amy would step in to shoulder the caretaking. They had a bereavement plan. Of all the 9/11 memorial services Doug attended, what most upset him were the families destroyed by an absent will. Amy—if nothing else—is a born mother. What's one more child? Amy is the kind of person who does death well, with catered platters. If Beth were to die, her body pinned beneath a party Jeep of camp counselors, Zach would be just fine. People are martyred in death. It's a tempting fantasy. Teens chanting *holy shit* over her contorted body as it bleeds, one girl pressing her cheek, flushed like a peony, plump as a soup dumpling Beth could slurp up whole. Like Zach's baby face when she pulled him from her breast, lips fluttering, suckling air. The nursing of nothing is what mothers called "self-soothing." How healthy he was, then, rosy and full, how the playgroup mommies fawned *You must produce whole milk* as Zach grew like a weed and she puffed with pride at her ability to sustain life. How Kelly Borden said *Motherhood is a little like dying* and how much Beth hated her for saying it. Not me, she thought; and later, how even Kelly Borden could speak the truth. Then she dried up, he faded, she had to supplement with formula, a known cause of allergies, and they could never be apart.

A car approaches from the other direction. Beth feels the vibrations through her legs. The engine slows for a country wave, arms fluid as silk scarves, then continues on.

Thankfully, she is closer than she thought. Back to the dirt, the final mile. Tucked among the overgrowth lies a rundown shack: *Bait, Tackle & Fly.* She pumps her arms up the hill, then collapses on the ground like a snow angel, spent, happy, so deliriously happy to be home at last.

Relief is short. She doesn't need a wristwatch to know she is late. Her phone is clogged with calls from Camp Shalom Yisroel. *Hello this is Este Fein.* The director does not call her Beth or Mrs. Chase but Mom. Hi, Mom. Hope everything's okay. *Baruch Ha-Shem.* Zach is fine. What a mensch. We're sending him home with Quinn Bowman's au pair. Your son has gone with Claire.

More messages. Doug, Amy. When she missed pick-up, camp must have tried all her emergency numbers. Or maybe camp called Doug who called her sister, triggering the chain of command. Ira on the tape. *Let me know what I can do, kid.* She must have listed his name, too. Beth grabs her keys, her purse. Hands shaking, she scribbles the address. She doesn't even know how she gets there, rancid, crazed, incompetent, selfish, so selfish, splattered in her own excrement.

Claire the au pair in terry shorts and yodeling braids. Beth doesn't wait for a welcome but rushes in, falls to her knees. What did you feed him? He has allergies. He could die, she chokes, but there is Zach, on the floor, happily thumbing video games. Like nothing. A little puffiness around the eyes, pink and watery from crying, she'd like to think, from missing her; from a minor airborne allergy, more likely. He barely looks up. Then: *Mommy! Angry Birds.* The game goes cheep, whee, cling, poop, ding.

TZVI

The advantage to being Tzvi: No one's looking for him. After the *mishigas* at the Bowl-A-Rama, the establishment closed for the season. He sold his last pill. Spit his last blood. It won't take long for another failed yeshiva *bocher* to step into his shoes, but that can't be his immediate concern. For the first time in his life, Tzvi feels a real sense of possibility. A fountain of hope burbling inside him. This rush—it is like flying. He has one final act. The Ninth of Av is approaching. This year it coincides with August 4th in the Gregorian calendar. There is so much to get used to. With time, he will. He buys sneakers with athletic tread and neon stripes. He strips the thin blanket from his bed. At eighteen minutes per mile, he can cover eighteen in a day. He allots two days for his pilgrimage to Murmur Lake. Let this be his lamentation: by the waters of Babylon he will lay down and weep. He will not forget thee, *mame*. And then he will go on his way.

PAIGE

Paige leaves late. She throws her life in a bag: handful of t-shirts, foam finger from last summer's county fair. Briefly, she considers her Beanie Babies, pleading eyes, birdseed bellies, but they are not coming. Fine, maybe the pig. She packs sandwiches, lunch meat slick but edible, has a final hot shower, hair tied, sweatpants rolled at the hips. In the kitchen, she rubs the eyes off a pair of potatoes wrinkling on the counter, dices and fries them with onions. Her mom is still out. Celebrating or drowning it.

Paige parcels out her funds. Road cash goes into her wallet, enough for a Motel 6 in the Carolinas; the rest gets zipped into her duffel. From a jelly jar she untangles her few items of jewelry: carnival beads, half of a friendship charm from Court McClain before she moved away in third grade. A tarnished skull ring, a lattice choke. She stretches it overhead, snapping the weave to her throat.

The mermaid park is about an hour from Tampa. With $2,563 she can carry a deposit, first month's rent, and a few weeks' grace. She also has a shit ton of fentanyl patches if need be, though she'd rather not start off on that route.

She steers the Toyota to the edge of town. Sure enough, Ira's car is in the lot of The Lion's Den; Kole's truck, too. She shuts her headlights and crouches low, gravel digging as she crawls between cars with her Swiss Army. It is less of a satisfying slash and more of a worm and weasel, no easy puncture, but once she's fought through his rubber, the unmistakable hiss, she is free.

For miles the only signs say POSTED: PRIVATE PROPERTY, but she knows the road by heart, taking the dark curves like a stunt driver, ears popping on the spiral descent into the valley. No one is around tonight. She slides out a smoke, straying toward the median as she scrolls for a playlist.

By the time she sees the animal it's too late.

Impact rattles her teeth, metal to white-knuckled flesh. Her head jolts, snapping back, her heart slams against her ribs, adrenaline floods her veins. It's a deer, all right. Typical. Her fender dangles like a broken arm, chafing against the wheel's rim. *Motherfucker.* At some point she'll have to turn into a gas station and try to hammer the part in place. Replace the brake pads that failed her. That will cost money. But her mother's shit bucket is still drivable. And the animal, from what she can tell, is still alive.

"Get up, girl," Paige urges. "It's just the wind that's knocked you."

Any other night, any other circumstance, she'd at least try to sideline the doe to safety. But tonight, it's all too much. If she drags the body, her entrails will leak, and Paige won't be able to take it, which means she will not leave. *Get back in the car,* she tells herself. *Drive.* Just then, the universe delivers. Tommy Potts and his pretty blue truck. Tommy Potts who can't put a thing out of its misery slows to a stop from the opposite lane. She hasn't seen him since the Bowl-A-Rama. He's limping, she's not sure why. He doesn't ask her where she's going and she doesn't ask him where he's been.

"Didn't see her coming."

"Sometimes they pop out from nowhere."

He toes the deer's side. The animal lifts her head six inches then lowers it to the road.

"It's okay, Paigebaby." His voice already miles away. "I'll tend to her."

IRA

Back at Murmur, he keeps to himself. All he's got is distance and hope, as if together they might forge a tenuous, neighborly sort of peace. He paces the cabin until he gets splinters, then dusts off the juicer, muscling down his foamy pulp, as if a better diet might cure him of his ills.

Overnight, Ira has aged. He stumbles to the lake, a walk as traveled as his hand to his member. He is a sloppy swimmer. *Jump* was the Lecher philosophy. Heather nearly died her first time, coughed and cursed and refused mouth-to-mouth. After that, she became a water baby. With Hillary he played shark, yanking her feet out from under her. Like a magician does a tablecloth, minus the ta-da. Instead of applause: *Go away.* Words like *I hate you.* Until there were no words. No more hugs for dear old Dad. Once they wrote letters. He saved them. Their estrangement born not from one big thing but from an accrual of things, which hurt worse. He doesn't know where he went wrong. Perhaps he should've kept things like *nice melons* to himself, but overnight they were juicy and ripe, and he was a man without filter. Soon as his daughters could erect boundaries, they did.

It is difficult to get close to people. Even with binoculars he can't see Beth, can only imagine her on the deck, standing over the sink, silhouetted in glass. He peers out his absurd little curtain, remembering the nights she was drunk and unhappy, in cotton so thin there were no secrets, warmth spreading through him like wine. Sometimes, a single look could hold the universe. Beth was radiant in that light.

He misses her drop-ins.

"Hey, you," she'd say. He'd hand over garbage. She spiked iced tea. They drank. Smoked grass. Laughed like teens. What should we talk about? Kid stuff. What if the sky is a planetarium?

What if the joke's on us, and we're just pawns in the great simulation?

And then she'd shut her eyes.

And say: I feel like this is and is not my life. Like I've already lived this life.

So he'd said: I remember you. Untrue. (Twenty-five years ago, they didn't even have renters.) Ira is a goddamn liar. But what's a twist in the truth between friends? It was clear this was what she needed.

Your mother, Elaine. How could I forget. Shapely woman. From the way Beth spoke, he could picture her, an enchanting if furious calamity of dark hair and pale skin, aggressively vulnerable, miserable in marriage, unfulfilled; he could practically taste the salty damp of her legs. Of course. The potter. Sat on the deck dipping her hands in clay, dripping a thin gray film, what's that called—slip, Beth said—yes, slip, molding her little Pygmalions, because isn't that it? Everything is an extension of the self.

Maybe she'd looked at him slant but she bought it. Memories have always been the bedrock of Murmur. Summers of firsts, wet dreams and menstruations. Couples got pregnant, got divorced, fell in and out love.

What was one more story?

Maybe, when it came to Chaya Bloch, what actually happened didn't matter. Maybe, like a good detective novel, the set-up was the hook. How she found herself here was besides the point. Maybe the water simply brought out the despair in people, drawing them like a force field to the deep. There was no way to anticipate the space a stranger takes up inside of you. Or what you take from a stranger. Maybe there were many angles to a story, open to endless interpretation. If he wanted closure, he'd have to write his own.

Murmur hasn't even sold, yet already he feels like he's trespassing. That's how fast a life changes. As a child, Ira was trained to eat like a rabid dog lest his food disappear before him.

Hurry, his mother said, as SS boots stomped upon her soul. Finish up. His father puttered from room to room as if he were forgetting something. Later, Ira would learn his father left in Europe a wife, children, a whole other life, shut one door but never truly opened another. It was not discussed, like reparations, once they arrived, were not discussed, as if one could ever discuss loss in terms of quid pro quo.

How do you grieve a place? Memorialize every blade of grass. Computer animation could digitize his fields, make them look real, realer than life. Only a matter of time until you can't tell the difference. In his mind he writes: *Dear Girls.*

What is there to say? He conflates because he does not know them, his children. Bubble butts bulging from tutus, tee-ball jerseys hung past their knees. They were in diapers and then they were grown. *I may not have been much of a father.* Where is he going with this? What does he expect? You were a wonderful father, Daddy! You took us to the mall. *I did the best I could.* Should he tell them he's dying? *From the moment we are born we are dying.* He wants them to be happy, to know themselves, to know love, even if love won't save them, not that they need saving. What do they need? *We're all just fumbling in the dark.*

The sale would grant them stability, at least. Instead of leaving them unwanted land, he'd release them from it, from obligation, cut geographical ties, do this much right.

In the morning, there is Noreen.

"Aren't you a sight."

He is wearing the pajama set the girls bought him a decade ago.

"Reenie." His jaw aches. "Am I glad to see you. Did you do something to your hair?"

Her hand flies up. He pulls the porch light. She flips her sunglasses and her face gives it away. She's been crying. Oh, kid.

Postcard sentiment is all he's got, a line from a song. *Sail on, silverbird. Sail on by.*

She slams the trunk. Purposefully, he'd chosen a four-seat convertible in case his daughters ever wanted to join him for a ride. They hadn't. What teenager wants to spend a weekend cooped up with their parents? How often did he and Viv gaze wearily into the fireplace? Noreen takes the stairs, fishing pole propped like a rifle, her unwieldy butterfly tattoo poised to take flight. How easy it is to miss what's right in front of you. She looks like she hasn't been home all night, but holy hell, is she beautiful.

"Be still my heart."

"Cut the crap, Ira."

"Listen—"

"No, you listen. Get your rod. The river is high from last week's rain."

NOREEN

In retrospect, Noreen knew all along Paige would leave her. Somewhere, in the deepest, more generous parts of her, she is happy for her daughter, for devising a plan and following it through, even though she wishes she'd been clued in. The mother always the last to know. Paige played her hand close and Noreen took the bluff. Her heart surges with pride, while the rest of her fritters with worry. And loss. And anger. And a sharp twist of envy for being left behind.

At The Lion's Den, Noreen sets out to get bombed with the same resolve she throws into everything. All is not lost. The fiasco at Murmur only increased the interest of Frank & Messina, who smelled blood in the water. But when their offer came through it was insulting. *Know your worth*, her card shark said, all those years ago. And yet, damaged goods were damaged goods.

She fingers the rim of her beer.

"Stroke it like the tease you are." Kole at the end. Hadn't noticed though she isn't surprised. Day drinking: never a good idea, except when you're out of ideas.

"Dream on, Kole."

For years, Kole would show up at the roller rink with a hot pair of jeans; the girls got younger but jilted him quick, so sometimes she took pity on him, snarled in his own heat. How alike they were at the core.

Nancy takes a long look at her credit card. "You know I can't, Reenie."

She can't argue, though it was worth a try. Kole pegs her with a cocktail square. "I'm talking to you."

Today she doesn't have it in her.

"Don't be rude. You and your girl. Someone ought to teach her a lesson."

"Good luck tracking her down."

"Are you aware that bitch slashed my tires?"

"Like hell."

"I'd recognize that rump from anywhere."

"Keep my daughter out of your mouth."

"Too late for that," he blasts over his shoulder as Nick throws him out.

Hours pass. She drinks until time runs together and Nick shoulders her upstairs to the abandoned rooming house to sleep it off. She wakes on the futon to a jury of kegs. How could she have missed it? No wonder Paige left. She pukes in the washroom, but can't eliminate the aftertaste. Everything she's pushed down has come up, acid burning a hole in her throat.

Then she is at the Troller house doing what she should've done long ago. "Get up, Mark. Grab your hat and lures."

The banks of the Neversink are flanked with canoes upturned like turtle shells: auburn, kelly green, the butter of a child's sun. Beneath the state line lies an addict's cave, which is all people talk and won't talk about, but it's still early enough along the bridge you could almost mistake the quiet for calm instead of despondency.

Noreen curls her toes through the shore. Ira doesn't know the first thing about trout fishing—*Reenie, I'm thumbs*—but Mark hooks him up with a tuft of rabbit fur, twisting the string around it, capping off his tie with a tiny, brass bead. Rolls up his pants and wades in, but the moss-slick bottom is tangled with tree root and Ira loses his footing, his nerve. Mark keeps his shoulders low and relaxed, swishes his lasso with grace. Noreen stacks stones by the river's edge, looks out on the island in the middle.

"Paige used to hop that cluster of boulders like they were on fire, called them something fancy."

"Archipelago."

"Even then she knew everything."

She cuffs a flat top and he says show me so they gather stones and skip.

"It's in the wrist," she says, placing her hand over his, stilling his tremor.

"What are the odds, Reenie, my tenant and your client."

"We should play the Powerball."

"World's smaller than we think."

"It kills me to think of Paige out there."

"Your daughter's not lost." He traces the inside of her forearm: 081891. Paige's birthday is soon. If only Noreen could reach her, if only Paige would pick up, she'd say: They win if you let the pain define you.

Ira says, "She'll come around."

A silver smallmouth writhes in its hook. Mark frees the bloody mouth, releases its iridescent body. Noreen smokes her cigarettes like they are her last. Mark pulls Ira to his feet. This is how to cast and whip. Ira is an old boy learning a new trick.

"Why are you throwing it back?"

"Doesn't belong to us." It's the first thing Mark says all day; the first words Noreen has heard from him in years.

They stay until the light changes. She wonders if the sunset looks the same or different in Florida, if Paige is watching the crushed blaze from her horizon. Overhead, an eagle dips.

"Ours is the only country with a bird of prey as its symbol of freedom."

"A birder after my own heart," Ira says.

They watch it, wings at full span, soaring down and up and in again.

"What's it searching for?" Noreen says after a while.

But the animal is not alone. There are two in the sky, tracing an infinity loop, a sideways crazy eight.

"Food," Ira says. "Sustenance, place to nest."

BETH

Amy is at the door, the Garden State's own Mary Poppins.

"I came as soon as I could." She is breathless in a fret of bags and Beth tenses immediately. How did she arrive so fast? Beth feels herself—sweaty, fecal—in the eyes of her sister. Amy lives for this. Forget lists, Amy is the type of person with a color-coded system for everything. There's no end to her busy. Her tween daughter, Sienna, stands at her hip.

"Give a hug to Aunt Beth."

"Zach's asleep. I was just cleaning." Beth aims her broom at a cobweb.

"Leave it. Spiders restore balance in the ecosystem." When did Amy become an authority on insects? Her sister beelines for the bathroom, threads the stopper, then plants herself on the toilet seat, as if Beth needs supervision to take a goddamn bath. While she soaks, Amy lights a cloying shrine of candles. They smell like Doug's shirts after an evening with clients. Amy's husband attends ball games and strip clubs with stunning frequency, too, staying overnight at their Manhattan studio rather than driving back to New Jersey. This is the sacrifice. In exchange, Amy gets her platinum line of credit and barre classes. If it bothers her, she doesn't show it. If she feels like an accessory, she's never said. If she's lonely, Beth's never asked.

The mirror fogs. When Amy takes a comb to Beth's wet hair, Beth gives into it.

"Don't stop." It feels good to be babied. Knees up, head back. Harder. It's like scratching a bottomless itch. She wants to bleed. Amy was already out of the house by the time Beth started tenth grade, leaving her to idle in cars, calling every other Sunday to "check-in." Check on what? A sisterhood deferred, before either had any real idea of themselves.

Are you okay?

Are you?

What?

Are *you* okay?

Yeah. I guess so.

Yeah. Me, too.

That last summer, before their family fell apart, they got along. Amy was not too cool for the car games they played as her parents stared stonily out the windshield. *Can the Catskills save a marriage? Stay tuned! Live at Five!* Beth flopped onto Amy's lap. Upside down they could entertain each other for hours, Beth's chin a manatee, a Ziggy cartoon scrawled on the flat of their fists, giggling, until their father said, "What's so damn funny?"

In the morning, Sienna takes Zach to hunt for newts. They concoct play-dough from cricket flour, dripping food coloring from bottles shaped like lawn gnomes. All the colors meld to brown. They seize upon a moldering mass of flesh, possibly a rabbit, long dead. Carrion splayed like prize safari; a twist of fur, muscle and bone.

"On guard," Sienna says, as they spear the remains and duel.

"Leave it," Beth says. "It may be diseased."

"If only Ivy were here," Amy says suddenly.

"Ivy?" Their half-sister is not even a passing thought. Beth can't remember if she's in college or out of college, if she graduated or dropped out. "That's random."

"She's doing peace work! In the Middle East! I've been messaging her on Facebook."

It feels traitorous. No one is close with Ivy. Who is Ivy to have such ambition?

"Let's call her."

They huddle before Amy's screen, heads pressed like conjoined twins, and there's baby Ivy on video, no longer a baby, armpits fluid as sea anemone, hair like boucle. She is in Dahab at the moment with her interfaith group learning Arabic, and she is glowing, flushed with youth, she just hiked Mount Sinai, and it was cosmic, beyond the beyond, you can't imagine a sunrise like this, save for the sherpas and busloads of tourists.

The connection punks out. When it resumes she's pixelated with audio delay. Beth reads lips. *I'll never leave.*

"Give me a reason." Ivy pans out to the Mediterranean blue, a round of huts strung in lights where they eat pancakes. Every culture has some version of pancakes and she's been living on crepes, lemon, sugar, hazelnut cream.

"War. Violence. Senseless hatred," Beth lists.

"Are you wearing sunscreen?" Amy breaks in.

"Oh my sisters." The camera bobbles over sand, foot, a hookah embossed with tiny flowers around which Ivy sits like a snake charmer. It makes Beth remember being nineteen. "I always knew you were jerks." Ivy sets her chin on her desert knees. Winks. Blows smoke to the sky.

IRA

Noreen drives. Ira is tired. Already he's regretting his decision to join Noreen in the city, but he's trying to be cooperative. The road roars. He clutches his cap. Noreen tries to smoke but the top's down. It's futile. They pass billboards for Cracker Barrel and GOD. When he wakes, they are idling in an oily swell of traffic outside the bridge.

First stop, Madison Avenue.

"Just like *Splash*." Noreen visors the glare, taking in thirty-six stories of steel and glass. Somewhere inside that armor are the offices of Frank & Messina.

"Sure you don't want me to come up? I make a good bad cop."

"I'm a big girl, Ira."

Viv opens the apartment door in her workout clothes. "Thought I smelled something."

"Knock, knock."

"Don't start."

"Who's there?" He prompts. "Butch."

"Butch. Who."

"Butch your hands around me and give me a kiss!"

"What you deserve is egg in the face."

"Come on, Viv, it's been a while. Indulge a sick man on his pilgrimage."

At a deli on the East Side, Viv orders him tuna on rye.

"You spoil me."

"A sandwich is hardly five star."

"What more can a person want?" He offers her a bite. Clumps plop out the bottom.

"You're still kicking."

"That's fresh. You should take that on the road."

"Why are you here, Lech?"

"You look great. Better than on our wedding day. The scuba suit, it's becoming."

"You look like dreck."

"I've lost my edge."

"That's not all you've lost."

"Have you heard from the girls?"

"I'm their mother. I hear from them all the time."

"I miss them."

"What do you miss?"

"How they used to climb trees." He holds out his wrists. She hands him a wedge of lemon and a wet nap.

"They never climbed trees."

"I remember scraped shins."

"Those were your shins."

"Viv, my mind's slipping. I'm an alta cocker in the woods."

"A little fear is good for you. Like sprouts."

"I'm thinking of getting out, selling Murmur. What do you think?"

"Don't come back here."

"You're not going to talk me out of it?"

"I'm done talking."

"We really did it once, didn't we? We had our laughs."

"Hindsight's a brilliant liar. You think we'd continue to populate the earth if women remembered *childbirth*, much less marriage? Amnesia is an adaptive skill." She polishes off his pickle.

He stretches his hands across the table.

"What's your secret, Viv?"

"Botox."

"Firecracker, I should marry you."

"Do you even listen to yourself?"

"History has been known to repeat."

"Over my dead body. Know what you need? A warning label: Don't shake before opening. Smoke at your own risk."

"I'm just saying."

"Don't just say."

"Do me a favor, dedicate a park bench in my name when I croak? Or better yet, turn me to mulch. I'd make a good fertilizer, a friendly house plant."

"Maybe you should try meditating." With that, she slips out of the booth. All her parts squeezed into those dance pants. You could bounce a coin off her backside. He grabs the strap of her purse. "There's so much still to remember."

"Make it up. It'll come out better in your head, anyway. And take care of yourself, would you? No one wants to *shtup* a *schlemiel.*"

He reunites with Noreen outside the Empire State. Men in sandwich boards peddle electronics, discount suits. Noreen fans herself with their flyers, eyes wide as a first-time carny, and it's that look of delight on her face that makes it all worth it. When was the last time Ira experienced anything close to awe? Not since the skyline changed.

The elevator is a cattle car of humanity.

"How'd it go, rainmaker? Make the mincemeat of Frank and Messina?"

"They weren't prepared for me, that's for sure."

"That makes two of us."

As they go up, Ira feels his stomach drop. Vertigo knocks him for a loop on the 102nd floor, and he's spinning, or maybe it's the building that's spinning around him. He palms the wall. Crowds push from the elevator bank to observe the new Freedom Tower.

"Go, take your selfie, Reenie, I'll wait here."

"Don't bail on me, now." She whips out a folder. "I got a contract!"

"Mazel tov, kid."

"Want to hear how I drove them up and up?"

He cups his jaw. He forgot to shave. "So that's it, then. The beginning of the end."

He calls his daughters from a payphone on the landing. Gum blackened over the asterisk key. Better chance of them answering if the number's not listed. Heather is on assignment in New Zealand. Her mobile goes straight to recording, inbox full. He can't even leave a message. Hillary picks up after seven rings.

"Can't talk now, Dad," which is how it goes. Never a good time. Voices compete in the background. She lives on one of these ritzy religious communes, with its prayer yurts and agave brush and feminist chapel called Miriam's Well.

"Can't I speak to my grandchildren?"

"Yoni, say hello to your Zeyde." Ira hears the phone scraping along the floor, his daughter's hiss. "Speak. SAY SOMETHING."

Nothing.

"Yonatan! All day he wants my phone for shoot-em-up games. Can we speak after Shabbos? I'm up to my elbows in dough."

"I'm selling Murmur."

An ambulance howls along 5th Avenue.

"Where are you?"

"Everywhere, nowhere."

"You have a place to go?"

"Remember? You found her first."

"How could I forget?"

"What did she look like up close?"

"*Dafka*, now you ask?"

"Just wanted to hear your voice, sunshine."

"There, Daddy. You've heard it."

On their way home, they stop at his parents' graves. The cemetery is located in a Vegas-like strip of morbidity off the Palisades, with streets named King David and Jabotinsky, as if designed to evoke the feeling of strolling around the Old City with a fresh falafel pocket. There is a funeral underway on the Avenue of Martyrs, an Astroturf mat warming the dusty mound. Ira reads off headstones, in blessed memory, loving mother father sister child. Survivor. Friend. They turn right at Levisohn, left at Glickstein. Noreen waits in the car.

Most of the mourners are Ira's age, with the younger generation awkwardly dressed in cardboard yarmulkes handed out at the entrance. Children weave through the rows in what looks like hide and seek, or maybe tag, extracting weeds around plots of those whose families have not paid for upkeep. Ira's parents are twenty steps away. A man—the son?—is reciting Kaddish in call and response, a split of fabric pinned to his lapel. Groundskeepers sport the nubuck of weightlifters. In coordinated silence, they slide the coffin from the flatbed. What a comfort, to witness a body's return. His parents were never as close in marriage as they are now. *Hello, mother. Hello, father.* He places a small stone atop each of them.

This is the tradition. One relative loosens the spade and shovels, then passes to the next who shovels and passes until all loved ones have dug, interning the dead with churned earth. Afterward there will be coffee, cake.

PAIGE

She's made it. Weeki Wachee Springs.

Lew Richardson has no spots for swimmers, but Paige impresses him with her passion, her Weeki trivia, and rendition of the original mermaid song (*We're not like other women, we don't have to clean an oven, we'll never grow old*), so he hands her a mop and tells her to soak up as much as she can.

His face is pitted like a coral reef. Paige will have to stay sharp. Lew sounds a lot like Tommy. Already he's grumbling about sharks. Takes her a beat to realize he means the Internet kind that pirate footage, and not the oceanic predator. Nobody's going to pay for a show they can stream for free. Don't expect a picnic. Girls, they come and go. With their wedlock sons, their environmental asthma. No one stays in the water for long. Let me guess, he says. Considering nursing school?

Meanwhile, she can play *Candy Crush* in her down time, read up on her scriptures. Lew says, I hope you know the Bible. Popular book around here. Jeremiah, Isaiah, in particular. Once a week the girls go for karaoke, helps if you sing.

The stadium glass is sixteen feet deep. Paige uses a ladder to clean it, waving to the bluegill through the glass. In this way, it's just like The Breakstone. She sweeps food wrappers from the benches, restocks the napkin dispensary, tidies the pyramid of gift-shop beer cozies and pinup calendars and crabs shellacked with google eyes. She swabs the deck of the rusty airboat, which courts guests down river, at an extra fee, for a glimpse of live gator or manatee.

Before the girls arrive, Paige slips into their dressing room. If there is shit in the toilet she cleans the shit. She clears toothpaste and ash from the sink. Brushes the scales on the fins to make sure all sequins are facing the right direction. She combs out the wigs. By the time the first group shows, Paige has their latex caps and fishtails ready. LeAyne, Savannah, Clarice, and Mishel toss her laundry, pajama shorts, their sons' soiled onesies. A flask goes around. Hashtag living the dream, they snort, glue waterproof eyelashes, collect twelve bucks an hour.

Paige catches the 2 PM show during her break. The narrative is the same, five times a day: mermaids frolic in a blue lagoon ruled by a harem prince. They laugh, sing, eat, drink. When they smile, bubbles rush like diamonds to the surface.

Paige stands by the tank holding towels.

"How do you do it?"

"Breathe." Her name is Mermaid Alicia. "Think horses and ice cream. The more relaxed you can be, the more natural you'll look. The audience comes for your story, not your life. Make sure to open your eyes."

All day long Paige watches her swim and swim. At closing, the sun is full blush.

BETH

They scavenge the county for yard sales, flipping over saucers for secrets. Amy handles Hummel figurines like a contagion. "One person's trash is another's trash." When she laughs, her forehead doesn't move. The owners look on from their lawn chairs. Zach wants a tricycle, a telescope, a studio recording of *Pete's Dragon*.

"Uncle Ira has a turntable."

"Who's Uncle Ira?" Sienna deliberates a hand mirror inlaid with shells. She makes a duck face, gives herself tongue.

No one leaves empty-handed. Beth goes *American Gothic* over a pitchfork, while Amy gathers farmstand cucumbers the size of clubs. They are women, with children. Theirs is a world without men, and it is easy to envision how this model might bear some lasting fruit.

Amy lights up the citronella.

"Remember when Mom made all those lopsided honeycomb ashtrays?"

"And then took up smoking, to give them a purpose."

"And then they cracked."

"They were awful to each other."

Amy stacks bowls. "No more than anyone."

Sienna, all braces and French braids, is more exotic than anything Shalom Yisroel could offer, so Zach skips camp to parade around in her shelf bras sized like bandage strips.

"We're twins!" he says. She frowns.

Beth says, "Why don't you tell her she doesn't need one?"

Amy says, "She wants to fit in. Half her class has their periods already."

"All that DDT."

"Don't be such a killjoy."

"Don't you think about it?"

"How the whole world's sped up?"

"How we're ruining it."

At least, the compost is worth celebrating. Beth's turned something into nothing. *Feel!* The soil is soft and rich.

"Damn," Sienna holds her nose. "You could hide a body in there."

Amy is less impressed. "I'm dying for a swim."

Not the *lake*, Beth protests. The pH is off from acid rain, she lies, how easily the lies slip out of her, so they visit a state park instead where a section of the waterfront has been partitioned off with pantyhose cups. Zach mimics his cousin, twisting hips, doing the *Sports Illustrated* hair flip.

"You're dead meat!" Sienna chases him to shore, rallying the surrounding children. Religious kids, local kids, they all bring buckets of sand. *More!* Sienna barks. She's a militant foreman. They bury his feet, his ankles and knees. Kids throw sand on his chest, some in the eyes, his throat, Zach sputters, but he loves it, he is a good mummy, neck and chin, an obedient mummy, he smiles wide, brave, eager to please, so brave, his enthusiasm bright enough to light up the entire eastern state.

Wind kicks up Beth's heart. *What if.* Any of those hands could've touched a Snickers, PB&J. There is such a thin line between being vicious and being kids.

She swats them away. "Break it up!"

"What are you doing?"

She doesn't answer but drops and digs until her child is free.

He pops up. "How do I taste?"

Beth wants to collapse. "Salty," she licks.

"Put me back in the oven. I'm not done."

Like that, the week is over.

Fast as they come, they go. The outlet mall is an hour and a half away, and Amy wants to beat out the weekend crowds for denim, puffer down, back-to-school.

As they pack up the car, Beth feels a hitch in her gut, her insides a knot. If she doesn't say something, she just might burst. If not her sister, then who? *I returned a child like a coat to the store.* Zach, if she's honest, she hadn't wanted, either, but it's strange, how the unwanted has invaded and spread inside her like pachysandra, crowding out room for anyone else. She was not in the market for a refund.

"I had an abortion," Beth blurts.

"Oh, bunny." Here comes the hug. "I've had three."

IRA

The animal is on her last breath. Someone had dragged her off the dividing line but left her on the shoulder.

"Why are you stopping? I have to pee like a racehorse."

"Hold your horses, Reenie."

Ira switches on his blinkers. The deer jerks beneath the floodlights, an involuntary movement. Been a couple days, gnats collecting in the crust of her lid. Her big eye stares at him glossy, afraid. He shushes her as if she's having a bad dream. His girls always came to his side of the bed, looming over him in ghostly nightgowns, until he carried them back down the hallway. Sometimes they curled up next to him. Not Viv.

The eye blinks.

Wasn't me, he wants to say, caressing her brown coat, unconcerned about Lyme or whatever else she might carry, although he feels some default responsibility as a member of the human race. The sorry animals were rampant as subway rats. She's pregnant, he sees now, as he strokes the pale swell of her belly. Dark teats protrude like fingers. It was late in the season for fawn.

"Wish there were another way, kid."

Ira cups her mouth, but she does not struggle. He tops the hold with his other hand. Two hands. One minute of pressure and she's gone.

Beshert is the word that comes to him. Meant to be. *Beshert* as the time he picked up Viv on Route 17 in his VW bug on her way back from Woodstock that summer. He'd been waiting tables all weekend and she was a mess. Almost drove past her, but her poppy blouse caught his eye, her chest opening inside him like morning petals and he told himself, *Take the risk. Let some sunshine in.* So he did and she had, end of story.

Vivian, the voluptuous Jewess from Long Island, whose family had been here since the pogroms, considered herself a Semite in bagels only (*what do ya call a seagull who lives by the bay*), took pity on Ira and his coarse speech. At 23 to his 21, she was worldly and wise, well-versed on sponges and diaphragms and spermicidal creams.

"What's with the Nazi car?"

Ira blushed. How quickly Viv saw right through him. Of course, that was the point: to piss off the old man. But his father was on the road and never noticed.

Earlier at the cemetery, he'd pulled a yarmulke from the glove, navy suede, the bar mitzvah of Viv's cousin's kid embossed in gold dust. His father told him you never know when you'll have to pitch hit for a *minyan*; to stand up and be counted.

The yarmulke is still in his pocket, creased in a wedge. He plops it over his bald spot, grabs the animal by the foot. Split hooves means she's kosher, not that he is, not that he's eating her, but it's odd, the tidbits of his upbringing that have stuck. With two hands he hauls her slowly toward the ravine, Noreen crunching after him. The air already cool. Before long, it would be autumn. The mourner's prayer is quick and insufficient. His chest aches. Together they shroud the body in fallen leaves.

NOREEN

Back in her apartment, she raises a victory beer to herself but the taste is bitter. The whole point of the sale was for her and Paige to celebrate together.

"We'll go to St. Barthes!" she'd told her.

"The 'h' is silent."

"Get those swimsuits that look like you took a bite out of them."

"Life doesn't work like that." Paige reached, always reaching, for the remote.

"I know how life works. We'll invest. Buy stocks. Google!"

But Paige would rather be God knows where. Noreen spills her beer down the drain. Her one job: to protect her daughter. She failed. She, who endured years of her brother only to betray her daughter by missing the signs, the myriad ways Paige tried to tell her: bed-wetting and tantrums, burning with urinary tract infections, with pinworms, sleepless in her skin, Paige scratching her eczema until she bled, bleeding herself with a safety pin along the ribs, torching Beanie Baby after Beanie Baby.

Noreen said, "Wash your hands."

Noreen said, "Everything you do reflects onto me."

Noreen said, "Kole's your godfather. He just wants to know you. Since when is that a crime?"

Kathy Troller answers the door as if no time has passed. She either isn't wearing a bra or needs a better one, her breast pooched at her middle, her perm over-treated. Noreen likes Kathy well enough. When she got together with Kole, Noreen was relieved, though she pitied Kathy her health, her hysterectomy, the tough luck of those who wanted but couldn't have a family.

"You're back," Noreen says. "Maybe now he'll keep his hands to himself."

"What did he do now?"

"Now, ladies. There's plenty of King Kole to go around."

Her blood curdles. She could wring his fat, pink neck. What would that solve? She'd only be screwing herself.

"Reenie! Tell me you've brought Christmas to July."

"Jackass, it's August."

"Kathy's just testy on account of her sister losing her foot."

"Diabetes. And now, can you believe, they're taking an eye. They'll take any part of you. Go in with one thing, come out with another."

"Ignore her."

"Soon I'll be gone completely."

"Knock it off. Me and Reenie have business. Go get us some ice."

"Get your own ice."

"That's not necessary." Noreen is trying to be civil.

The phone rings.

When Kole leaves to take it, Kathy says, "I'm going, for good, just so you know. I don't know how you put up with him for as long as you did."

The answer: Mark, in the window, where he always is.

"Listen," Noreen says. "I need to tell you, Mark. There's something you should know."

"I didn't know her by name," Mark says. He just volunteers it, low and even. Noreen isn't sure she's hearing right, so she steps closer, breathes up his cool basin smell.

Came in looking for directions. She was lost, she said. He helped her to get where she was going. That was it. She came into the shop. Lost, she said, and who isn't. Turned around, lacking an internal compass. He said, Follow me. Out the stripped door. Easier to show her himself. He was headed her way, besides. She trailed him, turning left when he went straight, her gated entrance strangled in barbwire. After that, he'd drive over after work and fish the river then pull into the gas station and wait.

During the week, she was alone with her children. He'd sit at the air pump until he glimpsed the silk top of her head covering. Red and blue swirls, what's that called? Paisleys.

They stood in line for an ice cream at the same time—but separately.

"That it?"

"Once she showed her real hair."

Kole enters, ice cubes chattering. In New York, Frank & Messina had made it clear they had zero intention of building on Murmur. They'd acquire the property because they could, because men like them collected land like Monopoly cards, which eventually, they'd cut up and sell off for scraps. Frank & Messina claimed every city resident wanted a piece of the country. "Where else are you gonna go when the streets flood, and the sky starts falling?" They were betting on planetary emergency. Until then, the place would lie fallow. Suddenly, it all feels wrong. Wrong to go through with this. To line Kole's pockets. To uproot Mark. *How can she possibly take away his one true thing?* The man belongs to Murmur.

"Hate to break it to you, Kole, but it wasn't in the cards."

Kole swallows, knocks back another, as if he doesn't hear her. "That was the bank," he says. "Thought for sure Mother would've adjusted the deed, being as I'm the only one who's done jack shit around here, but the property's still in my brother's name, you crafty mute bastard."

Kole lunges for Mark. Noreen tries to break it up and it's a clumsy scuffle. The tray topples, glassware flies and shatters.

Mark straddles his brother on the hardwood and wallops his jaw, over and over, until Kole cries uncle.

Mark shoots her a piercing look. "I don't need you defending me."

Noreen plucks a bloody shard from her hand.

Kathy stomps in. "You boys are still at it?"

"I can't win, Kathy. I'm beat."

"We're all beat. Stop rolling around and come cool off outside before the front moves in. TV says storms."

BETH

For days, it rains and rains and rains.

"There's nothing to do," Zach says.

"I'm not your circus monkey."

"Where's Ira?"

Beth puts down her shears. They are making superhero masks. Zach squeezes glue on his fingertips, peels the layers like dead skin.

"At some point you have to make your own fun."

He dumps out a jar of glitter all over the place. Back to camp he goes. Este Fein dismisses Beth's apology. "You think after nine children, I haven't left a few in a department store?"

Beth stands like a wet rag before her. Cover yourself, Zach preaches when she can't be bothered with more than a bikini, the human body is not for sale. Beth has so many questions. About ritual bathing. Unwavering faith. Community. The sects Ira called oil and water. Would a Satmar even know a Lubavitch? *Did you know her?* She studies the contours of Este's face: warm, open, well-fed. Their ages couldn't be far off.

"Join us for Shabbos, sometime."

Zach comes home with new rules: kiss the doorpost, bless the bread, drink wine on Fridays—that she's got covered. Never soak an animal in their mother's milk. Beth reminds him he's dairy free. Her son has questions, too. When will the *moshiach* come?

At Hand's Hardware, Beth scans the gardening section. Annuals or perennials? Flowers or vegetables? Plants or seeds? Zach shakes packets to the beat of Che Che Kule.

"Who can choose?" Beth says, more to herself than anyone, but an employee overhears her.

"What are your conditions?"

"How do you mean?"

"Sunlight, shade."

"I have all this soil."

"It's too late to plant now, but you can plan ahead for next season."

"I've never gardened before."

He hands her a book. "Think of it as a state of mind. What matters is your effort."

Could she ever do something simply for the sake of doing, without expecting to reap anything from it? Doug had handed her two folders: One with a housing contract, the other a letter of separation. This is the equivalency he draws. Sign here or here. He was moving forward regardless, securing his own oxygen mask. In the parking lot he'd said, *It's up to you.* Did she have an opinion on laminate flooring?

Last night Doug called.

What are we doing? she nearly said, but then he laid into her about the credit card bill.

"How could you not have noticed these unauthorized charges?"

"I was distracted."

"People take all kinds of advantage."

"I know," Beth said.

"At some point, you have to look out for yourself."

Tonight she calls Ivy. This is the future, hanging out on screens, in different time zones. Voyeuristic, yet interactive, sometimes frozen. What surprises her is how much she enjoys watching Ivy. Amy is right. She's like a new reality show, without the usual guilt that accompanies such pleasure.

Ivy's eyes narrow on the other side of the world. "Tell me, since you've got it all figured out." Beth can't tell if she's mocking or serious. "What's do you make of this mad sad bad world?"

"I'm pregnant." The minute Beth says it she knows it's true.

NOREEN

"Don't suppose you know about this?" Noreen snaps a postcard against her palm. *Weeki Wachee Springs, Where Mermaids are Real.* Cheesecake, wet lipstick, tropical print.

"What's it say?"

"The water's so deep no one's ever hit bottom."

"She's got a good head, that kid. Apple don't fall far."

Noreen slides her palms under Ira's shirt. He feels thin. "How'd you like to visit this fall? Never been on an airplane. My treat. Cheap seats in hurricane season."

After dissolving the deal, Noreen assumed she'd be crushed, but she feels unexpectedly good about her decision. There have been a couple of new bites out by Liberty, handful of murmurs, an online distribution outpost, college grads eyeing acreage for draft-horse farming and cannabis. Something will come along. Ira helps fill the void. He no longer kicks her out in the morning. If his cabin is cold, the bed is warm. They make a picnic and inspect each other for deer ticks. The mosquitoes stage an orgy on her. "Color me envious," Ira says, touching her love bites. "Everyone wants your blood."

IRA

For ten days and ten August nights, traffic is a trail of gold and red, a necklace of brake lights along the river. The Sullivan County Fair has been around for as long as Ira can remember and a hundred years before that, part carnival, part amusement park, part 4H club, complete with an enthusiastic auctioning off of the county's prime steer. His daughters used to live for rides of questionable safety, for fried food and spun sugar and fluorescent sand funneled into molds of flowers and fish, for live cover bands, for a dozen smaller stages hosting square dance, ventriloquism, exotic reptiles and saw-in-half magic.

Every summer, Ira does his afternoon comedy act.

This is no longer the Borscht Belt. For all the legends who've come through with their Take My Wife jokes, the region has retained little sense of humor. That's how Ira got picked. (This is his opening riff.) Who knew it was a thing, Jews being funny? Comedians didn't have to be tall or rich or handsome, merely fast with the tongue. Misery, not joy, lay at the crux of humor, and misery Ira had in droves.

Noreen picks him up. They're past discussion.

"How do I look?"

"The skinnier you get, the bigger your nose."

He sucks his teeth, tightens his belt. Calories slip off him, he can't keep food down, he's saddled with cramps at inopportune timing. One more symptom to check out. He's sick of doctors. He wears his Gordon Lightfoot shirt with the felt lettering.

"Don't know why I'm so nervous."

Noreen smooths his ponytail. "Well, your hair looks great."

"Shack up with me."

"Stick out your tongue."

"We're practically living together."

"Won't that cramp your style?"

"What style? Keep Murmur on the market, but in the meantime, maybe we'll even return to the big house."

"What've you done with my Ira?"

"I could use the company."

"Can we get a hammock?" Noreen says. "I always wanted to lie in one of those nets."

"They are never as comfy as they look."

The acoustics are terrible in the weapons tent, the buzz unnerving. It is a vendors' showplace but nothing is ever just for show. Every year he sees the end result, a mishandling, a failed safety, the accident reports reduced to a line or two in *The Monitor*, the county all but unfazed, as if violence were the price of freedom, and it was foolish to imagine things otherwise. Noreen calls the firearms beauts and Ira says are you crazy, woman, and she says crazy enough to fall for you.

"You're a real pistol."

"How else are you warding off predators?"

Ira throws up his hands.

"It's important to know how to protect yourself." With that, she takes off in front of him. Ira feels acutely aware of his circumcision. This is no place for him. Paige's boyfriend is running his hands up and down the display knives, custom Benchmades. Reenie never liked him, but she taps his shoulder, and he turns, dull-eyed. Ira remembers the tattoos. The kid calls her Miss Murphy.

"I'm not your kindergarten teacher, Tommy."

"Have you heard from Paige?"

"Not yet." Ira knows it's a lie. This morning Reenie received another postcard. *Don't Worry, Beach Happy.*

"I really got to talk to her, Miss. She's not picking up, you know, I'm just calling and calling. I don't know if her phone's disconnected or what, but I have to, it's important, I miss her something awful —"

His lips are ringed in orange soda.

She touches his arm. "I'll give you a shout when I do."

"Tell her it's important."

"Stop by sometime, Tommy. You need a haircut."

The kid pats his head as if it is separate from the rest of him. In bed at night Noreen has told Ira maybe she'll leave real estate entirely, open a hair salon, who knows, keep dreaming, there's no limit to what she can do.

"So you'll tell her, then. You'll tell her."

She nods.

His phone buzzes. "That's my cousin. Catcha later, Miss."

BETH

The parking lot is a mud pit. Last night, Beth stayed up listening to the rain pelt the roof like tossed coins. A cruel irony, to be back where she started, but the pregnancy stick is indifferent toward her freakish fertility. The pregnancy stick does not give a shit if the exterminator even finished. She'd peed until the lines swelled blue. So there. The mere sight made her morning-sick. At dawn, she went down to the lake. Shed her clothes and waded in slowly until she stood ankle, knee, waist deep, at which point, she dunked. This was the ritual: Once, twice, three times. With each immersion her ears glugged, canceling out the whole world. She concocted her own prayer. After, her arms opened out on the suface like a sail.

Zach was waiting for her back on land.

"I didn't want to wake you," she said, wrapping her naked body in a towel. In Zach's arms lay a rabbit, a scrawny-eared thing, its soft, trembling body nestled against his chest as if he were the mother.

"Can we keep him? Can we take him home?"

Beth did not say what home, where, who will care for it, it could be rabid, don't get your hopes up, animals like that don't stand a chance. Her pulse raced like an organ removed.

"Maybe," she said. "We'll see."

She's never seen so many guns. They look fake, like video games at a boardwalk arcade, their power abstract, impossible to size. They are so damn shiny. She clutches Zach's paw as they rove the aisles. Periodically they pass a display booth for lavender satchels, for wood carvings, handcrafted jewelry. Beth wonders who those sellers wronged to get exiled out here. Karma's a bitch, doesn't she know. Zach, of course, wants to touch every rifle, every automatic and semiautomatic, every knife and switch, he wants to twirl the nunchunks like a baton. His hand is a trigger. He pops off left, right.

"Howdy, partner," vendors call out to him. One man woos Zach with candy.

"Allergic," Beth says, steering. The man strokes his beard. Beneath his motorcycle vest is a T-shirt that says DON'T TREAD ON ME.

"Ma'am, we all have something that don't agree with us."

Outside the tent lies the real action, booths for root beer and temporary tattoos, the fairgrounds a muddy maze. There are all kinds of people: Camp people, religious people, farm people, people in wheelchairs, people pushing strollers, people in packs, leashed together, people speaking Yiddish, speaking Spanish.

There's Ailene, out the corner of her eye. Ailene sees her, too, but they avoid each other until they're standing in line for the merry-go-round.

"You weren't kidding when you said I hadn't lived."

"Come again?"

Beth drops it. "I wanted to thank your au pair. Is she here?"

Ailene waves her hand. "Eating herself into American oblivion."

"She was such a help."

"It takes a village."

Ailene looks tired with that baby strapped to her like TNT. Of course, you never really know what's going on in anyone's life. Beth wants to offer her something, but Ailene's already mounted her carousel horse. Going in circles makes Beth nauseous. She tries to spike like dancers do, only she was never a dancer. How can anyone focus on a single spot? From there it's the motorcycles, the tugboats puttering in a dirty pool, teacups that spin her green. She needs a break from all the spinning, so she sends Zach on the swings alone, legs pumping, face to the sun like it might anoint him. This is parenthood, the best-case scenario: hold, push, catch, love, let go.

They eat lunch from brown paper bags. Rice bowls, bottled water, packaged cookies. Beth scrunches the aluminum foil into planets. Zach flicks away Pluto. It's no longer part of the system.

Then along comes Ira.

"Hey," she stammers. Blood rushes to her face. "I wanted to—my outburst earlier—Ira, it was off-base to get all Edgar Allen Poe."

"You're human."

"Why didn't you just tell me the story?"

"Here's the story: A woman drowned. Are you better knowing?"

"I don't know."

"Not every sadness is yours or mine."

"I stole your notebook."

"Finders keepers."

"God, I mean, I really lost it."

"You look found to me, kid."

IRA

The curtain rises. Ira screws the microphone pole, spits into the fob, stares into the array of half-empty benches.

"Is there anyone out there? Smile if you can hear me!"

"Get lost, grandpa."

"Give me a chance. Like a mushroom on his first date, I'm a fun-guy!"

Camp counselors stand. Ira assumes they're counselors on account of their clipboards, backward sports caps, the counting of heads.

"I have special guests in the audience tonight."

Someone shouts, "It's one o'clock in the afternoon!"

"When you're my age it feels like bedtime already."

There's a groan, an awkward silence, as Ira watches another family shuffle into the pavilion looking for a respite from the heat.

"Did you hear about the circus fire? It was in-tents!"

A baby wails.

"You like that? All my life I've wanted to be a gas. My grandparents were gassed, and not of the laughing gas variety, mind you, so we could use some levity at home. I saw all the greats here. Danny Kaye, Henny Youngman, who got the laughs and the girls while all I got was *chazzerai*. Bad jokes? Plenty. But I had it backwards: life's not about what you get but what you give. That's the whole burn. And I don't mean gonorrhea."

No one laughs.

"So now I've got every disease in the book—except hypochondria."

The microphone pops.

"What goes up but never goes down? Your age!"

He's grasping now, he can feel it.

"As you see, I never gave up. Kids, never give up. Every year I come and make an ass of myself, pardon my French. But all good things end, even torture, so you'll be relieved to hear this is my last set. Oh I'm sure I'll find other ways to embarrass myself, just not on stage. I'm packing up like a *schmatta* salesmen I once knew, for greener pastures, as they say. If you'll indulge me a couple minutes I've got a few up my sleeve, hey, that's not funny, where are you going, can't you pity a putz on his last legs—*never trust atoms, they make up everything*—maybe take this schtick to the old folks' home where everyone will be too deaf and blitzed it won't matter how often I say cock and balls, they'll just go on stirring those helmets of ice cream until it all turns to soup."

"Boo!" Children megaphone hands.

"Get a life!"

"Go home, Jew."

"And there it is. Some things never do change, do they?"

This clears out the pavilion. As he steps off the platform, Zach jumps to his feet. In the back, Reenie whistles through her fingers. Beth rushes the stage.

"I didn't know you did stand-up."

"More like sit down."

"I think that's brave."

Beth offers her hand and he takes it, leaving Noreen standing right there. Zach slips his fingers into Ira's other hand as if he were his grandkid, and they swing him like a rope, past the bumper cars, the hog and dog races, where Kole Troller is betting on pigs, Britney Spareribs in the lead, Kevin Bacon a ham away. Ira gives him a neighborly nod.

"Who wants their name on a hat?" Beth says. The crowd swells, pushing them closer. He can feel her heat. Her side boob grazes his arm. He could reach over and grab her if he wanted. The way things are going, she probably wouldn't even resist.

"Know what? Airbrush without me."

The Ferris wheel looms large in the distance. Ira has a sudden, urgent longing to view the world from the rickety top.

NOREEN

Like a funhouse of mirrors, there's no way out. Jilted by Ira, she collides into Kole decked in camo and turkey feathers as if it's already hunting season. You, she says, turning headlong into Mark, whose body stops her like a wall. You, she says, wheeling, and there's Ira groveling, *Reenie, I'm sorry. I lost my head.* She sucks a colada, a plate of grease, and it's Kole again, rubbing Mark's shoulder like it's some kind of talisman as they gamble on the racing of pigs. *Give it up for Lady Hog-a!* There's Nick in the swarm, she thinks she sees Paige but it's her brother, of course, she'd never noticed, how identically they walked, Patrick and Paige. To avoid him she slips down the alley behind the gun tent and steps funny and looks down and there beside a crushed orange cone lies Tommy Potts, dirty mane mashed into straw, lips like earthworms, writhing, quivering, blue.

BETH

A broken grip and he's gone. Her worst nightmare: Zach has become lost in the crowd. He was here, he was just right here, then poof. *Not funny!* She shrieks. *Ollie ollie oxen free!* She has become that mother, the frantic one in Central Park, frazzled at the Natural History Museum. *Zach! Zachary! Zee! Wherever you are, come back to me!*

Fairgoers step in. *My son*—but her mind blanks on what he looks like or what he's wearing. Alligator rain boots. Strangers divide and conquer, they are good in a crisis, this stampede of heads and feet, they surround the haunted house, the animal pens. The weapons tent! *He is four* and her heart is wild. She races through every possibility, circling back, past the booth of feathered God's Eye and rigged games of chance, retracing her steps until sure enough, there he is, all along, her baby, as if he'd never wandered off, limp against a trash can haloed in bees.

One look and Beth knows. Zach's eyes wide as pennies, fear swirling like a five-cent top. He's ingested something. *How long has it been?* Time is everything. Time bucks all conception of time. Time stops like Zach's breathing will stop once his airway shutters. Already hives have forged an alarming topography on Zach's arms and fists. Here comes the swelling. His face a balloon. His voice: a struggle. One word.

"Mommy."

She doesn't say: Where were you? How dare you? Why would you ever leave me?

All she says is, "I'm here."

On her knees, she reaches into her bag. He slumps into her. She checks his pulse, cradling his skull in her lap, mopping curls as she digs deeper into the lining, where is that pen, she never stops talking, her voice soft and soothing, she is practically cooing, issuing casual assurances as if they're having a private cuddle and not lying in the muck in the middle of the Sullivan County Fair. This is nothing, okay. They are mother and child in pieta. Zach nods weakly. You are fine. *Whoops baby whoops baby baby baby baby baby.* Aren't we. You and I.

The fair falls away. Gone is the raceway, the pavilion. Gone is the scrambler, the pirate ship and Tilt-A-Whirl, which opens like a dollhouse on latch and spring. The pickle barrel retreats from view, as does the line for flavored popcorn, for fried dough, fried Twinkies, fried Oreos, rock candy. The stink of sugar. Smell of manure. It doesn't matter how careful she's been—how they'd steered clear of food vendors, avoiding the 4H tent—transmission is that easy. The source need not be known: Dust to fingers to tongue. *Give the woman room* she barely hears as the crowd bends around to watch her crack the emergency capsule with her teeth.

"I've got you," she says, and she does.

In the distance a band is playing. *The screen door slams, Mary's dress sways.* Somewhere, a junior baton troupe is marching, a football fight song skipping on the track. Beth angles her body so Zach won't see the needle. Hard to be afraid of what you can't see. His lids flutter, eyes roll to white, but when she squeezes his hand he squeezes back, *show a little faith there's magic in the night* as she jams adrenaline into the fattiest part of his little leg.

"Count with me." Like this, they rock to the rhythm, listing: five things you can see, four things you can touch, three you can hear until the ambulance arrives.

ACKNOWLEDGMENTS

When a book takes this long, the number of people who have buoyed me along, reaching out a hand when I was in deep, who've treaded beside me in the dark and cold, is extensive. I am flattened with gratitude by all the love, encouragement, commiseration, and support I've received by so many of you.

First and forever, to my family: Rob, Margot and Noah. Your remarkable spirits, perseverance, and hearts make me want to be a better person. Thank you for being my living life. To my sister and parents, who've had an unwitting front seat, and to the Feigs and Rosenthals who've watched me awkwardly dodge all writing-related questions at the dinner table and have intuitively understood to keep refilling my wine glass.

Thank you to Jerry Brennan, indefatigable wearer of hats: for your infinite thoughtfulness and care through every stage of this process. You do the job of ten people. And to Jenni Ferrari-Adler, for staying the course with such attentiveness, acuity, and grace.

To Elisa Albert, Catherine Chung, Seth Rogoff, Joshua Henkin and Adam O'Fallon Price—authors I deeply admire, who took the time to leaf through these pages and offer such generous blurbs. I cherish your words and am indebted to your kindness.

To all who've read drafts or snippets in various stages of undress: Gabe Habash, Andre Dubus III and the workshop at VCFA, Joanne Ramos, Jenny Halper, Julie Innis, Rachel Sherman, Emily Cementina, Aron Mesh, Sarah Kuntsler, Brian Zimbler, and to the remarkable Shayne Terry—for your indispensable counsel and insight.

To Karen Pittelman, who diagnosed my case of "storyitis" – you are my remedy. Zeeva Bukai who pointed out a POV hole in the 11th hour and gave me the courage to address it, Melanie

Pappadis Faranello who said maybe start with chapter 4, and to Alice Kaltman who saw the end before I did.

To places of influence and inspiration: the Vermont Studio Center, that rustic VRBO in the Connecticut woods with Melanie, the cabin in Narrowsburg, Camp Ramah in the Poconos, the Wayne County Fair, and to bungalow 3B. Thank you, Rosmarin's. Thank you, Route 17. Thank you, Honesdale Public Library and hot summer Wednesdays which took me winding through the sleepy towns of Sullivan County.

A perennial shout out to my mother, who arrives like Miss Clavel whenever I need her, making so much of this possible.

To Samantha Davidson Green, Dina Relles, Yvonne Conza, Erika Dreifus, Susan Kleinman, Courtney Rubin, Bob Hill, Josh Rolnick, Ben Tanzer, Meg Tuite, Brian Gresko, Nita Noveno, Maureen Langloss and Chris Gonzalez: for making me feel less alone.

To Avner Landes: for the marvelous *Meiselman* which led me to Tortoise Books.

To Penina Roth, for your sensitivity and invaluable feedback, and for championing my work with your formidable megaphone.

To Sarah Saffian—for listening.

To Esther Bukai for cover consultations.

To Autumn Watts of *Guernica*, and to Stan Rifkin (who years ago took a story for *Front Porch Journal* that would later become part of this book.) It was such a pleasure to work with you.

To Brooklyn friends and college friends, mom friends and high school friends, workplace friends and writer friends. To the internet. Anyone who's ever taken a workshop of me please know I've been a student of yours as well. To all who have listened to me agonize over this project for the past millennium and have managed to stand by me: you're the real heroes. Last, to every reader: I love you. Thank you for sticking here till the bitter end.

About the Author

Sara Lippmann is the author of the story collections *Doll Palace* re-released by 7.13 Books, and *Jerks* from Mason Jar Press. Her work has been honored by the New York Foundation for the Arts, and has appeared in *The Millions*, *The Washington Post*, *Best Small Fictions*, *Epiphany*, *Split Lip* and elsewhere. She teaches with Jericho Writers and lives with her family in Brooklyn.

About Tortoise Books

Slow and steady wins in the end, even in publishing. Tortoise Books is dedicated to finding and promoting quality authors who haven't yet found a niche in the marketplace—writers producing memorable and engaging works that will stand the test of time.

Learn more at www.tortoisebooks.com or follow us on Twitter: @TortoiseBooks.